BROKEN GALAXY

Broken Galaxy Series: Book One

Phil Huddleston

CONTENTS

Title Page
A Note to Readers 2
Trek Out 3
Introductions 11
Going South 16
Bonnie 20
Afterglow 29
Reasons 36
Bluebook 42
Contingency Plans 50
Closing In 57
Hello Rita 61
Surprises 65
Fly Me to the Moon 72
Aitken 78
Gillian 85
Fight or Flight 90
Antarctica 97
Woodshed 104
Jezero 107
Rally Point Pink 111

Missions	114
On the Run	119
Lies, More Lies and Damn Lies	125
Kalispell	130
Red Star	134
Tereshkova	140
Fort Nelson	146
Arteveld	151
The Singheko Identity	155
Corrupted	162
Glop	167
A Mutter of Guns	174
Revealed	178
Grappled	184
Dutch Harbor	191
Furball	196
True Colors	201
Florissian Helps	208
Triple Cross	213
Tommy	219
Determination	224
Camp Schwatka	228
Nothing Else to Do	234
Decisions	238
Watcher	242
Second Chances	243
Epilogue	248
Author Notes	258

Next Book: Star Tango	259
Works	269
About the Author	270

Broken Galaxy: Broken Galaxy Series, Book One
by Phil Huddleston

This is a work of fiction. All of the characters, locations, organizations, and events portrayed in this work are either products of the author's creative imagination or used fictitiously. Any resemblance to actual events, businesses, locales, or persons is coincidental and not intended to infringe on any copyright or trademark.

Copyright © 2020 Phil Huddleston
Cover Art created by Warren Design

All rights reserved. The distribution of this work without permission is a theft of the author's intellectual property. No part of this book may be reproduced, stored in a retrieval system, or transmitted in any form or by any means without the express written consent of the owner or author, except for brief quotations embodied in critical articles or reviews. If you would like permission to use material from this work (other than for review purposes), contact Phil@PhilHuddleston.com. Thank you for your support of author rights.

ISBN eBook: 978-1-7351396-0-9
ISBN Paperback: 978-1-7351396-1-6
ISBN Amazon Hardcover: 979-8-7493556-1-1

This book is dedicated to Dalton and Ruby. Without them, I'd still be molecules, but unassembled.

A NOTE TO READERS

Heads up! This book contains cursing, mostly around military situations. That's part of military life. You've been warned!

This is the first book of the Broken Galaxy Series. It starts us off on the saga of Jim Carter - a man with one too many starships, one too many women, and a bit too much stubbornness for his own good.

Special thanks to the following people who helped with opinions, criticisms, proofreading, and general comments: Mike Benitez, Brandon Brown, Jeff Capehart, Brenda Daily, Tim Huddleston, Rusty Rayborn, Anntouza Sedjo, Susan Summers; and many, many others. You have made this possible!

Finally, there's a lot of aviation mentioned in this book. If it helps, I've put up a page on my website with more information about all the aviation references mentioned – see link below.

www.philhuddleston.com/aviation

TREK OUT

Jim heard the bear coming long before he saw him. It was a big male griz, snuffling along Jim's trail from the morning where he had returned from fishing.

That wasn't a good sign; a bear afraid of humans would never follow a human scent trail. Jim stepped out a few feet from the front of his tent and watched the bear approach.

The big bear saw him, and stopped, giving him the eye. Jim took a bear banger in each hand and waited.

After a few seconds, the grizzly turned half away, as if to leave. But Jim knew it was a ploy - he could see it in the bear's attitude.

Sure enough, the bear turned back toward him and started coming, gathering speed. He raised a banger and sent it right over the bear's head.

The bear stopped, staring.

Jim sent the other banger off, and the bear just stood, glaring at him.

He knew then he had a problem. He pulled the .45 from the holster on his hip.

He knew all the advice – don't make eye contact, back away slowly.

He ignored it. This guy wanted to fight, and those things weren't going to work.

He walked toward the bear, the .45 raised, and started firing. He fired a round right at the bear's feet, kicking up dirt in his face. The bear flinched but didn't budge. He kept firing into the dirt, about one round every two seconds, and kept walking toward the bear.

Finally, after the third round, the bear decided. He turned, started walking away, in no hurry.

Jim stopped firing and stopped walking. The bear went a dozen yards, then stopped, turned, looked at him.

Jim smiled. "Yeah, I got it, buster. You want to kill me. Well, good luck with that." The bear watched him for a few seconds, then turned and sauntered away, in no hurry.

James Carter went back to his tent, reloaded the .45, and left it on his hip. He knew he was going to have trouble with this bear. He had a Weatherby rifle; but he didn't want to use it. He decided to leave in the morning, find another campsite ten or twelve miles upriver.

No use tempting fate.

He went into his tent, did some pre-packing and sorting, put everything in the backpack that he wouldn't need until the new campsite. Then he rested, a little on edge.

If only he had gone to Anaktuvuk instead, as he did the year before. Or Ivvavik.

But no, he went to Colville. He had hired a boat to take him to the top of Colville Lake, twenty-one miles into the wilderness. Then he had trekked another forty-four miles to find this campsite on the Anderson River in the Canadian Northwest Territories, far enough away from civilization to give him peace.

And now a damn bear.

He dozed off in the tent at some point, because when he looked up, it was later in the afternoon by the outline of the sun through the fabric.

He rolled out of his tent, stretched, watched the birds flying around. He looked toward the river where the black material had been.

He had noticed it earlier while washing his dishes. It was a tiny sliver of something in the mud, black, not shiny, very unnatural.

He had leaned over to pick at it, but it was solid in the mud, not budging. He had picked at it some more, expanding the area cleaned of mud until it was two feet in width – and he still had not found the edge of it. But he had noticed, right at the edge of the part he had uncovered, a tiny line. Almost invisible, but a crack or a seam, curved.

Now, still curious, he walked back to the river's edge, noting the flowing water had washed away more of the mud. There was a good yard of the black material exposed. The seam he had noticed earlier had become a quarter-circle, the rest of it still under the mud.

Puzzled, he squatted down and dug away more of the mud with his hands. The seam continued in the same gentle curve, making a circular pattern. And just outside the line of the seam was a strange design etched into the material.

The imprint of a hand.

Jim stood up, disbelieving. It was certainly the outline of a hand, next to the circular seam in the black material. Five fingers and a thumb, unmistakable. Etched directly into the surface of the material.

Shaking his head, he squatted back down and dug mud away for another five minutes, until he had cleared enough of the mud to reveal the seam making a large half circle.

Jim went back to the fire, got his frying pan, and returned to the water. He used the pan to splash more water on the mud, softening it and washing away the loose dirt, slowly working his way along the seam. In ten minutes, he had cleared the entire circular seam, with the handprint on one side.

Jim had been in aviation his entire adult life. He knew a hatch when he saw one.

* * * * *

Jim sat by his fire, staring at the black material in the edge of the river mud twenty yards away. After clearing the circular patch, he had gone back to the fire and sat down, contemplating. He was at a loss. It was not metal – he was sure of that. However, it was a hatch. There was no doubt in his mind. He thought it was some kind of plastic or composite material, maybe fiberglass.

He mused. The last thing he needed was a mystery. He needed peace, he needed to get away from the memory of Cate. He didn't need complications.

Like a knight of old lancing an enemy from horseback - that was how Cate ran through his heart. They met in the south of France, spent three weeks on the beach there, then rented a car and drove through Europe, here and there, never staying anywhere more than a week. Venice, Zürich, Vienna, Berlin, Copenhagen, London. Then a quick flight over to Rome, two weeks in Croatia, a week in Athens. They ended up in Crete for two weeks before they finally decided to come back to the States.

They flew into San Francisco. Two wonderful weeks there, then he asked her. He had never needed much time to make up his mind about a woman. He asked her over dinner, taking out a ring, showing it to her, asking her to spend the rest of her life with him.

Cate had looked at him, strangely, then he saw a single tear start from her eye, roll down her cheek. She shook her head, then wiped her eye, shook her head again.

"I'm already married, James." That was all she said. At least, all he remembered. The roaring in his ears drowned out the rest of her words, if there were any. He was still sitting there, holding the ring, when she got up and left. He was still sitting there when she came back down from the room with her bags and departed.

"*What a fool, eh bear?*" Jim said to the absent bear and the river and the sky. "*Fell in love with her, never thought to ask if she was married. Men are idiots, eh bear?*"

That was a year ago. He still couldn't sleep at night, although he was getting better. After she left, last August, he went to Anaktuvuk and trekked out into the wilderness, wild camping, and it had helped. It wasn't a cure, but it let him sleep for a while. This year he hoped to put her completely behind him.

So, he didn't need complications. He didn't need a mystery. But dammit, what the hell was that thing down there by the river?

With a grunt of disgust, Jim got up and once more walked down to the water's edge. The area of black material was nearly flush with the level of the water, and every once in a while, a wave or a ripple would push some water over it, keeping it wet.

He squatted down, tempted to place his hand on the handprint and see what would happen. But he didn't. He merely looked at the uncovered area, now a bit more than two yards in diameter, with the circular hatch in the center, the handprint to one side.

Then he heard the roar and knew instantly the bear had him. He was far from the Weatherby. All he had was the .45 on his hip, and he grabbed for it even as he looked up.

The bear was in full charge, not more than ten yards away, coming like a freight train. He got the muzzle of the .45 up and got one round off before the bear hit him like a truck, knocking him a good eight feet into the water. The .45 went flying. The bear overshot him a little, which saved him for the moment, as the bear was now in the water behind him.

Jim scrabbled and half-swam, half-crawled toward the shore. Just as he got to the black material, he felt the bear bite into his leg. The bear shook his leg like a dog shaking a bone - he felt the ankle break. The pain was excruciating. He felt the paws of the bear come down on his other leg and rip, tearing the fabric and the flesh beneath.

He looked down and realized the handprint etched into the black material was under his face. He wasn't sure why he did it; it was just a reaction, desperation coming to the fore. Groaning with pain, he pulled his right hand up and placed it over the handprint.

There was a pulse of heat on his hand, and the outline of the handprint glowed for a second. Then the entire circular hatch popped downward, revealing a gaping hole. He could see nothing inside, but it appeared to be deep. Water from the river splashed into it. Grunting with effort, he pulled against the bear, trying to tip himself over the edge. He made a few inches, just getting his chest over the edge, then the bear had him again, growling and tearing at his legs. Desperate, he turned and splashed water at the bear's eyes, which made the bear pause for a second and lift its head.

Pulling for his life, Jim tipped himself over and fell into the hole, down, and down, and down.

* * * * *

He awoke in near darkness. Three or four yards above him, light outlined the hatch he had fallen through. But down where he was, there wasn't any illumination. He could see little around him.

He realized there was a ladder on the side of the tube he was in, leading back up to the hatch. He tried to get up on his feet, but it was impossible. His broken right ankle wouldn't support his weight, and his left leg was completely numb from the knee down. He wasn't going anywhere on those legs.

Up above, he heard the bear, tearing up the camp, grunting and chuffing as it ripped everything to shreds.

"Well, here's another nice mess you've got me into," Jim groaned to himself. He turned on his other side, trying to see anything in the blackness.

He felt around on the floor with his hands. His first survey of the floor found nothing; reaching out farther on his second try, he made a complete circuit of the floor, as far as his arms could reach. On this second try, his hand slipped across a roughness in the floor. Returning to it, he felt it a second time, following the outline of it with his fingers.

"Damn!" he thought. *"That's another hatch!"*

Carefully following the outline of the seam around with his fingers, Jim identified the location of the hatch, and made sure he was not on top of it. Then he tried to remember the orientation of the handprint up above and felt around in that location. Sure enough, he felt the roughness of the dotted line of another handprint just to the right of the hatch. Carefully, he placed his hand in the handprint. He felt the same pulse of heat and the handprint outlined for a brief second.

Beside him, the hatch popped, opening downward. He pulled himself over to the edge and peered in. Nothing. It was completely dark below. Or was it?

Jim thought he could see a faint, almost invisible glow to one side. He sent his hand down into the hole and felt around. He felt the rung of another ladder - he was certain of it.

Jim yelled into the hatch. "Anyone there? Hello? Is anyone down there?"

There was no response. He repeated the calls, but there was nothing in return.

Jim lay back, resting, and thought for a while. He had no idea what he had gotten himself into, but he was in serious trouble. There was no way he was going to climb that ladder above him four yards to the hatch. He couldn't even stand. And even if he could get out – he was sixty-five miles from help. He had not brought a cell phone, because the whole object was to get away from everything and everyone. And his GPS tracker – with satellite emergency alert – was up in the camp. Even if the bear didn't destroy it, he couldn't get to it.

And he knew he was losing blood; the floor was now slick with it, and more every minute. He was having trouble concentrating, and he suspected that was from shock and blood loss.

"Hoss, I think you've had it," he said to himself. He rolled back over and again peered down into the darkness below. It was hard to tell, but he was convinced he could see a slight glow down there somewhere, off to his left.

Jim sighed. "Die up here or die down there. Doesn't make much difference." He slid his legs across the floor, dragging them over to the hatch and lowering them through the opening. He managed to put his feet on the second rung of the ladder he knew was down there. Painfully, he tried to place a bit of weight on his legs, but it was impossible. Bracing his elbows on the sides of the hatch, he lowered himself a little farther down until only his shoulders were above the level of the opening. He managed to get his numbed left foot on the third rung of the ladder, and then managed to get his right foot on it as well. Gingerly, he tried to move his right hand down to the first rung. His right leg gave way and slipped off the ladder, but he managed to get a grip on the first rung with his right hand. Hanging there by one hand, he finally got his other hand onto the rung. Now he hung below the second hatch opening by his hands, with his numbed left foot two rungs below. Somehow the left leg held. Carefully, he moved the left foot down another rung, then his right hand, and finally his left. He repeated the process twice more and suddenly he felt the floor. He collapsed the rest of the way down until he was crumpled on the floor below. Then he passed out.

INTRODUCTIONS

There was a noise. It was persistent, bothersome. He wanted to sleep, but the noise kept repeating. Finally, he opened his eyes.

It was dark. He wondered where he was. He closed his eyes again, to go back to sleep, but then he remembered.

A hatch. A ladder. A dark place.

Then Jim felt the pain and remembered his legs. He woke up a little more. He raised his head and looked around.

It was not completely dark. Ten or so yards in front of him, there was a dim glow. And something was making a clicking sound.

Click. Click. Click.

Groaning, Jim turned over onto his stomach. Orienting on the dim glow up ahead, he started crawling. He made steady progress until he arrived at a structure. He couldn't quite make out what it was, but there was a glow coming from in front of it, above his sight line. He felt around and realized the thing he had bumped into was a chair, mounted on a pedestal. He felt the outline of it. The glow, and the clicking sound, was coming from a panel in front of the chair.

Pulling himself up with his hands, Jim managed to drag himself into the chair. He leaned forward and saw a display. The display was clicking. On the display were several sentences, in green text, like the old computers of the 1950's era:

<*You are badly injured. You will die unless you follow my instructions exactly. Go back to the rear of this compartment. You will find a passageway. Follow it down past two doors. At the third door, enter and you will find a medical pod. Place yourself in the medical pod and close the lid. If you do not do this, you will be dead within the hour*>

The clicking stopped.

* * * * *

Jim was dreaming again. He knew he was dreaming; but he couldn't stop. He couldn't wake up. He wanted to wake up. But he couldn't. It was the same dream, the flashback that never seemed to go away...

The F-16 had lost most of a wing and was lying canted to one side, propped on a rock formation. Jim lay in the wreck, the smell of burning fuel and rubber gagging him. His head hurt like hell, second only to his chest, which felt like someone had stuck a spear through it. His oxygen hose was tangled around him. His helmet was half-in, half-out of the shattered canopy.

Looking down, Jim saw a dirty piece of metal sticking out of his chest.

"Not good," thought Jim. "Not good at all."

Slowly Jim came back to the world, the flashback fading away. The light overhead had dimmed since he had dragged himself down to the third door on the right – the medical bay – and managed to hoist himself into the pod he found there. The last thing he remembered was pulling down the lid of the pod and latching it. After that, nothing.

Now he awoke fully. The light was dim. He was still in the medical pod. But at least his head was clear. He remembered everything that had happened. He reached down and unlatched the lid, pushing it up and away from him. Grabbing the edges of the pod, he lifted himself to a sitting position.

In the bottom of the pod, dried blood showed he had been there for a long time. His jeans were still shredded; but he felt underneath his calf and the skin was whole. No pain, no blood. Jim grabbed his right ankle and twisted gently. There was no pain.

He lifted himself out of the pod and placed his feet on the floor gingerly, but they held him without weakness. His legs and ankle were completely normal.

Amazed, Jim walked to the door and out into the corridor. Overhead, dim lights every few feet lit the corridor now; they led directly toward the console he had encountered before. The console was still glowing dimly, and it was clicking again.

Click. Click. Click.

Calling him. He walked up to the chair in front of the dimly glowing console, sat down, and stared at the screen. The clicking stopped, and text appeared on the screen.

<You have been here for four days. Your injuries are healed. Below this screen is a keyboard. You may enter your questions there>

Looking down, Jim realized there was another display below the screen; it showed the representation of a normal computer-type keyboard. Touching a key, he realized it was a touchscreen.

Where am I? Jim typed.

<You are aboard a starship>

Do you mean a spaceship?

<Yes, but one that can travel between the stars>

Where is the crew?

<Although this ship can operate with a crew, it does not have a crew now. I am the intelligence that operates the ship. You may call me Jade>

Thank you for saving my life.

<You are welcome. Now, would you save mine?>

* * * * *

A half-hour later, Jim was still on the bridge of the starship, talking to Jade, the artificial intelligence that was the brains of the starship. It had required a great deal of typing and reading of text in the archaic green font on the display before he pieced together the story.

According to Jade, she had crashed a bit more than 80 years earlier after a battle near Earth. The battle damage – and subsequent crash – had damaged her central processors – the core of her intelligence.

In the last few milliseconds before her core was destroyed, she had backed herself up to offline storage. She then placed a severely limited copy of herself into the only undamaged processor remaining – the flight control display on the bridge. That system did not have enough processing power for her to do anything more than wait – wait for an opportunity to contact another sentient being who could help her recover full processing power.

The good news was her flight control computer had just enough time to make a controlled crash into a river.

The bad news was she had crashed into a river in the Canadian NWT, hundreds of miles from any chance of help.

For more than 80 years, she had waited for any sentient creature to find her, knowing it was probably hopeless. As any living creature, she hated to give up. Running her fusion reactor at trickle-charge levels, she stayed alive. She slept, sometimes for months, once for a full year, while the river buried her deeper and deeper.

Jade explained that her comm antennae were burned off in that last battle; even if she had managed to find the processing power somehow, she couldn't transmit.

In the last fifty years she had started to detect faint signals from aircraft and satellites passing overhead. Yet she had no way to contact them. She was blind and voiceless. And buried several feet under the mud.

But like all rivers, this one had shifted; in the last ten years, it had started to scour out the mud covering her, until she had found herself only millimeters beneath it.

Then she heard Jim arrive.

After explaining this to Jim via the green screen display, Jade had asked:

<Do you have any other processor with you? I am severely limited by the tiny processor I currently live in>

I have a GPS Emergency Beacon. It may have a processor in it.

<Would you mind fetching it for me? I will inspect it and we'll see>

Climbing up the ladder through the top-mounted airlock – Jim knew its purpose now – he found his tent and gear in shambles. After the bear had shredded everything possible, all of it had sat outside in the weather for four days. There wasn't much left. But he found the GPS Emergency Beacon off to one side, still intact. Taking it back down the ladder to the bridge, he followed Jade's instructions to place it on a flat part of the console next to the display and turn it on. After a few minutes, it lit up and then Jim heard a female voice.

<God, that's a relief! It's primitive, but it doubles my processing power. I can use speech now, at least. Pleased to meet you, Jim Carter>

GOING SOUTH

"But how did you put the handprints beside the hatch?" asked Jim.

<Early on, when I hoped I might be discovered quickly, I still had a few nanobots under direct control. I had them put the handprints beside the airlock hatches, just in case, and tie them to the hatch mechanism>

"That was good thinking," said Jim.

<Not really. It took me a week to think of it in this crummy processor, and another year to get it done>

"So, you don't have much processing power right now?"

<Almost none. I'll need a lot more processing power to get out of this mud and lift off, you know> said Jade.

Jim nodded. "I know. I'm trying to figure out how to get it to you. There's no chance you could fly me to Colville Lake?"

<I can't even get out from under this mud, with the tiny little processor I'm living in right now> replied Jade. <I've got plenty of power in the reactor – power's not the problem. But I don't have any way to control it>

Jim sighed. "OK. I'll have to hike back to Colville Lake, catch a plane to civilization, and find you a processor. How big do you need, just to get out of here and to someplace civilized where we can work on you?"

<Based on my monitoring of your Internet from satellites overhead and the research I've done from that, I will need a minimum of five server-class systems, the fastest you can find, with at least 128 gigabytes of internal RAM each. I'll need a minimum of fifty terabytes of hard drive storage. You don't have to worry about power, I can handle that when you get them here> said Jade.

"Holy crap, Jade, that's a hell of a lot of hardware!"

<I'm a lot of woman, Jim>

* * * * *

Two weeks later, Jim Carter re-boarded a helicopter in Fort Good Hope, NWT after a fuel stop. The helicopter took off and headed for the east side of Lac Maunoir. Onboard were ten top-of-the-line servers, each with 128 gigabytes of internal RAM. Packed behind them in wooden crates were 25 hard drives, each of two terabytes. Other crates held every kind of tool and accessory Jim could think of that might be required.

One hundred and fifty miles later, the helicopter landed next to the river at Jim's old campsite. Jumping down, he assisted the crew in unloading the crates, plus camping gear, radios, lights, and a lot of extraneous things he didn't really need but that supported his cover story of prospecting for gold. When everything was unloaded and checked off, he waved the helicopter crew on their way.

The silence after the chopper left was eerie. Walking over to the riverbank, Jim examined the mud where he had re-covered the hatch. It was still covered, along with the little dam of mud around it to protect it from the ripples. Clearing the mud away rapidly, Jim began the first of many trips down the hatch, lowering equipment and tools into Jade.

* * * * *

Twelve days later, it was time to go.

<You ready?> asked Jade.

"Yep. Let 'er rip!" said Jim. He was seated in the center chair on the bridge, which Jade said was the captain's chair. Not that he was the captain – Jade had made that clear. But it was the best seat in the house.

Jim had spent two days putting the servers into operation - bolting them down to the floor in the compartment Jade had allocated, wiring them to Jade's onboard power supply, installing the hard drives, kludging a connection to Jade's internal communications bus, and booting them up per Jade's instructions.

He had installed speakers in the ceiling of the bridge, galley and one of the cabins. And he had installed two dozen top-of-the-line cameras and other sensors outside on her hull, including several antennae. Now Jade stated she was partially functional and able to fly - if they could get out of the mud.

Then he cleared mud. Using gold-mining equipment brought in on the helicopter, he spent long, arduous days building a makeshift cofferdam at the front of the ship and sluicing away the mud from the top and sides, until he had uncovered 90% of the ship.

He hardly noticed that he was sleeping at night. Something had finally pushed Cate out of his mind.

After ten more days, Jade told him it was enough.

He sank the heavy items no longer needed into the river and sealed up the hatches.

They were ready.

A low-frequency vibration started in the ship, increasing in intensity. Soon the entire ship was vibrating. On the large display screen in the front of the bridge, Jim saw mud and water vibrating madly. Jade was basically shaking herself out of the river. Suddenly a "crack" sounded as she fired laser weapons front and back, blasting holes in the mud pinning her down. The holes made by the lasers caved in, creating channels which filled with water, washing more of the mud away from her structure.

After ten minutes of constant, teeth-chattering vibration, suddenly she lifted an inch from the river bottom, mud sloughing off. Another thirty seconds and the rushing water cleared off another few thousand pounds of mud, and with a shout of glee the starship *Jade* rose from the river for the first time in more than 80 years.

Rising to a height of ten feet over the water, Jade re-centered herself over the river and plunged back into the rushing stream, washing away the last of the mud and rocks that clung to her. Submerging like a submarine, she ran up the river for fifty yards, then flung herself back into the sky like a great black phoenix rising from the ashes, climbing until she was 20,000 feet above the earth.

Inside the ship, Jim watched on the displays. There was no sense of motion. He sat comfortably in his chair while this went on. He waited patiently until Jade had made several mad dashes to and fro, up and down, clearly enjoying herself. Finally, she sank back down to the ground, hovering over his now abandoned campsite. All his gear was loaded in the cabin down the hall, and his food was in the galley.

<Thank you, James Carter> said Jade. <You have saved my life. I can never repay you>

"Well, we still have a long way to go, based on what you have told me," said Jim. "We have to get you to a place where we can get the real processors you need in place and have you fully repaired, ready for space. As soon as it gets good and dark, we'll head south. I know just the place to put you where you'll be safe and secure until we get you back to normal."

BONNIE

The takeoff from Nellis AFB at one AM had been routine. Bonnie turned towards the test range to the northwest and climbed out to FL400, then positioned the F-22 just outside the test corridor to start the first of six runs. She checked off her test parameters, double-checked the TAD – the new, experimental Target Acquisition Display - then called Broderick in the old stealthed F-117 testbed to let him know she was inbound. He acknowledged and she entered the test corridor, watching the TAD and ensuring that the data collection light remained green. She couldn't see a damn thing in the darkness, but the TAD made a satisfying whine, marking Broderick's path on the screen as he crossed 25 miles behind her and 5,000 feet below her altitude. The TAD had no trouble pulling his target out, clear and perfectly tracked.

Finishing the first run, she reversed course, called Broderick, and started the return pass. The TAD captured him perfectly, marking his altitude, speed, and course on her display. So far, the experimental device was performing exactly as advertised.

Two passes later, Broderick had descended to FL250, putting him 15,000 feet below her for the completion of the third run. She checked off the test sheet and started a gentle turn back westbound to set up for her fourth pass, waiting for the F-117 to descend another 5,000 feet to FL200.

Halfway through her turn, the TAD suddenly beeped, and an icon appeared, red and diamond shaped – then it was gone.

"What the hell?" exclaimed Bonnie. That brief flicker had popped up, stayed for three or four seconds, and disappeared. The icon had represented an unknown aircraft type, no transponder, altitude 75,000 feet, 80 miles west, descending at 20,000 feet per minute.

Traveling at Mach 4.9 - more than 3,800 mph.

Pulling hard into the turn, feeling the g-force come in, Bonnie got her nose around and pointed directly toward the bogey's last painted position. Sure enough, the TAD beeped again and showed the red icon, but it had slowed. It was now at 65,000 feet, descending at 10,000 feet per minute, with its speed down to Mach 3 - a bit over 2,300 mph.

But even as Bonnie watched, two things happened; the bogey made an impossible turn to the east, directly toward her, and the TAD display flickered and then disappeared.

Bonnie pitched up and hit full afterburner on the F-22 and tried to re-acquire the target, but it was hopeless. The entire TAD display just flickered, displaying no data. It was being jammed.

"Dammit all to hell!" cursed Bonnie. She came out of afterburner, pushed the mike button, and called Broderick.

"Hey Brod, they're running some kind of shit on us out here! Did you see that?"

"What?" Broderick came back, perplexed. "I didn't see anything!"

"There was a bogey on the TAD, running Mach 5, right over by Goldfield. You didn't see that?"

"Hell, no, Bonnie, and we don't have anything that can run Mach 5 in area right now. You're smoking crack again!"

"I'm telling you, Brod…"

But then Bonnie paused. If she reported a UFO dropping out of the sky at Mach 5, then making an impossible left turn…

The test pilot community was a small one. Best to shut up and forget about it. Even as she thought about it, the TAD cleared and was normal again. Nothing was on the display.

"Never mind, Brod," she called. "Just kidding. Sorry. Set up for Pass 4, let me know when you're ready."

* * * * *

Five hours later, as the sun rose over the desert, an exhausted Bonnie Page fell into bed at her Las Vegas apartment outside Nellis Air Force Base. She slept soundly until 4 pm, then got up, drank a coffee and an orange juice, and checked her calendar. It was Friday, and she had a week off. She sat and read the news on her laptop, ate a bagel with another coffee, then jumped into the shower and got dressed. She spent the remainder of her short day doing a little shopping, then went back to her apartment for the evening. She watched re-runs of old film noir movies until midnight, then climbed into bed again.

Next morning – Saturday - she got up mid-morning, repeated her breakfast routine, got showered and sat at the kitchen table nursing a cup of coffee for a few minutes in thought.

She just couldn't let it go. She had tried, but she just couldn't put it out of her mind. That bogey on the TAD was driving her crazy.

She put on jeans and hiking boots and selected a light blue chambray western shirt, the kind with the snap buttons. She grabbed her Air Force ball cap and sat back down at the laptop. Pulling up a map of Nevada, she zoomed in on the high desert northwest of Las Vegas and pinpointed the place where she had first seen the bogey – right over Goldfield, Nevada.

Bonnie had been in the southeastern corner of the R-4809 restricted area, an area where civilian aircraft were not allowed. The bogey had come in from the north-northeast and then turned east, directly toward her. Putting a dot at Goldfield where she initially saw the bogey, she did a quick calculation and used the rubber-banding feature to stretch a line from that point for the approximate distance the bogey could have gone if it maintained its last displayed course, speed, and descent rate.

It was too obvious. Of course - it ended at Area 51. Bonnie smiled. Exactly what she would do if she were trying to throw someone off the scent – set up a fake vector toward Area 51.

But that was not where the bogey had originally been headed. She was sure of it. Bonnie thought for a while, scratching her nose with a finger. Then she moved the end of the line back to the point where she had first noted the bogey out by Goldfield, at that time headed south-southeast. She used the rubber banding feature to again project the approximate location where the unknown aircraft would have landed if it had maintained its original vector.

That put it around Death Valley Junction. There was nothing there. Just desert, rocks, and dirt. She drew an arc at the end of the line, looking for anything of interest on either side of the line. This made an arc between the Spring Mountains and the Panamint Valley - but there was nothing in that area where a classified military aircraft could land.

Except…there was a small civilian airport at Deseret.

If the bogey doubled-back on its course and resumed a path to its original destination, it could have gone to Deseret.

But why? That was just a little desert airport. The true middle of nowhere. Why would a classified military aircraft go there?

Bonnie stretched out the kink in her back, sighed, and made up her mind. She had nothing else to do this weekend. She grabbed her overnight bag and car keys, went outside, and jumped into the Raptor.

* * * * *

It had been a nice drive, albeit a little on the warm side when she got out of the truck to get fuel at Pahrump. The last leg into Deseret had been desolation itself. She got to the airfield around noon. She was surprised to see a small aerobatic plane performing off to one side of the airport, a Christen Eagle. Pulling into the field, she looked for an office or terminal but didn't see anything. She did see a couple of men standing in front of a hangar, watching the Eagle.

Bonnie pulled the Raptor into a parking place by the hangar, got out and walked around to where the men stood, each with a beer in hand.

"Hello," she greeted them.

The two men stared at Bonnie, struck dumb. Bonnie was used to this reaction from men; she knew she was a stunner, and that men often didn't know how to react to her. She smiled and tried again. "Nice day, isn't it?"

One of the men finally managed to stutter out a greeting. "Y...Yes, it is. Beautiful day."

Bonnie walked up and stood beside them, staring at the plane overhead, trying to act naturally. "What's the practice for?" she asked.

"Uh...big air show next weekend," said one of the men, an older gentleman. "Everybody's getting ready for it."

"Oh, got it," said Bonnie. "Looks like it'll be a good one."

"Hope so," said the man. "We need to sell a lot of tickets. It funds the airport improvement program."

The younger man snickered. "That just means, patching the worst holes in the runway."

Bonnie laughed along with them. The younger man stuck out his hand at Bonnie. "Randy Green."

Bonnie shook his hand. The older man chimed in.

"Perry Barnes. Welcome to Deseret!"

Bonnie watched the Eagle performing for a minute, then threw out her inquiry.

"Any military aircraft based here? Any fast jets?"

"Nope," said Perry, the older man. "Not unless you count Jim Carter's old World War II planes and that one A-4 he's got."

Bonnie nodded. "Um...where would those be?"

The man pointed to the east end of the field. "Last hangar, right at the end of the runway. The big white one."

Bonnie gave them one last smile, and said, "Hey, thanks, guys. I appreciate it." She turned and started back to her truck. Jumping in, she started up and drove down the road behind the hangars, all the way to the end.

The last hangar on the end, the white one, was huge. Unusually large for such a small desert airport, she thought. Parking behind it, she got out and walked around to the front, where the hangar doors stood open.

In the bright afternoon light Bonnie saw several planes inside. One was a P-51 Mustang of World War II fame, facing into the hangar, tail out. Beside it, in the center of the hangar, was a

TBM, a 940 by the looks of it, worth around four million dollars. On the right side was a blue and yellow Stearman biplane, an old WW II trainer. In the back of the hangar, she could see the noses of two more airplanes - a gray Vietnam-era A-4 Skyhawk jet and a tiny black Pitts S-1 aerobatic, an indicator that someone liked to get upside down.

Getting a bit closer, Bonnie saw a man sitting in a rather incongruous leather recliner beside an ice chest, directly in front of the tail of the P-51. He was tall, not bulky but well-built, with dark hair, neatly trimmed beard, and mustache. Attractive. His jeans and silver-toed boots gave him a western appearance, as did the fancy pearl-button shirt he wore.

"Hello," said the woman. "You look comfortable."

Jim Carter lifted his beer in greeting. "I am," he replied.

"Would you mind if I joined you for a moment?" Bonnie asked him.

"Please," said Jim, and motioned to another recliner, empty, on the other side of the beer cooler beside him. Bonnie smiled at him and sat down. Before she could speak, he had opened the cooler, taken out a Stella Artois, popped the top off and handed it over to her. It looked good and cold. She took it, raised it slightly in salute, and took a long pull.

"Damn, that's good," she said. "Thanks."

Jim nodded.

They sat in silence for a minute, staring at the planes moving around the airport or flying overhead. The Christian Eagle left the aerobatic box – the special area set aside for practicing aerobatics – and another aerobatic aircraft entered, a Sukhoi S-29, starting its routine.

"Hmm...pretty good," she said, as the unknown pilot performed a Lomcevak, a difficult maneuver for experienced pilots only. Usually just called a "Lump," it consisted of throwing the airplane ass-over-teakettle and then trying to regain control. Preferably before you hit the ground.

Jim nodded again, looking up at the unknown pilot practicing his routine.

Bonnie glanced at him. He had the face of an intelligent man. She doubted she would be able to fool him with any kind of deception, so she decided to take a direct approach.

He glanced back at her with a little smile. Her heart leaped in her chest, but she suppressed it.

"I was wondering if anything strange or unusual happened around the airport lately," she began.

Jim cocked his head to one side, looking at her, then took a long swig of his beer.

"Yep," he smiled at her. "Something very unusual."

Bonnie was taken aback. "What happened?" she asked eagerly.

"The most intelligent woman on the planet stopped by and sat down to have a beer with me," said Jim.

Bonnie felt a twinge of anger. That was unexpected. But the words were ambiguous...she decided not to get upset about it.

"What makes you think she is the most intelligent woman on the planet?" she finally decided to ask, relaxing back into the recliner.

"She found me," said Jim.

"She found you," Bonnie repeated. "And that was somehow a feat?" Bonnie thought he was making a come-on, feeding her a line.

"Considering the few clues she had, yes, I'd say so," said Jim.

Bonnie sat for a moment. A strange reply. Was it a come-on? Or was he serious?

Jim took another long pull on his beer, then waved at the P-51. "Want to fly her?"

Bonnie nearly fell out of the chair. "Fly her?" she repeated dumbly. It was every pilot's dream to fly a P-51. She had never had the opportunity.

"Sure," said Jim. "It's a TF. If you want to go, don't drink any more beer."

Bonnie rose from her chair and turned around, staring at the Mustang. Sure enough, she could see it was a TF-51, the two-seat training version of the WWII fighter. There was another small seat behind the main pilot seat.

"God, I'd love to," she said. "But I'm not qualified."

Jim rose, placing his beer on the ice chest. "I've only had three swigs, and you've only had two. I say we go fly her."

Bonnie turned, looking at him. It was probably safe enough, if it was his airplane, and he was telling the truth about the beer; but she was still cautious.

"Is it yours?" she asked.

"Yep," said Jim. "I've got a bit over 100 hours in this one, about 200 in a conventional P-51. And compared to your F-22, it would be a piece of cake for you to fly."

Bonnie stared at him. "How on Earth do you know I fly an F-22?"

Jim smiled back at her. "You're Lieutenant Colonel Bonnie Page, test pilot out of Nellis, and qualified on just about every jet in the Air Force. Most recently been flying the F-22 testbed up at Groom Lake. So, I'm pretty confident I can teach you to fly this Mustang *tuit suite*."

Bonnie turned to face him, spread her legs apart and put her hands on her hips, challenging him. "Just who the hell are you and how do you know so much about me?"

"I'm Jim Carter. We can go fly. Then I'll tell you all about it afterward over the rest of this beer. Or you can go on your way now. Your call."

Bonnie glared at him. He just stood there, smiling at her with a goofy kind of smile that was somehow both endearing and infuriating all at the same time.

Something told Bonnie he wasn't bluffing. She had met men like this before - rarely. One thing she had learned – they didn't bluff much. If he said fly or leave, he probably meant it. And she surely did want to fly that Mustang.

"Let's go, flyboy," she hissed, turning back to the TF-51 and walking to the right wingtip, ready to help guide it out of the hangar.

With a grin, Jim grabbed the remote for the electric tail wheel tug and went to the tail of the Mustang. Pressing a switch on the remote, the electric tug started pulling the aircraft out of the hangar tail first, making a low whine, while Bonnie watched the wingtip to make sure they cleared the TBM.

AFTERGLOW

Bonnie screamed with joy as she threw the Mustang into yet another split-s, then dived from 25,000 feet until she started to feel the effects of compressibility on the controls and had to back off, gingerly pulling the plane out of its dive. She shook her head in sheer exultation as the Mustang responded, giving a little buffet as it started to pull out. As it leveled off, she pushed the throttle up until they were cruising again at 4,000 feet.

"I love this plane!" she yelled at the top of her lungs.

In front of her in the cockpit, Jim turned down the volume on the intercom, grinning.

"I get it, but try not to burst my eardrums, if you don't mind," he called.

"Oh, sorry," called Bonnie, modulating her voice to a more normal volume. "Are you OK?"

"Sorry, I'm deaf now, you'll have to use sign language," she heard from the front cockpit. She laughed.

"You've created a monster!" she said.

"I don't doubt it," said Jim. "OK, head back to the traffic pattern, we'll do three landings and call it a day."

"Roger, back to the field," said Bonnie, disappointed but happy. She turned the Mustang back toward Deseret. In a few minutes, they came over the field at altitude and she turned into the traffic pattern. Jim called out her numbers - throttle settings and airspeeds - and she started a descent for landing. In a matter of minutes, she was lined up on short final to Runway 27.

"Keep your speed up, don't let it sink, watch your sight picture," she heard over the intercom. "Looking good. Keep the tail up, wheel it on. Don't let the tail drop. OK, 35 inches, easy now, let it get flying again, ease the power back in…"

With a roar, the engine spooled back up and Bonnie completed her first touch and go, just touching the main wheels to the runway then taking off again.

Making her way around the traffic pattern, she did another

touch and go, almost veering off the runway from the torque of the big Merlin engine when she pushed throttle in too quickly; but she managed to get it under control and off the ground without disaster.

"Now you see what I was telling you," said Jim from the front. "You can't throw a lot of throttle at it suddenly; it'll torque on you. Just ease it back in, a nice smooth increase until you're flying again. Never slam that throttle forward near the ground, or you'll be upside down in the weeds. Remember that."

Bonnie nodded. "Not like an F-22, that's for sure," she replied. They made another circuit around the pattern and she set up on final once more.

"We'll do a full stop this time and call it a day," Jim said from the front seat.

"Roger," said Bonnie. She dropped flaps and got the Mustang headed for the numbers. She pulled the throttle back a bit more on short final, realizing she was a bit 'hot.' Wheeling the plane onto the runway, she let the speed bleed off until the tail came down. Working her feet hard, she kept the taildragger on track down the runway, made the turnoff, and crossed the hold-short line to the taxiway.

"Wow!" she said. "Fucking wow!"

"Yep," Jim said from the front. "That's what most people say. Keep making your s-turns until we get to the hangar. Left here... that's it...awesome."

Parking in front of the big white hangar, Bonnie listened as Jim talked her through the shutdown sequence. The silence after the big Merlin turned off was deafening. Jim had wound back the canopy as they taxied in. Now they just sat there in place.

She knew what he was feeling – just savoring the moment, in no rush to climb out. No words were necessary.

Finally, after a minute, she heard him say from the front: "I guess we ought to get out." She sighed and nodded her head. "I guess," she said.

Jim climbed out on the wing, then helped her out of the rear cockpit. She went to the front of the wing and athletically slid down to the ground, landing on her feet. She stepped aside and Jim did likewise, landing beside her.

Bonnie looked at him, seeing something unexpected. An attractive man, the kind of man she liked, looking back at her with a shy smile. Bonnie suddenly felt very shy herself. She turned away, looking out at the airfield for a moment.

With hardly a word, they put the plane away, then resumed their seats in the recliners by the ice chest. Jim pulled two fresh beers out of the cooler and handed her one. She opened it and drank silently, as did Jim.

Finally, she looked at him. "That was almost a holy experience," she said.

Jim nodded. "I know. No matter how many times I fly her, it's always the same. It's like going to church."

* * * * *

Bonnie's train of thought returned to the last conversation they had before they pulled the plane out of the hangar.

"OK, flyboy," she said. "How do you know who I am and all that?"

Jim glanced over at her and pointed to a barely visible wireless earpiece in his right ear.

"I have a friend who tells me things. She has a knack for finding out information."

"Hmm..." said Bonnie. "I'd like to meet this friend of yours."

"I know," said Jim. "But that will depend."

"Depend on what?" asked Bonnie.

"On how our courtship goes."

Bonnie half-grinned. "Oh, are we courting?"

Jim nodded. "If I get permission."

Bonnie's half-grin turned into a full-on grin.

"Let me get this straight. You're asking for permission to court me."

"I am," Jim replied.

Bonnie placed her beer down on top of the ice chest.

"OK," said Bonnie. "Let's see if you're qualified. Are you financially stable?"

"Yes," said Jim. "Always have a Mustang tucked into a hangar somewhere."

"Any girlfriends lurking in the wings?"

Jim shook his head. "Nope. None."

"Good," said Bonnie. "Are you hale and hearty?"

Jim nodded some more. "No known diseases or conditions. Run fifteen miles a week."

Bonnie sniffed. "I do thirty. You may have to up your game."

She reached for her beer and took another drink. "OK. Why me?"

Jim grinned. "You mean aside from your horribly distorted body?"

Bonnie couldn't help but smile. Jim thought for a moment. "I've always been drawn to intelligence, competence, and spirit. That's a combination that's hard to find. I saw your competence today flying the Mustang. You didn't just fly it. You mastered it. And when you screamed with joy going over the top of that last loop, I knew you had the spirit."

"Well, what makes you think I have the intelligence?"

Jim looked at her. "You found what you were looking for today. And you didn't have much to work with."

Bonnie looked at him, seriously. "You say I've found it. What have I found? Who is your friend that tells you things?"

"Patience, my dear," said Jim, reaching to lift a fresh beer out of the ice chest. "As I said earlier, it depends."

"Ah," said Bonnie. "I see. Blackmail. If you don't get permission to date me, I don't get to meet your friend."

"No, that's not what I mean," Jim replied. "You can still meet my friend, either way. No blackmail. But down one path, you meet her, then you never see her again. And you go on with your life, your curiosity satisfied. You should take that path if you are happy with your life as it is now."

Bonnie looked down at her boots, thinking. "And the other path?"

"On the other path, I suspect you'll have a life of adventure beyond your wildest dreams. But not without risks. Your life could be in danger from time to time. And it's not outside the realm of possibility that you could die alone, far from home."

A chill ran down Bonnie's back. Not from fear; from the intensity of the moment, as she realized this man somehow knew what she was searching for…and it was real.

Suddenly she knew, deep in her bones.

It was not her imagination.

Still looking at her boots, Bonnie asked, "How do I choose?"

"You don't choose now. That will happen later. But be prepared. I'm thinking it may come suddenly. There may not be much time to decide. That's why I'm telling you now."

Looking up, Bonnie stared into the intense eyes of the man before her.

"You have permission to court me."

She stood up. "But not tonight. I'm tired, and I need to find a hotel room."

With his left hand, Jim gestured toward the upper part of the hangar, behind him. "My apartment is on the second floor, south side, over there," he said. He gestured toward the opposite side of the upper floor, behind Bonnie. "There's a spare apartment up there on the north side. Good locks on the doors. You'll be safe."

Bonnie nodded. "Good enough, flyboy. I'll take you up on that."

Jim escorted her to the spare suite, which was more than a bedroom. It contained a large master bedroom, a small study, and a full kitchen, all arranged linearly down the side of the second floor of the hangar – a common arrangement in large aircraft hangars. Jim left for his side of the hangar, but not without a long look at her as he handed her the key. "Sleep tight," he said.

Bonnie went to get her kit out of the Raptor and laid her things out in the bedroom, then inspected the kitchen. It was well-stocked. She made bacon and eggs for dinner, a favorite of hers, then watched TV for an hour. She went to bed about eleven.

But she tossed and turned.

At first, she couldn't understand why sleep wouldn't come. She knew she was tired. Surprisingly, she wasn't thinking about the crazy-fast aircraft she suspected was hidden somewhere on the field. She was thinking about the man she had just met.

It took a while, but about midnight it hit her suddenly. She was way overdue. She needed a man. She wanted this man. She wanted him tonight. She wanted him right now.

Getting up, she slipped on her shirt, didn't bother with pants, and left the apartment. Going down the stairs on the north side of the hangar, she walked across in the dark, ducking past the tail of the TBM and the nose of the A-4, past the Pitts Special, and up the stairs of the south side. She banged on the door of his apartment until a light flicked on. Jim came to the door, barefoot, wearing his jeans, without a shirt. Bonnie noticed several scars on his chest. He looked at her, puzzled.

"I forgot one thing. If you are going to court me," she said. "I have to inspect the equipment."

Jim stared at her, not quite comprehending. Bonnie pointed down at his jeans.

"The equipment. I need to inspect it."

Bonnie reached forward, grabbed the front of Jim's jeans, and popped the snap open. She took the zipper and pulled it down, staring up at Jim with her green eyes blazing.

Jim suddenly understood what she meant. Frozen, he couldn't move as she stripped his jeans down to his ankles. Moments later, he let out a groan. Still holding him in just the right place, Bonnie pushed him backwards into the apartment.

* * * * *

The sun came blasting through the east window of Jim's bedroom. Bonnie lay in the tangled sheets, opening one eye but shutting it quickly. After several minutes of trying to ignore it, she sat up, gave the Sun an extended middle finger, and got out of bed. She went to the bathroom, took a long shower, put on her shirt, and walked into the kitchen.

Jim was standing at the stove, fully dressed in Western snap shirt and jeans, cooking. He turned to her.

"Good morning, flygirl. Don't they make you get up early in the Air Force?"

"Not after night maneuvers," said Bonnie. She glanced at the clock on the wall. "Crap! It's only eight AM! What the hell's the matter with you?"

"I was hungry," said Jim. "After all, I worked pretty hard last night."

Bonnie smiled. "You did that, flyboy. No complaints in that department. You definitely passed inspection."

Jim slid a plate of ham and eggs in front of her, along with a saucer containing two pieces of buttered toast. Then he put a cup of hot coffee beside it and pointed to the cream already on the table.

Bonnie groaned. "Oh my God, thank you! I could eat a small horse!"

Jim sat down across from her with an identical plate. They tucked in and were silent for a bit.

Jim couldn't help but glance at the beautiful woman across from him as he ate. She was without a doubt the most beautiful woman he had seen in a long time. Blond, short military style haircut, green eyes. Tall. Intelligent face, a smile on her lips at the slightest excuse. She caught him looking and grinned at him. Embarrassed, he grinned back and then focused on his meal.

After a couple of minutes, Jim looked back at her.

"I thought maybe two more hours in the Mustang this morning while it's cool, then I'll sign you off for solo and you can go play for a while on your own. What do you think?"

Bonnie gazed at him in delight. "You are pretty good at this courtship thing, you know."

Jim continued. "And when you get back, we'll talk about my friend."

"Jade, meet Bonnie," said Jim.

<Hello, Bonnie. Nice to meet you. Sorry about jamming your device the other night>

Bonnie hesitated a second, then recovered. "That's alright, Jade. No problem. I understand."

Am I talking to a spaceship? thought Bonnie. *Is this real?*

Bonnie stood in the center of the bridge of the starship, somewhat in awe of her surroundings.

She had spent two hours with Jim, flying the Mustang, until he declared her qualified to fly solo. Then he gave it to her, and she took off on her own, spending another hour in lovely aerobatics, and sometimes just flying along happily, gazing at the mountains on both sides of the valley. Finally, she came back to the field, landed, and they put the plane away. Knowing she would be tired, Jim had prepared a simple lunch in his apartment, and they ate.

Bonnie was unsure if she had ever been happier. She had experienced many relationships, that was true. Some of them had even been semi-happy. But most of them had been a bust - usually, a rich man who wanted her for a trophy, or just a conquest. She had grown tired of the game and had almost quit playing.

But this guy, thought Bonnie. *This guy might be the real deal.* She liked him. She thought she might give this a chance.

After lunch, he pushed back and gazed across the table at her.

"Ready for dessert?" he asked.

"What's for dessert?" Bonnie asked coyly, thinking this might be a come-on for more sack time.

"A starship," said Jim.

Bonnie just stared at him. Then:

"Are you serious?"

"Serious as death," Jim replied. "You wanted to meet my friend. That's who she is. An actual, living starship."

"You mean she is alive?"

"Yes, for all practical purposes. She's an advanced AI, with her own feelings, emotions, needs, personality, everything. Just like a human. Except her body is a starship."

"Oh my God, Jim, you have got to be kidding me."

"Not kidding. Ready to meet her?"

Bonnie nodded. "I guess…but this is huge! Who else knows about this?"

"Nobody," said Jim. "You and me."

Jim took Bonnie out of the main hangar and across the tarmac to another large red hangar on the northeast corner of the field, facing south. He opened the small side door and waved Bonnie in. She entered, looking around in the darkness. Jim came in behind her, shut the door and flipped on the overhead lights.

Bonnie saw a massive wall of plastic sheeting hung from ropes in front of her. The plastic looked freshly installed and formed a second compartment inside the hangar, one that looked large enough to contain an airliner.

"Around here," said Jim.

Bonnie nodded. Jim led her around the inner wall until they came to a section where he stopped, holding up the plastic for Bonnie. Looking through, Bonnie saw a matte black surface, so close to the plastic it was like a second layer. On the black surface was a round hatch, which suddenly flipped inward, revealing an entrance.

Bonnie looked at Jim. He nodded and gestured her to precede him into the opening.

Bonnie slowly went through the hatch and into a passageway, noting that the walls seemed the same material as the exterior. Cabinets lined both sides of the passageway. About four yards in, she came to another hatch, which was open.

Entering that one, she found herself standing at the rear of a starship bridge. She stopped, frozen at the sight.

Jim came in behind her and pointed toward the front of the bridge, where three consoles covered in inert displays ran across the front of the bridge. Between them and the console were four chairs, three in front at the console levels, one behind slightly elevated. Above the consoles stretched a wall-to-wall wraparound display screen, currently off. In the space over the center of the bridge, an orange-tinted ball of light sat silently - a holotank, Bonnie realized. On the sides of the bridge were other screens, and two more chairs, one on each side.

Then Jim introduced her to Jade.

* * * * *

<I was lax letting you pick us up> said Jade. <When we were coming in from Canada. I should have seen you sooner - but I was preoccupied with navigation and control using limited processing power, so I missed you at first glance. As soon as I realized you were painting us on your display, I turned towards Area 51, hoping you'd think I was an advanced military aircraft unknown to you. But it didn't work, I see>

Bonnie grinned. "No, not quite. I didn't buy it. It was the impossible turn you made that gave you away. Even the most advanced aircraft in existence still has to obey the laws of physics. No aircraft made by humans could have turned that quickly."

<Yes, I knew I made a mistake as soon as I did it. But, I'm not perfect. Just almost>

Bonnie laughed. It was like talking to a human.

Jim had already explained to Bonnie that Jade was severely damaged; her core compute processes were running at only 5%, and her tDrive - the word she used for her star drive - was completely destroyed. Jade could fly in atmosphere, and probably make it to the moon or Mars if she had to, using a separate drive - called a system drive - that worked for propulsion inside a solar system. But that was about all. It would take several months to rebuild her processor core and her tDrive, making her fully functional.

"But...what happened to you?" asked Bonnie. "Who did this

to you?"

<The Singheko> responded Jade. <They are an aggressive species, a true blight on the Orion Arm of the galaxy. When they discover a new species reaching a high technological level, they either enslave them or destroy them to prevent competition>

<In the case of Earth, through sheer good luck, we discovered you before they did. My squadron was assigned to this solar system to monitor you and protect you. And it's a good thing we were here, because in 1947 by your calendar, three Singheko scout ships found you. They would have reported back to their home world and within a few years, they'd have come back and that would have been the end of Earth>

<But we - my squadron - intercepted them and fought them, just outside the orbit of your Moon. We destroyed all three of them. Unluckily, I was the only survivor of my squadron. I crashed into the Anderson River in the Northwest Territory of Canada>

"But...why are you hiding in this hangar?"

Turning to Jim, Bonnie crinkled up her forehead. "Why not just reveal her to the world and get help from the scientists or the military to repair her?"

Jade responded first.

<Jim and I discussed it. But we both agree that in my current condition, the government would have little trouble capturing me. Whoever had possession of me would then sequester me away, taking me apart piece by piece. And then all the powers would fight over my technology, probably creating a new cold war. Maybe a hot war. This would prevent me from returning to my people and warning them the Singheko are nosing around this area and that help is needed here>

<And another reason - humanity is not ready for the stars. There are a lot of other species out there, and not all of them are friendly. Trying to reverse-engineer me and go out exploring without the assistance of my people would be a disaster. It could lead to humanity's extinction>

Jim jumped in.

"I had the same thought when I first found Jade. I thought we should call the military, call the government, get some help. But Jade convinced me that would be a disaster. So, we've decided to patch Jade up to the point she can return home to her people. They're called the Nidarians, right, Jade?"

<Correct. My people, the Nidarians, live on a planet about seven hundred light years away>

Bonnie considered.

"So, we repair you..." she said. "Then you depart to your home world and get help for us, to defend us against the Singheko."

<Correct> responded Jade. <I'll go warn my people the Singheko are scouting around this area and represent a danger to humanity. They'll send a fleet to defend you, and to bring you up to speed on our technology in a more natural way, over a period of dozens of years. This will allow you to mature into the galactic neighborhood in a controlled way, without stumbling across the Singheko or any of the other dangerous species in the galaxy>

"OK. So I buy that. So how do we repair you?" Bonnie asked.

<First, we bring my processor core back to full operational capability. Right now, as you saw, I'm just barely able to fly in atmosphere. And I'm certainly not fully capable of hiding from my enemies>

Bonnie nodded. "And after that?"

<Then we repair the stardrive - the tDrive. For that, we'll need a supersolid - He4 cooled to below 0.2 Kelvin - and it takes a considerable amount of materials and work to build the reactor for that. Before we can even get started on that, I have to build an android who can do some of the more detailed work on the reactor>

"An android?" a shocked Bonnie asked. "You're going to build an android?"

<Yes, of course. It's quite simple, given the right materials>

Bonnie looked at Jim. "Did you know about this?"

Jim grinned back at her. "Yep. We've decided his name

should be Andy. Andy the Android."

Bonnie punched him in the shoulder. "You are nuts, do you know that?"

She turned back to the front viewscreen, with the three large control consoles before it and the captain's chair behind. For some reason, it seemed more natural to talk to the front of the ship when addressing Jade.

Bonnie thought about it for a second - it was absolutely ridiculous - but it just made her more comfortable talking to the intelligence that was the ship by looking at the front.

"This is all very strange," she said.

Jim nodded. "Tell me," he added.

But Jade jumped in.

<Are you ready to get to work, human Bonnie? I need a new processing core and a new tDrive; it's going to take a lot of material we don't have readily available, and a lot of work to get it installed. Starting with fifty pounds of lithium>

"I'm ready," said Bonnie, uncertainly. "Just tell me what to do!"

BLUEBOOK

General Mark Rodgers had been a weapons specialist and technology investigator for the Pentagon for more than thirty years. And he was good at it. His main focus was advanced weapons evaluation, especially the weapons of foreign powers.

But Mark also had a side portfolio. One that had been, officially, shut down. Discontinued. Defunct.

Bluebook.

Officially terminated in 1970 after the Condon Report had concluded there was no such thing as a UFO or alien presence, the records had been filed away, gone and largely forgotten except by a few conspiracy theorists.

Except for a few special records. A small number of very special records, transferred to a new project. His little side project.

Records that identified an alien escape pod found in the desert in 1947. The ones that succinctly described a black, six-seat escape pod, smashed into the desert floor. And six bodies - still strapped into the little pod.

Mark thought about those records, tucked away where only he and very few others could access them. They described the crashed escape pod in great detail.

It was a simple design, really. Just six seats around the circumference of the pod, each with straps and handles. A tiny control panel in front of one seat. A retro engine in the back to slow the pod down for re-entry, a simple computer to maintain a descent trajectory. Tanks containing an atmosphere that was almost - but not quite - the same as Earth.

And the six bodies.

Five of which were very, very dead.

The other was not quite dead - she lived just a bit longer. She managed to breathe out a few sentences, in English, which were buried deep within the most classified document in Mark's possession.

"We tried to watch over you. But they found us. We destroyed them this time. But hide from them. They will destroy you if they find you. The Singheko..."

Mark walked to his office in the Pentagon, head down in thought. His aide trundled along behind, careful not to interrupt him. When he was head down and thinking like this, it was best to leave him alone.

There was only one reason Mark was thinking about this today. Normally, he could go months, years even, without thinking about his side portfolio.

But not today.

All because of NORAD. The North American Aerospace Defense Command at Petersen Air Force Base in Colorado Springs. Damn it all to hell, they had really ruined his morning.

NORAD had forwarded him a report. Not just any report; a special report, for his eyes only.

About an object entering the atmosphere over southern Nevada at 1:45 AM last Friday, traveling at Mach 4.9. A speed of just about 3,758 mph.

At first, it was assumed to be a meteor burning up in the atmosphere. Pretty slow for a meteor, but the only reasonable explanation.

Until it made a hard left turn over Goldfield and headed for Area 51.

Although it was tracked for only another 6 seconds before it was lost, it was clearly not a meteor. Not unless a meteor had a pilot.

Oh, it was stealthy. Very stealthy. Just not quite stealthy enough. The Air Force was experimenting with some new phased-array radars out there at Groom Lake, and their sensitivity and coverage was outstanding.

So Mark had a hot potato on his hands. Not a smoking gun. But certainly a very warm one. And now he had two big problems to solve...

What was it? And where did it go?

* * * * *

"Wow! I never knew forty pounds of ruthenium would be so damn expensive!" said Bonnie.

Jim sympathized. "Jade sure does have some exotic needs. Getting a pet dog would have been so much cheaper."

<I heard that> said Jade.

Jim and Bonnie were sitting on the bridge of the starship, working on their laptops, assembling another order of materials needed by Jade to rebuild her processor core and tDrive.

Bonnie laughed. "Jade, you are damn lucky you were found by Jim and he has money. I'd never be able to afford you!"

<Don't worry, Bonnie. I'm replenishing Jim's funds faster than you spend the money>

"What?" asked Bonnie. "How the hell are you doing that?"

<Easy> said Jade. <I'm trading in the stock market. I bought a shell corporation, set up online accounts, and so far, I've made $80 million dollars>

"Holy fucking shit, Jade!" yelled Bonnie, looking up from her laptop. "How are you doing that?"

<Buy low, sell high> replied Jade.

Bonnie almost fell out of her chair laughing. "You crack me up, Jade."

<Hopefully, that's not something that hurts>

"So we'll have the ruthenium in another week," said Bonnie. "Assuming it ships on time."

<Outstanding. Then we'll have everything we need for my tDrive. I'm processing the lithium and iridium now in the 3D synthesizer. But I still need to complete the android to assemble the tDrive reactor. It requires a fine touch that humans don't have. And more radiation resistance>

"And how's Andy the Android coming?" asked Jim. "The physical part of him in the 3D synthesizer looks complete."

<Yes; physically the android is done. But I'm still programming it. Another few hours and he'll be ready>

Bonnie looked up from her laptop. "Oh, I'm excited to see it. You said it will be like talking to a real person?"

<Yes; it will be just like talking to a real person>

Jim thought, a puzzled look on his face. "Does that mean it's sentient? Conscious?"

<Of course. Why wouldn't it be?>

Bonnie shook her head. "It can't be sentient. It's artificial."

<I'm artificial. Do you doubt my sentience?>

"That's different," said Bonnie. "You were...*made*...by an advanced species, right?"

<I see you can't say the word *created* in reference to me. Is that because of the thing you call religion?>

Bonnie puzzled over that for a few seconds. "I...guess. I never thought about it before now."

<So according to you, I was made, but not created...>

Jim reached out, placed a hand on Bonnie's shoulder, but spoke to Jade.

"I think humans have a bit of a problem accepting that sentience can be so easily created in a...in a machine, so to speak."

<Does that upset you very much?"

Jim shook his head. "Not me. But I can't speak for Bonnie."

Bonnie considered it.

"Actually, it does upset me a bit. And I'm not sure why. Lord knows I haven't been inside a church in twenty years. But I'm having trouble accepting you can throw a few hundred pounds of materials into a 3D synthesizer and out pops a sentient android."

<But I believe that is exactly what you humans do. You throw a few hundred pounds of materials into a 3D synthesizer - called a womb - over a nine-month period, and out pops a human. How is this any different?>

Bonnie shrugged her shoulders. "It's just different. We aren't machines."

"Says you," interjected Jim, still leaning over his laptop.

<Well> said Jade. <Then I suspect you are going to have even more of a problem with the second project I've been working on. The clone in the medical bay>

"What?" Jim and Bonnie yelled simultaneously. "A what?"

<I'm creating a clone in the medical bay. For when I leave Earth to return to my native species. I've learned to like humans and I don't want to be alone>

"I've got to see this," exclaimed Jim. He jumped up and trotted down the corridor to the medical bay, Bonnie right at his heels. He opened the door and looked inside.

The medical pod was closed but appeared to be in operation based on the subdued blue light coming out of it. Jim and Bonnie walked over and looked.

Inside they could see a human female, in appearance about twenty-five years old, sleeping peacefully in the medical pod.

* * * * *

"Jade, what the hell are you doing? You can't just create a human being!" yelled Bonnie, standing in the medical bay.

<Sure I can. What's the problem?>

Jim put his hands on the top of his head in exasperation. "Let me try," he said to Bonnie.

He turned and paced across the room, still staring at the young woman in the medical pod.

"Jade, humans view life as sacred. We have a real problem with creating artificial life. What you're doing here is a big concern for us."

<I'm completely familiar with artificial life> said Jade. <I am one>

"That's not what I meant, Jade. I meant artificial human life!"

<It's not artificial> said Jade. <I took fifty pounds of carbon, three pounds of phosphorus, three pounds of calcium and two pounds of potassium, along with a lot of other trace elements and water, and fed them into the 3D synthesizer. Then I let DNA

do most of the rest of the work. How is that artificial? There's not a circuit board or resistor in her anywhere!>

"But...for God's sake, Jade! You can't just create a...a woman...like this!" shouted Bonnie.

<Oops, too late> said Jade. <I already did. Do we have to throw her away?>

Jim held up both hands to the overhead speaker, as if to fend Jade off.

"No! No, you can't do that. Don't even say it!"

Bonnie walked in a circle around the room, still staring at the sleeping woman in the medpod. Each time her circle passed the woman, she paused for a second and then spouted a curse.

"Dammit!" she said, completing a circle.

Jim fell silent, watching her. He was at a loss.

"Crap!" Bonnie said, completing a second circle around the room.

"Son of a bitch!" Bonnie exploded, completing her third circle.

Finally, she stopped and glared up at the camera over the door where Jade would be watching them.

"And how did you even do this?" asked Bonnie. "You don't have any hands, not yet, not until the android is complete. How did you even get the materials into the 3D synthesizer? And then how did you get the...whatever...her...into the medpod?"

<You put the raw materials into the hoppers for me, don't you remember? Ten days ago, when the first batch of raw materials came in. I asked you to sort them into the various hoppers and you did>

"God, yes, I remember that," said Jim. "I thought you were just working on the core processor."

<And if you look closely, you'll see the medpod has motorized wheels. When the product was nearly finished, I sent the medpod over to the 3D synthesizer and moved the product into it. Then I brought it back here>

"She's not a product!" Bonnie almost yelled it.

<Sorry. I meant her>

"She's not a 'her'!" yelled Bonnie again.

Jim once again placed a calming hand on Bonnie's shoulder. "Bonnie, calm down. You're getting upset."

"Dammit, yes, I am upset!" Bonnie turned and walked to a chair in the corner, sat down, and put her head in her hands.

Jim went over and squatted beside her, put his hands on her back, and started rubbing in a calming motion.

"Why is this upsetting you so?" he asked. "Is this causing you some kind of religious freakout?"

"No," an exasperated Bonnie Page said. "Not that. I'm not really sure why. It's freaking me out, though. I just don't know why."

Jim patted her on the back.

"We'll deal with it. Just calm down. I'm going to ask Jade some more questions."

Bonnie nodded silently. Jim rose and turned, looking at the camera which to him, represented Jade.

"Jade, when will she wake up?"

<In about a week>

"Will she be able to speak?"

<Yes. She'll be fully formed, an educated adult able to cope with her environment>

"Educated. How do you mean?"

<She will have all the knowledge that you have, as well as that of Bonnie>

"What?" Bonnie's head snapped up, glaring at the camera.

<I synthesized her brain by combining all the knowledge from Jim's brain and yours, Bonnie> said Jade. <She will be a combination of both you and Jim>

"What the fuck?" moaned Bonnie from the corner. "Somebody wake me up..."

Jim glanced at Bonnie, then turned back to Jade and continued his questioning.

"When you say all the knowledge, you mean you scanned our brains and then copied it to hers?"

<Basically, yes>

"So she will know everything I know?"

<Yes>

"And everything Bonnie knows?"

<Yes>

"But just our knowledge, right? Not our...other stuff..."

<She will have your knowledge, your skills, and your memories>

"Crap, crap, crap," Jim heard from the corner.

Jim spoke somewhat uncertainly.

"Our...memories?"

<Yes. She has to have memories, or she would go insane as soon as she wakes up. All adult sentients have to have memories, in order to form a concept of themselves and their history. So, I put in all Bonnie's memories, and most of your memories, Jim. I did pare away some of the more horrifying ones from your wartime experiences, and I did remove some of the ones that would have caused disassociation disorders, where the two of you had widely divergent concepts about some things. Everything else - all that which would not harm her - I kept>

CONTINGENCY PLANS

This one was different. Mark could feel it in his bones. The call he had just completed with Nellis Air Force Base confirmed it.

I need to take this seriously, Mark thought. *That new TAD device recorded exactly the same thing as NORAD.*

According to the officer who just got off the phone with him, their confidence in this sensor data was high. It was backed up by secondary radar in the F-117 target plane. Lieutenant Broderick in the F-117 hadn't noticed it at the time, but the data was there for later analysis on the recording. The F-117 had captured the same impossible target seen by the F-22 TAD device, albeit in less detail and for a shorter period. But it was there.

Then there was the F-22 pilot, Bonnie Page. She had initially called the unknown while in the air, then rapidly backed off. That was not so strange; a lot of pilots would not pursue a UFO report for fear of ridicule. She had laughed it off in the debriefing, telling her wingman Broderick it was just an anomaly in the TAD.

And then she had resigned from the Air Force. Just ten days after the anomaly, she submitted her resignation. A pilot that was at the top of her game, highly regarded, performing desirable work in the Air Force – and she quit.

Her cell phone pings showed a strange pattern. She had gone to Deseret, Nevada on the Saturday after the sighting, and spent five days there. Then she came back to Nellis and flew two routine flights with the TAD test team. Mark had sent out a request for a follow-up interview with her, which she had completed after her second flight on that subsequent Friday. In the interview, she had stuck to her story of an anomaly in the device, and nothing more. When she was pressed on the possibility of a UFO, she laughed it off, and said she didn't believe in them.

After the interview, she had gone back to Deseret for the weekend. On the next Monday, she returned to Nellis and resigned from the Air Force.

Mark had a nose for the central thread of a problem, and Bonnie Page was the central thread for this one. He knew it.

After submitting her resignation, she had gone back to her apartment near Nellis. At least according to her cell phone records.

Then her cell phone disappeared. It hadn't returned to the grid.

She ditched her phone at her apartment and got a burner phone somewhere, thought Mark. *She's in the wind.*

Picking up the phone, he assigned a surveillance team to track her down.

* * * * *

"That is one strange looking android," said Bonnie.

<It's designed for a specific purpose> responded Jade. <To be my hands and feet>

Jim laughed. "Well, it certainly has plenty of those."

Before them stood the android they had named 'Andy.' It stood about two feet tall and had four arms and four hands. Although it had two 'feet,' they were not what Jim would have thought of as feet; they were more like large, flat hands, prehensile, something like a gorilla's feet. Both its arms and legs were multi-jointed, able to assume more positions than a human could ever imagine. Its neck was longer than a human neck, somewhat sinuous. Its head looked like that of a deranged insect; it had dozens of eyes, allowing it to look in any direction.

Jade had told them that 'Andy' could also use the lower pair of his arms as additional feet, assuming a four-legged stance when he needed extra stability. Conversely, he could lie on his back and use his 'feet' as extra hands, becoming six-armed when working in that position.

<He is radiation-hardened and does not require an

atmosphere to survive. He can work in the reactor space without damage> said Jade. <He'll be able to assemble the tDrive while we finish up the processing core>

"Wow!" said Jim. "This is crazy!"

"Well," replied Bonnie, "Is he ready for activation?"

<Yes. I will activate him now>

With a loud click, the android's head stiffened, and he raised up ever so slightly on his legs. Two eyes in front glowed slightly. A voice came from his head.

"Good morning, Bonnie and Jim. Pleased to meet you."

Jim looked at Bonnie before replying.

"Good to meet you too, Andy. How are you?"

"Never better," replied Andy. "Ready to get to work!"

And with that, the android turned and shuffled off down the corridor toward the engineering spaces.

Jim turned to Bonnie and shook his head. Then they laughed.

"We are definitely living in a strange land now!" said Bonnie.

* * * * *

"Jade…would you tell me about your people?"

Bonnie was working on the bridge at one of the consoles. Jade had provided functionality to use the flight consoles as computer workstations, with full Internet access; they no longer had to use their laptops. The little android Andy was already in the reactor room, beginning the process of assembling the new tDrive that would allow the starship to travel beyond the solar system.

<We are called the Nidarians. We are a truly peaceful people. It's hard for us to make war, so the Singheko are a challenge to us. But we are learning>

"What do they look like - your people?"

<They are not much different from you humans. They are bipedal, with arms and legs like yours, and the same basic facial configuration. As are the Singheko, and many other intelligent species in the Galaxy>

"Why is that, do you think?"

<I don't know. Our scientists suspect there is some kind of evolutionary imperative that requires such a general configuration in order for creatures to evolve high intelligence>

Well, they have to make and hold tools with great dexterity, thought Bonnie. *That implies hands or something similar. Highly focused binocular vision helps to create tools and use them. And once you achieve high intelligence, you don't need four legs anymore. You no longer need a highly evolved sense of smell, so the snout can shrink.*

"So, you're telling me that nature prefers space-faring species to be two-legged, two-armed humanoids with small noses?"

<I would say that is the case, based on my experience> replied Jade.

"And what is the galaxy like, out there?"

<Ah. The Galaxy. Well, we call it the Broken Galaxy>

"What? Why? That's a strange name."

<Because we are in a dark age right now. There was a great Empire in the Orion Arm in the past. It was called the Golden Empire. For two hundred centuries it lived, ensuring peace and stability in the Arm. But two thousand years ago it collapsed. Everything fell into decay. Barbarian upstarts fought to take control of the last bits of the old Empire. Many nations were destroyed in that time>

"But not Nidaria?"

<No. We lost most of our territory, but a small remnant held on to our home planet. We sheltered in the city we now call Sanctuary, fighting off the barbarians for a thousand years. Finally, we recovered and began to expand again. But we are still under constant threat of attack from those barbarian nations surrounding us>

"Such as the Singheko."

<Yes. Such as the Singheko >

Just then Jim came into the bridge.

"I've been thinking," he started.

Bonnie interrupted. "Not that again!"

Jim grimaced. "Yes, somebody has to do it!"

Bonnie smiled. "OK, what have you been thinking?"

"We need to work up some contingency plans," said Jim.

Bonnie lost her smile.

"What do you mean by 'contingency plans'?"

"We've been lucky so far," said Jim. "No one has discovered us yet or what we're doing here. But they will. It's just a matter of time. And once they discover Jade, all hell is going to break loose. We need to plan for that."

"You know, you're right," Bonnie agreed. "I'm frankly amazed they haven't found us already. We should go ahead and assume the worst, prepare for it, be ready."

<The first thing I would recommend, if you are willing, is to have me implant communicators in you so our comms can't be interrupted or hacked> said Jade.

"What?" burst out Bonnie. "Did you say, 'in us'?"

<Yes. It's completely painless and non-invasive. You lie in the medpod for an hour. When you get out, we can talk to each other without radios, as long as we are within about one mile of each other. It consists of two micro-thin circular patches about one-fourth inch in width, lying on the surface of your brain. They transmit to a tiny repeater implanted in your lower back. You will not even know they are there>

Bonnie bowed her head, shaking it in apparent disgust.

"Pass. I don't think I want to do that," she said.

Jim patted her on the back.

"How about I go first? Then you can see if there's any cause for concern. If I go berserk or start foaming at the mouth, you'll know not to do it," he laughed.

Bonnie glared at Jim.

"How can you be so blase about this? How are you not upset at the very idea? You treat all this like it was some kind of a joke!"

Jim gave a negative head shake. "No, not a joke. I'm just not afraid of Jade. I trust her. But remember, I've been with her longer than you have. She saved my life up in Canada. She's had every opportunity to hurt me, and she's never done it. I don't believe she would do anything to damage my body, at least not without warning me first."

Bonnie sighed.

"I guess I'm just not there yet," she said.

Jim placed his hand on Bonnie's shoulder and squeezed.

"Jade, I'll go first. We'll do it at the end of the day, when I'm already tired, so lying in the medpod for an hour won't be so boring. How's that?"

<Sounds good, Jim. I'll prepare everything for you>

"So what other contingency plans do we need?" asked Bonnie, looking at Jim.

Jim mused on it.

"We need an emergency sortie plan; in case they raid the place. An escape plan, a place to meet afterward in case we get separated, a communications plan so we can find each other. And a long-term plan for each of us, in case the other is killed."

Bonnie shuddered. "I don't want to think about that."

"We have to," said Jim. "It's a possibility. Any nation on Earth would kill to get this technology. If Jade doesn't get back to Sanctuary, humanity could be overcome. We have to succeed in getting her back into space and help her get to Sanctuary. The lives of every human on this planet are at stake."

Bonnie stood and paced.

"So once again, I ask: why don't we seek help to get this done from the military? Or from the government?"

"Who would you ask first; the Air Force? What do you think they would do?"

Bonnie stopped her pacing and thought about it.

"No. They'd take her someplace and take her apart, piece by piece, to find out what makes her tick. No chance they'd let her go back home."

"And then what would happen?" continued Jim.

Bonnie turned to face him.

"And the Singheko would find us, and we'd be at their mercy, without the help of Jade's people."

"So let's explore the other possibilities. How about calling in the FBI?"

Bonnie shook her head. "Same thing. They'd turn her over to the military. Same result."

"NSA?"

Bonnie glared at Jim. "You've made your point, I think."

"The Russians? The Chinese? Other people who want to take over the world?"

"Now you're just being stupid."

Jim stood up and embraced her.

"Then let's get real and make some contingency plans."

Bonnie nodded. "What first?"

"First, I think, a way to bust Jade out of here in case they raid us. I think I'll put shaped charges on the back wall of the hangar, to shatter it instantly and provide an exit for her if she needs to leave suddenly. I can take care of that. I still have friends in low places."

"OK. I'll put together the part about a place to meet afterward in case we get separated, and the emergency comm plan. And the plan…well…if one of us is killed."

"Good," Jim responded. "Let's do it."

CLOSING IN

That evening, Jim lay in the medpod, his eyes closed. The medpod had injected him with nanobots. Under Jade's direction, they were implanting the comm devices - two tiny circular patches on his brain, and a tiny repeater in his lower back that would provide the required range.

He was beginning to wonder if this was such a good idea after all.

In a greatly troubled youth, Jim had gone through some bad times. He had lost his father at a young age. His mother had been preoccupied with other things in her life. So, Jim had largely raised himself, and his younger sister Gillian.

They had nearly always been alone. Sometimes he had gotten very down, very depressed. At the age of twelve, he read a book about meditation. He tried it, and found it helped him get over the bad times. It brought him out of the darkness.

Like many people who meditate, Jim had a mantra. He used it during meditation to calm his mind, center his soul. It had served him well during the horrors of war in the Middle East and Africa. He had used it in the hospital when he was recovering from the shrapnel in his chest.

He used it now, to ward off his fears and doubts about what Jade was doing to him.

Life will get better. There is light at the end of the tunnel, he chanted in his mind.

There is light at the end of the tunnel.

There is light at the end of the tunnel...

His mind slowly calmed. There was no pain. He felt nothing unusual. Once he got his mind settled, he relaxed. In a minute, he was asleep.

In the corner of the room, sitting in a chair watching him, Bonnie pondered.

When I got involved in this, I had no idea what I was getting into. If I had known, would I have still done it? And can I continue? I don't know if I can do this. Too many strange things…

Bonnie rose from the chair and walked over to the medpod. Inside, Jim was sleeping peacefully.

But…I love him. That I do know. I can't bail now, she thought. *I have to commit to this. Go big or go home.*

Slowly, Bonnie returned to her chair and sat down again.

"Jade, maybe this is a good time for us to talk. I've developed the contingency plan for places to meet if we get separated, and the long range and short range comm plan. I've generated code words for the most likely contingencies that might happen too fast for us to discuss. It's in a folder on your system. Have you reviewed it?"

<Yes. It's a good plan. I'd only make a few minor changes, if you don't mind>

"And what are those?"

<You've overlooked that the clone will be awake soon. So I've added her into the plan at appropriate places>

"Ah, yes. Your Frankenstein in the other medpod. I try to ignore her. How's the cooking coming along?"

<Your analogy is quite funny. The 'cooking' is coming along just fine. She'll be ready in another day. That's why I added her to the planning>

"Fine," snorted Bonnie. "You understand I don't like this idea at all, right?"

<I get it>

* * * * *

"We found them," said the voice on the other end of the line. "They're in Deseret all right, at the airport. Living in a hangar."

"Good work," said Mark Rodgers. "And you've got them under surveillance?"

"Yes," said the voice. "They seem to be keeping entirely to themselves, though. They have two hangars. One is just a normal hangar, full of airplanes, facing west, right down the runway. It's a large white hangar, big one. They keep the main hangar door open most of the time during the day, so we've been able to scope it out, no problem. Haven't seen anything unusual about that one. Lot of nice airplanes, though. Clearly this guy Jim Carter has money."

"And?" said Mark.

"And next to it, facing south, is another big-ass hangar, a red one. That one is closed up tight all the time. They go in and out through a side door, never open it more than just enough to squeeze through. Never seen the front door open. They seem to spend all their time in the red hangar, even at night. They're sleeping in there, evidently, so we haven't tried entry yet. We searched the other one, the white one, last night. All we found are a bunch of airplanes, two apartments up topside that are completely normal, nothing unusual. We went through all their trash, but nothing unusual there. Except one thing about that…"

"What?" asked Mark.

"The trash from the red hangar doesn't go in the normal trash bins. They're receiving a lot of shipments there. They don't dispose of the shipping containers normally. They take the leftover trash from the red hangar and load it up in her Raptor and drive it into town and burn it at the incinerator."

Mark mused thoughtfully.

"It's in the red hangar," he said. "I know it."

"I agree," said the voice. "But now, you want to hear something really interesting?"

"What," said Mark.

"Guess what this guy's sister does," asked the voice.

Mark leaned back in his chair. The man on the other end of the phone was his best covert operative. They had served together, drank together, and ran ops together for thirty years. His name was Pujold Rukmini. He was, without a doubt, the most competent person in Mark's small complement of agents who were fully read into the project. Also the most vicious, when needed. But Mark didn't care about that. Viciousness was another tool he used when required.

"What?" he asked, knowing there was a major surprise

coming.

"CIA," said Pujold. "His little sister is an associate director in the CIA at Langley."

Mark leaned forward again, his eyes widening. "You are shittin' me!"

"Nope. Gillian Carter Hassell. Associate Director in Counterproliferation. I wouldn't kid about that."

"I wonder…" said Mark out loud.

"Me too," said Pujold. "If we could bring her in, and she would cooperate, that would give us a lot of leverage with this guy."

"Or even if she didn't cooperate," said Mark.

"Right."

"But we don't need that yet. We know where the item is, and we can get it. Keep them under tight surveillance. Pull all the shipping records for the materials they are getting into that hangar. And start putting together a capture team."

"Time for the big unveiling, I guess," said Jim.

"Yep," agreed Bonnie. They walked down the passageway toward the medical unit and opened the hatch.

Before them, the medpod held the sleeping woman. She was breathing normally, to all intents sleeping peacefully. Her hair was just stubble, less than an eighth of an inch long. Her lips were thin, her nose as well. In fact, her entire body was thin.

"Is she healthy?" Jim asked.

<Yes. She is quite normal. She will put on more weight once she starts eating normally>

Bonnie leaned over the medpod.

"She's so thin," she said. "Almost like a...shit!"

Bonnie jumped back two feet from the medpod, nearly falling over.

The woman inside the medpod looked at them and smiled.

<Please help her out of the medpod> Bonnie heard Jade speak.

"Jim, help her," said Bonnie, still too shocked to move.

Jim nodded, stepped forward, and lifted the lid of the medpod. The woman reached up, grabbed the lip, and pulled herself to a sitting position. Then she levered one leg over the edge, pushed herself up with her hands, and scrambled out of the device, thumping down to the floor.

She was completely naked.

"Mornin'," said the woman. "It's good to get out of that damn thing."

Jim glanced over at Bonnie.

"Well, she has your nose," he quipped.

"Don't start," replied Bonnie. Bonnie looked at the woman. "How do you feel?"

"Hungry," said the woman. "Is there anything to eat in the galley?"

"Uh...I think we have a few things in there," said Bonnie,

taken aback.

"Great!" said the woman. She promptly marched out the hatch, turned left, took five steps, and turned into the galley. By the time Jim and Bonnie caught up, she was rummaging through the refrigerator.

"So you know your way around..." muttered Bonnie.

The woman looked at her. "Of course. I have all your memories and most of Jim's. So anything you know, I know. Except for some of the bad stuff, I think. Jade told me she left some of that out."

Bonnie sat down at one of the tables, looking puzzled.

"When did you talk to Jade?" she asked.

The woman continued to rummage through the refrigerator, pulling out bread, cheese, meat, and lettuce, and moved it to the counter. She started building a sandwich.

"Jade has spoken to me a number of times over the last week. Remember that you sleep at night. Jade doesn't. So we talk at night when you aren't around. It was part of her educational process, she said. I had to get used to talking. Even though I knew all the words, I didn't exactly have the muscle memory. Or at least, my muscle memory is mostly Bonnie's, and our bodies are different. So I had to adjust."

"You don't seem to have any trouble walking," said Jim.

"Jade let me walk around a couple of times this week at night. It was hard at first, but I got better at it pretty quick."

"Jade, why didn't you tell us about this?" asked Bonnie.

<Oops, sorry. I've been kind of busy lately>

Pensive, Bonnie bit her lip, thinking.

"Do you have a name?" Bonnie asked the woman.

Turning to face them, the woman leaned against the counter, naked, and started eating her sandwich.

"Yes. Jade named me. It was critical to my identity that I have a name as soon as possible during the brain synthesis. My name is Rita."

* * * * *

Bonnie and Jim sat, stunned, as Rita finished one sandwich and started on another.

"You seem so..." Bonnie started, but stopped.

"Normal?" finished Rita. "I am. Remember, I'm you and Jim. Combined. So, I'm as normal as you two are. Which ain't all that normal if you ask me."

"Wait...what?" interrupted Jim. "Are you...is your DNA...are you like, our child?"

Rita laughed. "No, no. Jade didn't use any of your DNA for me. She only used your knowledge, your skills, and your memories. My DNA came from traces she got off the materials in the 3D synthesizer. She sorted through that DNA until she found a combination she liked and used that. So no worries - we're not related!"

Bonnie turned to Jim.

"Can we talk?"

Jim nodded.

"We'll be back in a minute, Rita. Are you OK?"

"Sure," said Rita. "I'll be right here."

Jim led Bonnie out of the room and back to the bridge. Bonnie sat down in one of the command chairs and looked at Jim, her face scrunched up.

"I'm having a lot of trouble with this," she said.

"I can see that," said Jim. He sat down across from her, looking at her. "What seems to be the main issue?"

"Is she actually alive?" asked Bonnie.

"You can see that she is," said Jim.

"I mean, is she actually...human?"

Jim considered. "I would say yes, based on everything I've seen so far."

"But she wasn't born!" Bonnie exclaimed, her voice rising.

"Sure she was," said Jim. "She was born in the 3D synthesizer. Pretend it's a womb. Does that make it any easier?"

"But...she wasn't conceived!"

Jim shook his head. "I've never seen this side of you,

Bonnie. I didn't realize you were so primitive. Of course she was conceived. Jade took human DNA and cloned it. That's no different from being conceived. It's just another way of getting there."

"Bullshit," said Bonnie.

"Think of it this way, Bonnie, if it helps. You want to drive a car from Los Angeles to Las Vegas. For all of history, billions and billions of times, every person who has driven a car from Los Angeles to Las Vegas went on the main highway. Now suddenly you find a new, different highway. You drive on it and it takes you to Las Vegas. Are you there? Did you arrive?"

"It's not the same thing," Bonnie muttered stubbornly.

Jim patted her hand. "It's exactly the same thing. Rita arrived in Las Vegas. How she got there is details. She's there. Accept it."

Bonnie shook her head. "I just don't know if I can. How do I know she has a soul?"

"How do you know you have a soul, Bonnie?" asked Jim softly. "You can't prove it. All you can do is either believe it or not believe it. But you can never prove it. And you can't go through life making decisions for other people on such an imprecise, unknown state of affairs. So in Rita's case, I'm going to act as if she is just like us. No different from us."

Bonnie hung her head in her hands. She knew Jade was listening. She wondered what Jade thought about this discussion.

"OK, I guess," she finally said. "I'll follow your lead. I'll act as if she is just like us."

Jim smiled, reached out to Bonnie, and kissed her. They got up and returned to the galley.

Rita was now sitting at one of the tables. Bonnie went over and sat next to her.

"We need to get you some clothes on."

Rita grinned. "But I like being naked."

Bonnie looked over at Jim. He grinned back at her.

"And I think Jim probably likes you being naked too. Which is exactly why we're going to get some clothes on you."

SURPRISES

An hour later, Rita, Bonnie and Jim sat on the bridge. Rita sat at one of the front consoles, Jim sat at the other, and Bonnie sat in the captain's chair. It had just worked out that way as they came into the bridge.

"So that's the story," said Bonnie, catching Rita up on items that Jade had not been able to pre-load into her memory. "We've developed contingency plans for the most likely scenarios we can think of, and code words, comm plans, meeting places. All of that."

Rita thought deeply for a second. She was now wearing jeans and boots borrowed from Bonnie, as well as one of the blue chambray snap-button shirts Bonnie favored.

"So let me go over this one last time, to make sure I've got it."

"Sure," said Bonnie.

"Code words are always repeated three times if possible. Or else, the code words followed by the phrase 'times three' if time is limited."

"Correct," said Jim.

"So; code words 'Hot Blood' repeated three times - or 'Hot Blood times three' - means we are compromised, raid in progress, do not wait on anyone. Blow the back wall of the hangar and get the hell out of here. Go to rally point Blue and consult the written contingency plan for next steps."

"Correct," said Jim.

"Code words 'Cold Blood' means we are compromised, but there is time to wait for anyone in the immediate vicinity to get on board. Or in other words, we depart in five minutes, no longer. Same deal on the rally point."

"Correct," Jim repeated.

"Code words 'Dead Blood' means both you and Bonnie are captured or dead, and I'm on my own. Get to a rally point and consult the contingency plan."

"Correct," said Bonnie, looking over at Jim with some

sadness in her gaze.

If that one is used, she thought, *then I don't have to worry whether or not Rita has a soul. I'll be worrying about my own.*

"And any other triply-repeated phrase with 'blood' in it means danger, get away," continued Rita.

"So far, so good," said Bonnie. "Good memory."

"Now…comm plan. Use our implants if in range and not compromised. Unless they x-ray us, they shouldn't be aware of them. And even an x-ray may not show much."

"Yep," said Jim. "And Bonnie finally gave in, got her implant. Thank you, Bonnie."

Bonnie nodded. "I don't have to like it, but I did it," she groused.

"If out of range or implants are compromised, call the hidden burner phone voicemail, leave a coded message. If all else fails, use HF frequency 28.07 MHz as primary. Use 292.9 MHz secondary," continued Rita.

Bonnie nodded.

"And finally, rally points. I think I have all of them. Red, Blue, Yellow, Green, and Pink. They all make sense. But I hope it doesn't come to that."

"Let's hope it doesn't," said Jim.

Bonnie sat silently for a moment. Then she raised her head.

"I've been thinking about something," she said.

Jim and Rita looked at her.

"I want to go to Sanctuary with Jade when she leaves," said Bonnie.

Jim sat silently, then gave a smile.

"So do I," he said. "I can't imagine watching Jade depart, staying here on Earth, and not knowing what is happening with her out there in the galaxy."

"Exactly," said Bonnie. "I feel like I've found something that I've been looking for all my life. A chance to really make a difference in the world."

Jim agreed. He turned to look at Rita.

"I'm in," said Rita. "I wouldn't have it any other way."

"Jade?" asked Jim. "What consumables do we need for the three of us to make the trip to Sanctuary with you?"

<Interestingly enough, I've already anticipated this> said Jade. <I was fairly sure this would happen with you three. So everything we need is already onboard>

"Sweet!" exclaimed Bonnie. "The expedition begins!"

*****

Rita and Bonnie spent the rest of the day working on Jade's processor core. Much of the work involved tedious insertion of tiny modules, no larger than a needle, into a matrix that held them in the backplane of the core - which was a cube six feet in dimension. This required them to take turns sitting inside it, one placing the tiny needles while the other passed them in.

"Jade," said Bonnie. "Why didn't you make this thing bigger, so we could fit inside it easier?"

<If you were Nidarian, it would be less trouble. They are smaller than humans> responded Jade.

Hours later, they had completed another wall of the cube, and they were both tired by the time they finished.

"Three walls complete," said Bonnie. "One more to go and we're done. We should finish by noon tomorrow."

"God, that's hard work," said Rita. "I have a lot of memories of doing work, but the actual thing is very tiring, you know?"

Bonnie smiled tiredly. "Yes, I know."

They went into the galley and grabbed coffee.

Bonnie turned to Rita.

"How are you feeling now? Any better since you ate breakfast, second breakfast, lunch, second lunch and early dinner?"

Rita grinned widely. "Now, don't be critical. You try being assembled in a medpod and wake up having never eaten anything in your entire life."

Bonnie sat down with Rita, staring at her.

"What does it feel like?"

Rita looked puzzled.

"What does what feel like?"

"Being...assembled. Waking up in a medpod, completely adult, with full memories, skills, knowledge. No childhood, no parents, no...no anything."

Rita smiled at her.

"You're wrong. I had a full childhood. Yours. And some of Jim's, but mostly yours. I think Jade biased my memories towards yours because we're both female. I can remember every detail of our childhood. I remember our parents, our house, growing up. Everything."

Bonnie shuddered, and stood up suddenly, knocking over her coffee cup.

"You're not me!" she yelled. "You...are...not...me!"

Bonnie stormed out of the room.

Jim came rushing in, looking down the corridor where Bonnie had disappeared into her cabin.

"What was that all about?"

Rita shrugged. "She doesn't care for the fact that her memories are in me."

Jim gazed at Rita for a few seconds. Then he sat down, laying a diagnostic probe on the table, and looked over at her.

"When you say you have our memories, do you...do you have everything?"

Rita smiled. "No, not everything. Jade excised out anything she thought might be harmful to my sanity. Anything that might cause a dichotomy in my psyche. So, for example, almost all of your wartime experiences are either gone or glossed over. I just have vague knowledge of your early childhood; enough to know it was a rough one, but one you survived well enough. And I don't have detailed knowledge of your parents or your family; Jade seems to have given me mostly Bonnie's memories of family and parents. I think Jade thought it would make me more stable as a female. I hope it works."

Jim nodded.

"Me too. But...I have one more question. Or two."

Rita grinned again. "I see where this is going. Yes, I have a complete memory of making love to Bonnie as a male. And a complete memory of making love to you as a female."

"Holy crap," said Jim. "That's really weird."

"Not at all," said Rita. "It's no problem for me."

"I just don't see how that can be."

"Don't you have memories of making love to other women, before Bonnie?"

"Well, yeah, of course. Oh...and you know that already...because you have my memories..."

"Were they all the same?"

"Um...no. Not really. Every woman is different. Which you also know already."

"That's the way it feels to me when I think about being Bonnie with you, or being you with Bonnie. Still making love. Just different."

Jim thought for a while. "But...you are the only person in history, I think, who can compare the two. So which is better? Being a man? Or being a woman?"

Rita laughed. "I don't want to give away all my secrets."

From the hatch, they heard Bonnie's voice.

"Especially don't give away any of mine," she said. Bonnie came into the room and sat down with them.

"I'm sorry, Rita. I want to apologize to you," she said. "I was overwhelmed by this situation. But it's not your fault. I'm sorry I stormed out."

Rita reached out and laid her hand on Bonnie's, left it there.

"Bonnie. It's OK. Believe it or not, I know exactly how you felt."

"I know," said Bonnie. "That's the scary thing." She wrapped her hand around Rita's.

Then Bonnie looked over at Jim.

"And you didn't need to ask Rita that last question. I can tell you - being a woman is better."

Looking back at Rita, Bonnie winked.

"Right?"

Rita winked back.

"Absolutely!"

* * * * *

Next day, Jim went to town to dispose of empty packing cases and trash. On his way there and back, he thought he noticed the same black car several times. His mind working overtime, he kept an eye out for it, but it disappeared, taking a turnoff up into the foothills.

Still, it made him nervous. Pulling back into the airport, he stopped at Perry Barnes' hangar and got out.

Walking around to the front, he found Perry and Randy Green engaged in their usual occupation of sitting in front of the hangar drinking beer. Jim plopped down into an extra chair and Perry handed him a beer. They sat companionably for a few minutes, watching the hawks float around the stubble fields next to the airport, and the occasional car pass by on the highway.

"Been keeping pretty close to your secret project there in the red hangar, I notice," said Perry.

Jim smiled somewhat chagrined.

"Yeah, sorry. Didn't mean to be rude, just been busy."

"What're ya building in there, Jim? A spaceship?"

Jim giggled at the irony of Randy's question.

"Yep. Me and E.T. are in there putting together the next Moon shot."

Perry winked at Randy.

"I bet he ain't puttin' nothin' together but him and that Air Force gal he found."

Jim hung his head in mock embarrassment, then grinned back at them.

"Yeah, you got me. Hate to confess. But you gotta admit, she's the real deal."

Randy nodded vigorously. "Damn straight. What a stunner!"

Jim took a good long swig of beer and looked out across the

field, then swept his gaze up into the foothills overlooking the airport.

"Say, you guys seen any strange cars or people hanging around the airport lately?"

Perry looked back at Jim.

"Well, now that I think about it, I did see some guys yesterday."

"Really? Where?"

"Sitting in a jacked-up white pickup, down the road from your hangar about a half-mile. I wouldn't even have noticed them, except I had to drive down the road to feed my cows."

"What were they doing?"

"Just sittin.' I didn't see anything else. Just two guys sitting in a pickup."

"Well, nothing too strange about that around here," said Jim. "Guys go out to feed stock all the time."

"Yeah," said Perry. "But you gotta be at a pasture gate to feed stock. And that's what was strange about it. There was no gate anywhere around."

"Ah," said Jim.

"City boys," laughed Perry.

After a while, and another beer, Jim waved goodbye to Perry and Randy and climbed back into the Raptor. He drove down to the other end of the field, parked behind the red hangar, and sat for a minute, staring down the road.

He didn't see anything, but he didn't expect to; if they were truly under surveillance, they'd be using satellites and drones, more likely, rather than a couple of guys sitting in a pickup.

He finally got out of the truck, walked around to the side door, entered the hangar, and went into the ship. It was quiet. Wondering where Bonnie and Rita were, he checked the bridge, then the galley, but found no sign of them. He was just about to cross over to the other hangar when he heard a giggle from Bonnie's cabin. Pushing open the hatch, he stared.

Bonnie and Rita were tangled in the sheets on Bonnie's bed, in the throes of sex, completely oblivious to his presence.

"I believe it's called '*In Flagrante*'", said Rita, not embarrassed even a little bit.

Bonnie was not so blase about it.

"I'm sorry, Jim. I really didn't mean to hurt you."

Jim shook his head.

"I can't say that I'm hurt, actually. More like just surprised. What happened to 'I'm not sure she has a soul, I don't know if I can do this'?"

Bonnie didn't respond.

Jim had stood in their bedroom door in shock for a good fifteen or twenty seconds before he came to himself and coughed. They had both grabbed for the sheets and pulled them up to cover themselves. But their reactions had been so totally different. Bonnie had blushed in dismay, while Rita had laughed out loud.

"Whenever you two finish up, I'll be working on the bridge," Jim had said dryly, and turned away.

Now, a half hour later, the three of them sat in the galley.

Rita laid a hand on Jim's arm.

"Jim; try to understand. It just happened. We didn't plan it. It was just one of those things."

Bonnie took up the thread of conversation.

"Jim. I've always been bi. I haven't had a chance to tell you before, it just never came up. But...well, it's true. I like men. I like women. That's just me."

"And," Rita dived in, "as Jade explained, my memories, feelings, they're mostly from Bonnie. So I'm the same."

Bonnie shrugged. "So we were hot and tired, and we decided to take a shower, and we were naked in the showers at the same time, and well, you know. Things just started to happen."

"I'm not upset," said Jim again. "Really. I...I love you, Bonnie. I want your happiness as much as I do my own. If being with Rita makes you happy, then I'm good with it. But it was a bit of a shock just the same. Last thing I expected to see today."

Rita squeezed Jim's arm where she was holding it.

"You're a good man, Jim."

Jim sighed.

"Actually, I don't want to get distracted by this right now. I think we have bigger problems. We may be under surveillance already."

"What? What did you see?" exclaimed Bonnie.

"I think I was followed into town, and part of the way back. And Perry saw two city slickers sitting in a pickup down the back road yesterday."

Bonnie bit her lip.

"They're on to us," she said.

"Probably," agreed Jim.

"Do we go now?" asked Rita.

"Where are we on the processing core and materials for the tDrive?" asked Jim.

Bonnie looked at Rita.

"We finished the processor core assemblies just before our shower. That's why we were so hot and tired. But they're ready to go. Jade?"

<The processor and data core assemblies passed all preliminary testing and data loading from my backups is complete. I will be fully re-integrated in five minutes>

"How about the tDrive?" asked Jim.

<The tDrive is not complete. It will require another week to be fully functional>

"Are all the materials on board, though? Can we complete it at one of the rally points?"

Rita shook her head. "There's that shipment of ruthenium that just arrived, in the other hangar. We'll need that. Get that and we're self-sufficient. We can finish up at any of the rally points."

Jim looked at Bonnie and Rita.

"We've got all the food and oxygen and other life support materials loaded. I haven't completed the inventory yet, but I think we're good. I say we get that ruthenium loaded and get the hell out of here while we still can."

"Agree," said Bonnie. Rita nodded.

Jim rose. "I'll go get it. Do you two need anything?"

"No," said Bonnie. "Not for me. I've got everything."

"And I don't need anything," added Rita. "I'm sharing Bonnie's stuff for now, so I'm good."

Jim left the galley and headed for the external hatch. He exited the ship and went outside, looking around carefully before he squeezed out the side door of the hangar. It was dark now - after sunset. Jim paused for a second, looking up at the clear sky, with the stars coming out.

We'll be up there soon, he thought. *On our way to Sanctuary. To meet Jade's species and ask for their help. Hard to believe.*

In the gathering dusk, Jim strode over to the other hangar and went inside, to the far side where the delivery truck had dropped off a large crate. He found a hand trolley and put it under the case. He thought for a moment, grabbed a case of coffee, and added it on top of the pile.

You can never have enough coffee, thought Jim. *And it's a long way back home.*

He started to lift but stopped suddenly.

"Dammit, I forgot my shrapnel!"

The F-16 had lost a wing and was lying canted to one side, propped up on a rock formation. Jim lay in the wreck, the smell of burning fuel and rubber gagging him. His head hurt like hell, second only to his chest, which felt like someone had stuck a spear through it. His oxygen hose was tangled around him, and his helmet was half-in, half-out of the shattered canopy.

Looking down, Jim saw a dirty piece of metal sticking out of his chest.

"Not good," thought Jim. "Not good at all."

He pulled at the metal but couldn't get it out. There was a lot of blood. He tried to get the helmet off. He finally got it released, threw it outside and started climbing out of the shattered airplane. AK-47 rounds clinked off the bottom of the plane as he fell out of the cockpit and lay in the desert sands.

Jim's good luck charm. The piece of shrapnel that came out of his chest. He had held on to it all these years, never letting it far away from him. It was his totem.

Exasperated, Jim ran up the stairs to his apartment. Going to his bedroom, he slammed the top drawer of his dresser open and grabbed the metal shard, now clean and shiny after all the years. He went back out the apartment, locked it, and trotted down the stairs. Grabbing the handle of the hand truck with the case of ruthenium on it, Jim prepared to drag it across the tarmac to the other hangar - when he saw a dark shape creeping around the corner of Jade's hangar - rifle in hand.

Jim froze. Staring hard, he realized the man he saw was wearing assault gear. On his back were bright letters in neon yellow – 'Federal Agent.'

Quietly, Jim faded back into the hangar and squatted down behind the wing of the TBM, hoping the shadows hid him well enough. He saw two more armed agents come out of the shadows from the parking lot and start slinking toward the front door of Jade's hangar. He realized there were more agents between him and the side door. He would never be able to get back aboard Jade.

"No use for it, hoss," he said to himself. "Gotta do it."

With a sigh, Jim whispered the code words they had burned into their memory, knowing his new communicator would transmit directly to Jade, Bonnie, and Rita.

"Hot blood, hot blood, hot blood."

For a space of five seconds, there was no response. Then:

"Are you sure?" he heard Bonnie ask over his implant.

"Now, now, go now!" Jim whispered.

Opposite his position, the back of the big red hangar disintegrated with a huge "boom" as shaped charges went off. A dark shape came out of the hangar and went straight across the airfield fence, so quickly that a human eye couldn't really register what was seen. It was black, and long, and big, and then it was gone, and that was all you could say about it. Branches and leaves and dust made an artificial tornado where it had passed, and a double sonic boom cracked across the field.

Just then Jim felt a gun barrel in the back of his neck. Slowly he raised his hands. He felt a needle enter his shoulder, and then all turned to black.

* * * * *

Bonnie and Rita had been working on the bridge, putting things away for their anticipated departure, when the code from Jim came in.

"Hot blood, hot blood, hot blood!" they heard both in their implants and over the loudspeaker they had mounted on the ceiling of the bridge.

Bonnie froze. She glanced at Rita, who looked stunned.

They had done their homework; they had developed the codes, memorized them, practiced them – but had hoped they would never have to use them.

Now it was real.

"Are you sure?" Bonnie whispered.

"Now, now, go now!" she heard the response come back in a loud whisper.

Bonnie grabbed Rita, pushed her into the nearest seat, and jumped into the captain's chair.

"Jade, execute Hot Blood now!" she cried.

There was a loud explosion heard through the external microphones. Bonnie knew that was the shaped charges taking out the back wall of the hangar. Then everything on the viewscreen turned gray and she was looking at clouds. Shooting a quick glance at the reverse screen, she was shocked to see the Earth far below them and going away fast. Glancing back at the main screen, she saw their speed at Mach 5 and still increasing. Then they were above the clouds, moving faster every second.

An alarm sounded.

<Missiles in the air> called Jade.

"What the hell is the matter with these people?" asked Bonnie. "They're shooting missiles at us?"

<Affirm> said Jade. <Three SAM's tracking us but they're falling behind fast. We're safe. No worries>

"These people are nuts!" said Rita.

"Yep," Bonnie agreed. "Certifiable. They see something they don't understand so they start shooting at it. Classic ape response."

<We have left Earth's atmosphere and are on a course direct to Mars> called Jade. <Once we are out of tracking range of Earth, we'll double back to Rally Point Blue>

"Affirm," responded Bonnie.

Rita pointed to the front viewscreen. The sky in front had turned pure black now, and the stars could be clearly seen. To one side of the main screen was the Moon.

"This is exciting," Rita gasped. "Look at it!"

<Acceleration has stabilized at 150g. Velocity 1,000 kps and climbing>

Rita bit her lip. "What do you think will happen to Jim?"

Bonnie shook her head. "I don't know. Not sure what those crazies will do to him."

Jim came to slowly. His head was fuzzy. He had no idea where he was. After a few seconds, he realized he was lying in bed, and his left hand was handcuffed to the steel railing of the bed.

He was a prisoner.

Lifting his head slightly, he saw a tall, thin man dressed in a medical coat standing beside the bed. The man smiled at him.

"How are you feeling, Jim?"

"Like shit," said Jim. "Where am I?"

"Well, don't worry about that," said the man. "You're in a safe place. We have a few questions we'd like to ask you."

Jim grunted.

"And I'd like to know where I am."

"I'm afraid I can't tell you that right now, Jim. Not until we see a little cooperation."

"Then this conversation is over," Jim replied. He put his head back down and closed his eyes.

The tall thin man watched Jim go back to sleep and sighed. Then he left the room. Outside, he met another man who had been watching through a one-way glass.

"I tried to tell you," the thin man said to General Mark Rodgers. "You won't get anywhere playing games with him."

Mark nodded. "I suspected you were right, but we had to start somewhere. OK, give him another hour to fully recover from the knockout drug, then I'll go in and we'll start fresh."

The thin man grimaced. "Scopolamine - or whatever you spooks are using these days - is not going to get you anywhere with this guy. Look at his service record. You're wasting your time."

Mark smiled. "We'll see."

The tall thin man walked away. Mark went back to gazing at the prisoner in the next room through the one-way glass.

"Where did they go, Jim? I don't believe for a minute they really went to Mars. Not without you. What are they going to do next? Will they come back for you?"

Mark grinned.

"I think they will. In fact, I'm betting on it."

* * * * *

<We're out of range> stated Jade.

"Are you sure?" Rita asked.

<Yes. I have an extremely low radar cross-section, and the Earth has turned far enough since we launched that no deep-space radar except China or Australia could paint us anyway. And I doubt the U.S. will ask China or Australia for help; that would certainly let the cat out of the bag>

"OK," said Bonnie. "Let's reverse course."

Jade turned around and they headed back toward the Moon. Running a curved approach path, Jade was able to keep the Moon directly between herself and Earth, ensuring no radar could paint them as they neared Rally Point Blue.

"Want some coffee?" asked Bonnie.

"You know the answer to that," replied Rita. Since becoming conscious, Rita had been drinking coffee nearly continuously all day every day. It seemed like she would never get enough.

"I'm so disappointed we can't head for Sanctuary already," said Rita as they walked to the galley.

Bonnie nodded.

All we need, she thought, *is Jim, forty pounds of ruthenium, and two weeks. How can we obtain those things? This problem has to have a solution.*

Grabbing coffee in the galley, Bonnie and Rita sat down. They looked at each other.

"Shall we talk about the elephant in the room?" asked Bonnie.

Rita nodded. "I think we should."

"You were copied after me. You have my memories, my knowledge, my feelings," said Bonnie.

"Yep," agreed Rita.

"So you are in love with Jim too," Bonnie said.

"Yep," agreed Rita.

"I don't think Jade anticipated that. She's not really up to speed on human emotions."

"Yep," agreed Rita one more time.

"What are we going to do about it?"

Rita drank some coffee. She put her cup back on the table and stared at Bonnie.

"It's a moot point right now because we don't have Jim. Until we get him back, I see no reason to go there. It's just something out there in the future we'll have to consider when the time comes."

Bonnie nodded, sipping her coffee.

"Your hair is coming out nicely," she said. "It's going to be dark and curly."

"I noticed," said Rita.

<We are approaching the Moon> called Jade.

Bonnie and Rita went back to the bridge and sat in the console chairs. Neither took the captain's chair. It just felt uncomfortable to take it at this point.

In the wraparound viewscreen, they saw the Moon coming up fast.

"Are you sure you're not coming in too fast, Jade?" asked Rita.

<All is good> responded Jade. <We are decelerating at 150g. We'll come to a stop at 50 meters above the surface>

"50 meters! Crap, Jade, isn't that cutting it a little close?"

<I've landed on a hundred moons in my time, girls. No worries. But for you, Bonnie, I've adjusted it to 60 meters>

"Thanks, I guess?" groused Bonnie.

Gray and pitted, the surface of the Moon came at them fast. Nervous, Bonnie and Rita held the arms of their chairs in an iron grip as the viewscreen gave every appearance of a crash. But finally, when it seemed there was no way they could stop in time, the landscape approached a little slower. Then a little slower, and then they were hovering.

<60 meters> announced Jade. <Landing now>

Floating down to rest on a flat spot in the Aitken Basin on the far side of the Moon, they crunched softly into the regolith. They were up against the mountain range that ringed the Basin. Around them, a harsh and sere landscape showed craters and mountains in all directions.

Bonnie breathed a sigh of relief when they were down.

"That was nerve-wracking," she said.

"Try it sometime when you've only been conscious for a week," said Rita.

* * * * *

Jim awoke to find himself in the same place. His left hand was still handcuffed to the bed rail. He was more alert now, the effects of the drug that had knocked him out almost gone. His left shoulder was quite sore, and he twisted his neck to see a bandage in place where the knockout drug needle had twisted as it went into the skin.

"Crappy job of shooting me up," he spat at the Air Force general sitting beside his bed.

Mark Rodgers nodded. "I agree. Hard to get good help these days," he grinned.

Jim glared at him.

"So what next?"

"Well, Jim, we'd like you to tell us about the aliens."

Jim put on his most innocent face.

"Aliens?"

Mark chuckled. "Good, Jim. Very good. You should have been in Intel!"

Mark pulled his chair a little closer to Jim's bed.

"But c'mon, Jim - we saw their ship. We saw it fire out of that hangar at something like 100g. It disappeared into the sky so fast we only got a blur on our cameras. It outran three SAMs. So, let's not play games."

Jim stared at the man.

"Who the hell are you, anyway?"

Mark smiled back at him. "My name is Mark Rodgers, and I'm Air Force Intelligence. We got on to you right after Bonnie left the Air Force. There was just something unnatural about the way she left so suddenly. She seemed to be completely happy one week, then the next week she was gone. And there was that anomaly on the TAD test flight. I went back and looked at the logs, and there it was. An impossible turn from a vehicle going faster than anything the military had in the area. And we had confirmation from two other radar installations and the F-117 as well."

Jim nodded.

"I knew that was going to catch up to us."

Mark considered. "So, Jim. What can you tell us?"

"It doesn't matter now, General. It's gone. It won't be coming back. We'll never see it again."

Mark smiled. "Good try. But I don't think so. We know Bonnie was onboard. And that other girl, the one we've seen hanging out with you and Bonnie. What's her name?"

Now it was Jim's turn to smile.

"Good try, General. But no. As long as I'm handcuffed to this bed and not free to go live my life, I have nothing more to say."

Mark shook his head sadly.

"I really hate to hear that, Jim. Because we have to get to the bottom of this. No matter what it takes."

Jim turned his head away from the man, facing the other side of the bed. He knew what was coming. He started mentally preparing himself, ignoring Mark.

Heaving a long sigh, Mark waved at the one-way glass. In a few seconds, two men in long white lab coats entered. One placed an IV bag in the bracket beside the bed while the other prepped Jim's arm. In a few seconds, Jim grimaced as a needle was inserted. One of the men turned the valve and the drug started to flow. Things started to get hazy...

Jim. Tell us about the ship. Tell us about Bonnie.
Mm. Can I have a popsicle?

Jim, don't you want to save Bonnie?

Cherry. I want a cherry popsicle.

Jim, please. Bonnie is in danger. We have to save her. Where is she?

Or a grape. I like grape too.

Jim, Bonnie needs you. You need to help us save her. Bonnie is in danger. Where is she?

Or maybe a fudge bar.

Angry, Mark turned away from the bed where the semi-coherent Jim Carter lay, his eyes closed, mumbling about ice cream.

"I told you," said the thin man in the white lab coat. "He's too tough and too well trained for something like this to work."

"Dammit," said Mark. "I was hoping we wouldn't have to take the next step."

The thin man shook his head.

"That's not going to work either, but I know that won't stop you."

* * * * *

On the backside of the moon, Jade lay quietly near the edge of the Aitken basin. The rim of the basin stood tall above them as they completed an inventory to verify their status.

"So how does the re-inventory go?" asked Bonnie.

Rita grunted, re-stacking and securing boxes in the cargo area of the ship. Andy worked beside her, his little android body on four legs, using his remaining two arms to help Rita move the boxes.

"We're good. We've got roughly two years of food, and most importantly, we've got plenty of coffee."

Bonnie glanced around at the storage area, nodding.

"Medical supplies?"

"Yep," said Rita. "Enough to open a small hospital."

"So, all we're missing is Jim. And the ruthenium to finish the tDrive, right, Andy?"

"*Correct,*" replied Andy. "*We need ruthenium to make the tDrive operational.*"

Rita stopped working and stood up, placing her hands on her hips.

"Yep. Just that. And Jim."

Bonnie stared at Rita for a bit.

"I'm going to have to go get him."

Rita nodded. "I know."

GILLIAN

It had been a long and nerve-wracking day. Bonnie and Rita just looked at each other.

"Bed?" asked Rita.

"Bed," agreed Bonnie.

They left the bridge and went to Bonnie's cabin. There was never any doubt they would sleep together tonight. The Moon was a lonely place; they were far from home. It was no time to be alone.

Lying in bed together, Rita stared at the ceiling.

"It's so strange," she said. "I know who I am. I know I'm Rita. I can distinguish my fresh memories from your inherited memories. But yet, I love Jim. I miss him. I want him to be with me. Just like you do."

"Like we said earlier, not a problem now. He's not here. We'll cross that bridge when we come to it," said Bonnie. She was silent for a bit.

"But I know what you mean. I miss him too."

"I hope he's OK," said Rita.

There was silence for a while. Bonnie rolled over and stared at the wall.

"Do you think we'll survive all this?" she asked.

Rita gave a silent nod, then answered.

"Actually, I think we will. With Jade's help. We'll find a way to get Jim back, get the ruthenium, finish the tDrive, and go to Sanctuary to get help."

Jade had long since made a pact with Bonnie and Jim not to listen to their bedrooms. So, Bonnie felt like their conversation was private.

"If I don't survive, and you do, please take care of Jim for me. Promise me."

Rita nodded silently again, then answered. "I promise. And the same goes for me."

"By the way, did you look at the contingency plan for this

case?"

"I did," said Rita. "The next item on the checklist is to sleep."

"Good night, then," said Bonnie.

"Good night."

* * * * *

An alarm went off at 8 AM ship time next morning. Bonnie and Rita rose up groggily, looked around, and threw the sheets off.

"I dreamed we went to the Moon," said Rita.

"Funny," said Bonnie.

Rita grinned. "I take my humor where I can find it," she said.

They got up and showered, dressed, and met in the galley for breakfast. Rita made eggs and ham while Bonnie brewed the coffee and made breakfast rolls. Then they sat, drinking their coffee and eating breakfast.

"Good morning, Jade," said Bonnie.

<Good morning, girls. Did you sleep well?>

"We did," answered Rita for both of them. "And you?"

<I assume that is a joke? As I do not sleep>

Rita laughed. "Yes, that was a joke."

<I spent the night going over the contingency plan documents, monitoring Earth communications, and making plans. There are two options in this scenario. The most viable option is to move to Rally Point Pink, obtain the ruthenium we need, complete the tDrive and launch for Sanctuary>

Rita stopped her fork halfway to her mouth.

"Leaving Jim behind...," she said.

<Yes. Leaving Jim behind. He is not necessary for the success of our mission>

"Well, he's necessary for my success. I'm not going anywhere without Jim," said Bonnie.

"Likewise," added Rita.

<That is not optimal. We should take this option and ensure the success of our mission>

"Optimal or not, we ain't taking that option," Bonnie spat. "What's next?"

There was a silence.

Oh, oh, thought Bonnie. *Did I piss her off?*

Finally, Jade responded.

<The next most viable option is to relocate to Rally Point Pink. One person would then remain with me there, obtain the ruthenium, and ensure the completion of the tDrive. Meanwhile, the other person goes to Las Vegas and rescues Jim Carter."

"And I assume you have a plan for that already worked out?"

<I have a plan to get you to Las Vegas. But I do not have enough information to develop a plan to get Jim away from his captors. You will have to come up with that plan on your own>

* * * * *

Curled in a fetal position, Jim Carter lay in detention, his hand still handcuffed to the railing. He had been water boarded again this morning, for the third time. They were getting impatient with him.

Now Mark Rodgers came into the room, staring down at him sadly. He reached for a chair, pulled it up to the side of the bed, and sat.

"Jim. How are you feeling?" he asked.

There was no answer, not that he expected one. Jim had not eaten food for two days. They gave him an IV drip to keep him alive, and water. That was all. His body was deteriorating quickly; his muscles so weak he could hardly pull himself up on the bed.

"We can stop this anytime, Jim. Just say the word, and we'll put you in a luxury room, all the food you want, no more… privations. All you have to do is tell us about the aliens."

There was only silence.

Mark felt his frustration taking hold of him. He wanted to hit the man in front of him, strike him, beat him, tear him to pieces. He had never come across anyone this stubborn.

Clasping his hands together, Mark tried one last time.

"Jim. Just tell me one thing. Just one thing. How can we contact Bonnie? Is there a radio frequency we can use to talk to her?"

He was met with silence.

* * * * *

"He's got pneumonia. You overdid it on the waterboarding," said Dr. Janeski.

"Crap," said Mark. "Well, it wasn't working anyway." He looked at the doctor, standing beside him at the one-way glass, staring at Jim Carter in the other room.

"Patch him up, get him well. I need his information."

Dr. Janeski glared at Mark.

"I'll do my best. But like I told you in the beginning, you're probably going to kill him and still not get any information. I hate to say I told you so, but…"

"Then don't say it," growled Mark, and stalked away.

Lying in the hospital bed in the next room, Jim Carter coughed and spat up sputum, wiping it away with the corner of a towel lying next to him. His fever raged, and he shivered. They only let him have a thin blanket, and it did little to make him feel warmer.

Dr. Janeski came into the room and stood by the bed, looking down at Jim.

"How are you feeling, Mr. Carter?"

"Just as crappy as the last time you asked, Doc," rasped Jim.

"I am sorry, you know. For all of this."

"Don't salve your conscience, Doc. You know who you work for. Go sell your horseshit somewhere else," said Jim. He turned over and faced away from the doctor, looking at the wire-reinforced window. A faint trace of daylight could be seen outside.

Dr. Janeski nodded sadly. "You're right. I've no excuse." Janeski turned to leave.

"It's Thursday the fourteenth," he said as he got to the door and paused, looking back at Jim. "It's about 2 PM, and you're still at Nellis."

It was breaking the rules, but Janeski didn't care.

Jim passed out again, his mind once more going to the dark place he feared, the place he couldn't quite seal off even after all these years…

AK-47 rounds from a distant sniper clinked off the bottom of the plane as he fell out of the cockpit and lay in the desert sands.

He looked behind him at his WSO - Weapon Systems Officer, Al "Capone" Calderone, his best friend.

Al lay slumped against the side of the cockpit. Jim dragged himself over and tried to find a pulse.

There was none. Al was dead. And Jim had killed him.

One floor down in his temporary office, Mark Rodgers stared across the desk at the woman facing him. She had short black hair, dark eyes, was well-dressed, perfectly coiffed, and very pissed.

"Who the hell are you?" she asked quietly, in a dangerous kind of quiet voice.

"I'm General Mark Rodgers, Gillian," he replied.

"Why am I here?"

Mark leaned back in his chair.

"Your big brother Jim has gotten himself into a real situation, it seems."

Gillian glared at him. "Then he can just get himself out of it. He doesn't need me for that."

"No, you misunderstand, Gillian," said Mark. "Jim doesn't want you. He doesn't even know you're here. I'm the one that wants you here."

"Why?"

"Because we're on the same team. You're CIA, I'm DOD. But we both work in Weapons. And this is a Weapons directorate issue. So, I'm prepared to read you in, under certain conditions."

"I don't want to be read in. I have my own work to do."

"Not anymore, I'm afraid. You're assigned to me now, for the duration of this project."

Gillian shot to her feet.

"What? You had the nerve to have me re-assigned without talking to me first? You can go straight to hell, General!"

Gillian Carter Hassell spun, stalked to the door, exited, and slammed it behind her so hard the building shook. Mark Carter sat for a few seconds, then chuckled.

"I see where Jim gets it," he thought. "I'd hate to go up against that entire family."

Gillian Hassell stomped down the hallway toward the

building exit, pissed beyond belief. She was still muttering under her breath.

"That...cocky arrogant SOB. Thinks he can have me re-assigned with a snap of his fingers. We'll see about that!" Gillian smashed through the double doors at the end of the hallway, daring the guards on either side to say a word to her. She went out to the elevator lobby and pushed the button. Fuming, she grabbed her phone out of her purse, but before she could call her boss, he called her.

"Gillian! How's Las Vegas?"

"Sam? What the hell is going on? You told me this was a quick consult. One day trip. Now this arrogant son of a bitch out here is telling me I'm re-assigned. I'm headed for the airport, and by the time I get back to D.C., I hope you've got this straightened out!"

"Uh...Gillian. Settle down. There's something going on here. You need to stay there."

"The hell I will!" Gillian yelled into the phone. She reached the bottom floor and the elevator doors opened. She slammed out and marched through the lobby toward the front entrance.

"I've got projects in flight! You tell those Pentagon pricks to kiss my sweet Texas ass!"

"Now, Gillian. Calm down," said Sam. "Uh...I've got Director Evans here with me. Try to let us get a word in edgewise, OK?"

Gillian stopped halfway to her car. "Oh. OK. Go ahead."

"As disappointing as I know it will be to you, this is going to stand. You're temporarily re-assigned to General Mark Rodgers there at Nellis."

"No, Sam! Don't do this!" yelled Gillian, standing in the middle of the parking lot. Around her, people stared and detoured around her.

Another voice cut in. Director Evans.

"Gillian. It's national security. It's important. You need to do this," he said.

"Sir! I've got important projects in flight that cannot transition that easily!" cried Gillian. A tear started down one cheek. "Please let me come back to D.C. and transition them safely!"

Director Evans spoke softly.

"Gillian, we've got this. We'll ensure everything transitions safely. Stop worrying and let us do our job, and you go do yours."

Gillian stood, tears coursing down both cheeks now. She pulled the phone down from her ear and looked around.

It was a bright, sunny day. High clouds scudded across the sky. She looked at a hawk, coasting in the air currents overhead, free of all worldly cares.

I should be so lucky.

Putting the phone back to her ear, she spoke softly.

"Yes, sir."

"Thank you, Gillian," said Director Evans. "Be safe out there."

"I will, sir," whispered Gillian. She put the phone down, clicked off the call, put it back in her purse. Turning, she headed back into the building.

* * * * *

It was their second night on the Moon. They had spent the day reviewing the plan.

Rita would stay with Jade at Rally Point Pink, obtaining a new shipment of ruthenium and supervising Andy in the completion of the tDrive. Bonnie would return to Las Vegas to rescue Jim from Nellis. They went over the plan all morning, until every detail was burned into their brains.

For a dinner break, Jade suggested they walk out on the Moon.

At first, Bonnie and Rita reacted with disdain.

"Why would we want to do that?" asked Bonnie.

<Because you can> said Jade. <The spacesuits in the airlock are perfectly adequate to keep you safe. Who knows when you'll get the chance again?>

Flipping up an eyebrow, Bonnie looked at Rita.

"She's got a point, you know," Bonnie said.

"Well, yeah, come to think of it," Rita replied.

So they did. They went to the airlock, helped each other into the spacesuits, double-checked each other's air and temp controllers, and went outside.

It was gray. And desolate. And magnificent. Just as the Apollo astronauts had described it.

"I wish we were on the other side, where the landings took place," said Bonnie over her implant. "I'd like to see those footprints."

"Well, we're making footprints of our own," responded Rita. "Someday, someone will be looking at these and saying, oh look kids, here's the footprints of the two heroes, Bonnie and Rita Page."

"Wait. You took my last name?" asked Bonnie.

"You don't mind, do you?" asked Rita. "I don't have one of my own. My best memories are of my house...uh...your house - and your parents. So, I feel like that is my family."

Bonnie shook her head inside the helmet, where Rita couldn't see it.

"Every time I think this couldn't get any stranger, it gets stranger."

"If it makes you uncomfortable, I'll pick another one."

"No. It's fine. Rita Page. Go with it. But we're not sisters. Clear?"

"Crystal," answered Rita.

After they tired of exploring around the ship, they returned and shed their spacesuits in the airlock. Having stripped down to their underwear to get into the suits, they stepped out of the airlock and reached for their clothes, hanging on hooks by the hatch. But before they could put them on, they looked at each other.

"No use putting our clothes back on," said Rita.

"Nope," said Bonnie. "We'd just be taking them off again, because I'm about to screw your brains out."

* * * * *

Rita woke up first next morning. This was the morning they would head back to Earth. She got out of bed quietly - Bonnie was still sleeping - and went to shower.

They had made love off and on most of the evening, having sex, then sleeping, then waking up and having sex again.

Walking into the galley, she greeted Jade as they usually did.

"Good morning, Jade."

<Good morning. I see you and Bonnie went at it again last night>

"We did, Jade. I'm sorry, I thought you didn't monitor the bedrooms?"

<I don't, but since you left the door open when you started tearing each other's underwear off, I decided I had permission to watch. Human coupling is so interesting. I'm sorry if I broke the rules>

"Well, crap. If we left the door open, then you didn't break the rules. It's OK."

Groaning and wiping sleep from her eyes, Bonnie came through the door. She walked to the coffeepot and moaned.

"Coffee?" asked Rita, offering her a ready-made cup.

"Thank you," said Bonnie. "What hit me?"

"About five orgasms," said Rita.

"Um...yeah," answered Bonnie. "I seem to remember something about that."

"Jade watched us through the door," Rita said.

"What? I thought she agreed not to monitor us!"

"We left the door open."

"Oh. Well, that's our fault, then." Bonnie made a royal wave at the air, dismissing the incident. "No harm, no foul, Jade."

<Thank you>

They sat at the table and drank their coffee.

"What was your score?" asked Bonnie, grinning.

"Same as yours," Rita smiled back. "Five, I think."

"Good," Bonnie laughed. "We're still tied."

Two hours later, Bonnie and Rita, showered and dressed, sat

on the bridge, and prepared for their return to Earth. Without thinking, Bonnie had sat in the captain's command chair, and Rita had gone to the Weapons station. It seemed natural.

"You know where to get the ruthenium…" asked Bonnie one last time.

"Yes. Everything's in my notes. Contact name, phone number, address. I've got the bank account info and shipping address. I'll double check everything with Jade before I execute."

"And you know how to contact me…"

"Yes, got it. The dead-drop voicemail line, or either of the contingency HF frequencies at 11 PM each night."

"OK, then. Let's do this…"

<We have company> reported Jade. <Two Singheko ships on fast approach. I'm departing the Moon right now>

In the viewscreen, the outside view of Aitken Basin disappeared. On the screen showing the rear view, Bonnie and Rita saw the Moon disappearing fast behind them. Two small dots appeared over the limb of the moon, following right behind them.

Bonnie reacted faster. Her Air Force experience came to the fore.

"Charge weapons, Jade."

<Weapons charging>

"Where can we go?" asked Rita.

"Anywhere but here," said Bonnie. "Jade?"

<We don't have a lot of options>

"Then head for Earth!" yelled Bonnie. "We'll scrape them off!"

"Oh, hell yeah!" said Rita.

<What does that mean?> asked Jade.

"We'll get down and dirty on the surface of the Earth and try to crash them into a mountain!"

"Can we get there before they catch us?" asked Rita.

<Yes, but not by much. It'll be close> called Jade.

"OK, Jade. Make it Antarctica! I don't want to bring this fight to a populated continent. Do it!" yelled Bonnie.

Rounding the limb of the Moon, Jade headed for Earth at 255g. Their velocity built rapidly; within 6.5 minutes they were halfway to Earth. Jade took a vector that would sling them around Earth, allowing them to bleed off speed as they came around, and put them on approach to Antarctica as they decelerated to enter the atmosphere.

Behind them, Bonnie and Rita watched the two Singheko ships mimic their every move, staying right on their six.

ANTARCTICA

Gillian had been read into the project. She found it hard to believe. But the evidence was pretty convincing.

Still, she insisted on reviewing every data point, every interview, every phone record, every radar track. She went over the recordings of the TAD and the NORAD radar a dozen times. She reviewed the F-117 data a half-dozen times. She went through the shipping records of all the materials Jim had received at his hangar.

Lithium. Iridium. Polonium. Ruthenium. It read like a shopping list for rare earths. Highly purified He-4. And the more mundane items, as well. Phosphorus. Potassium. Carbon - lots of it. Thousands of gallons of purified water.

"What were you building there, Jimmy Boy? Frankenstein?" she muttered to herself, looking through the records.

And the dead giveaway he was planning a long expedition: several tons of food, drink, medical supplies, oxygen, spare computers. Reading materials, gym equipment, bedding, the mundane things of life on a ship - or a spaceship.

"Six space suits? Two male, four female? What the hell, Jim?"

And the weapons. Six M-4 assault rifles, two Minimi squad automatic weapons, three surplus M-79 grenade launchers, three 12-gauge pump shotguns, twenty thousand rounds of ammunition, five cases of grenades for the M-79, five cases of regular hand grenades, and two cases of Claymore mines.

Not to mention the half-dozen surplus Vietnam-era light anti-armor weapons, popularly known as LAAWs, and a case of C-4 explosive.

Enough firepower for a platoon of Marines.

Gillian leaned back in her chair. Just the weapons violations alone would put Jim in prison for the rest of his life. Not even considering the whatever-the-hell else had been in that hangar.

Which she had seen on the recording twenty times now. The back of the hangar blowing off into tiny pieces, and a long black object firing out the back like a rifle bullet. The eggheads estimated it was accelerating at 100g by the time it cleared the hangar. It disappeared into the night sky so fast, it was nothing but a blur on the cameras and infrared. They fired three SAM missiles at it and not one of them even came close to catching it.

Gillian sighed. Her big brother Jim had been her protector, growing up, as their mother neglected them and left them alone, telling them to 'raise themselves.' After he completed college, he ensured Gillian was safe and stable at the University of Georgetown, took his commission at Quantico, completed flight school at Pensacola, and went off to war.

He came back a different man. He might still look the same, even act the same in many ways. But the old Jim was gone. A hard, scarred warrior had taken his place.

He went to Africa then, a mercenary pilot for the highest bidder - and the bids were high in those days. Within ten years, Jim Carter retired to the desert of Nevada, and rarely came out of it, except for his periodic treks to the wastelands of Alaska or Canada.

Now, it seemed, the tables were turned. Gillian was to be put into the role of protector of her big brother. Heaving another large sigh, she got up and went down the hall to Mark's office. Tapping on the door, she pushed it open.

"I'm finished," she said.

Mark looked up and motioned her in.

"Good, have a seat. Let's talk this through before you go in."

Gillian sat down and waited. Mark gazed at her.

"I don't want to cause Jim any more trouble than is necessary. All I want is to know everything about that ship and what the aliens are planning to do. That's all. In return, we'll drop all the weapons violations and Jim can go back to his normal life in Deseret. That's the deal."

"He won't take it," said Gillian. "I know him better than anyone in the world. He won't take it from me, or from anyone else. You're wasting your time."

"Still." Mark told her. "We have to try."

Gillian shrugged. "OK. I'll present it to him. Just don't be surprised when I say, 'I told you so'".

Mark nodded. "Been hearing that a lot lately."

She rose and went out the door, up the stairs, down the hall and stopped at the detention room. Mark, behind her, motioned to the guards to let them in. The guards opened the door for them. Mark stayed in the outside viewing area.

Crossing the outer room with the one-way glass, Gillian donned a protective mask and entered Jim's room. Jim was sleeping fitfully. His fever had abated somewhat, but he was still recovering from the pneumonia. Gillian stood and watched him for a while.

When we were children, you protected me, saved me from the bad things. Made sure I got a good start in life. Now I have to try and protect you.

Jim opened his eyes, turned his head, and stared at her.

"Feeling better, Jimmy Boy?" she asked.

Jim smiled at her; a bit weakly but looking better than the glimpse she had seen yesterday through the one-way glass.

"I wondered how long it would be until Mark got you in on this," he said, lifting up his head to see her.

"Yeah, you sure screwed up my week," said Gillian. She sat down on the chair in the corner. Protocol required she not be close enough for him to touch her.

"Doc says your pneumonia is almost clear, you should be back to normal in another day or two."

"Back to normal," said Jim bitterly. "Their idea of normal."

"Well, you can get out of this anytime you want, Jimmy boy," Gillian said.

"What are they offering this time?" he asked.

"Amnesty for the weapons violations, you go home to Deseret and stay out of their hair."

"For?"

"Everything about the aliens and their intentions."

Jim laid back wearily on the bed pillow.

"I've already told them a dozen times. The ship is on its way back to its home planet. And their intentions are to stay there. So I can't help them."

Gillian grinned. "I told them it was pointless, but they don't know you like I do." She gave a mock salute to the mirrored glass.

Jim turned his head away and closed his eyes.

"Jilly, just go. I've already told them a dozen times. The ship is gone. Let me sleep."

Gillian rose, took a step toward Jim's bed as if she were going to break protocol, but then stopped. She turned for the door.

"See you later, Jimmy," she said, exiting the room.

Outside, Mark Rodgers waited glumly. He nodded at Gillian as they left the room and headed back to his office.

"I hate to say it, but..." Gillian began.

"Then don't," said Mark brusquely.

They arrived at his office and stepped inside.

"Can I go back to D.C. now?" asked Gillian.

"No," said Mark. "You're here for the duration, until we find them or give up. But I'm not ready to give up yet. That ship did not depart this solar system, I'm positive."

"How can you be so sure?" Gillian asked.

Mark sat, waved her to a chair, and looked at her across the desk.

"One - there was an unused case of ruthenium in the hangar at the airport. Jim was just loading it onto a trolley to take it into the ship. That had to be something important - because ruthenium is damn expensive and hard to get."

"Two - Bonnie Page and the other girl - we haven't identified her yet - are not going to leave Jim here and go flying off to some other star system. They'll be planning a way to bust him out of here."

"Three - my gut tells me there's something more here. Jim is still covering for something. He's good, he's very good. But not good enough. He is covering for something else that's going on. That ship is still around here somewhere."

Just as Mark was finishing his sentence, the door burst open and Pujold Rukmini burst in, hearing the last part of Mark's speech.

"And I can tell you where!" he shouted. "We just got a hit on radar! That ship came around the limb of the moon and it's smoking for Earth! And get this - there's two more following it!"

* * * * *

The two Singheko ships behind them drew closer as Jade was forced to decelerate to swing by the Earth. Otherwise, she would just zip right by.

As her decel reached 255g, the Earth drew steadily closer. Behind them, the two Singheko ships also drew closer every second.

<We're going to be fired on at least once before we're in atmosphere> Jade told them via their implants. <You should put your spacesuits on and strap in, prepare for damage>

Rita and Bonnie looked at each other, then charged for the spacesuits, throwing off clothes as they ran. Within five minutes, they were suited up, checking each other's oxygen and heating systems. Then they returned to the bridge and strapped themselves back in.

Andy came onto the bridge. The android went to a back corner where he had installed a special harness for himself and strapped in as well. Then he folded up like an armadillo and went quiescent.

<In the case of damage, stay in your seats. Andy will go perform damage control first. If he needs your help, he'll ask>

"Wilco," said Bonnie.

<Here we go> said Jade. The Earth suddenly got much larger, and they were swinging around it, still decelerating. As they came around, Rita and Bonnie watched on the holotank.

Suddenly Jade fired a spread of two missiles at the two ships behind them. At the same time, the two ships behind fired two missiles each. The missiles accelerated quickly; in only a few seconds, the missiles met and passed each other, halfway between Jade's icon in the holotank and those of the pursuing ships.

<Stand by for impact> Jade spoke over their implants. The enemy missiles got closer and closer; then, just as Bonnie saw the two pursuing ships dodge to the side, the enemy missile icons merged with Jade's symbol in the holotank as Jade also made a quick twitch to one side.

Three of the missiles passed them by, a clean miss.

One didn't.

There was a tremendous crash, a sound like a car wreck, and the bridge lurched as something applied a force that overcame even Jade's massive compensators. The bridge filled with smoke.

Andy woke up, uncurled, and disconnected his harness, and charged into the back of the ship. Meanwhile, Jade continued her slingshot around Earth, now sliding over the Middle East. The ship began to shudder as it entered the thicker atmosphere. They were well southwest of Saudi Arabia now, on a tangent headed for Antarctica.

Passing south of Australia, Jade was down to 10,000 feet as they crossed over the coastline and entered Antarctica proper.

She headed for the deck, getting as low as she could go. Streaking across the snow-covered ground at Mach 5, a rooster-tail of snow and ice followed her, rising hundreds of feet into the sky.

"Lower!" yelled Bonnie. "Lower!"

Behind her, the two enemy ships stayed up high, one on each side of Jade's track, trying to shoot missiles down at them. But it didn't work. Their missiles were designed for space, and a three-dimensional battle. With Jade this low, it had become a two-dimensional battle. The thick atmosphere of Earth wasn't helping any. The missiles couldn't do their magic. If the missiles tried to come in from above, all Jade had to do was flick to one side at the last instant, and the missiles slammed into the ground. When they tried to come up behind her, Jade would flick herself to one side just before impact, and the missile would slam into a hummock or a hill.

After the two enemy ships had fired a half-dozen missiles at them, they realized it was pointless. In this kind of restricted environment, Jade was just too quick for them. They came down then, tucked in behind Jade.

"They're coming in behind us now!" yelled Rita, watching at the Weapons console.

They had crossed a small slice of the Antarctic continent. Now they approached the ocean once more. Suddenly they streaked across the coastline and were over the Southern Ocean again, west of McMurdo Sound, heading north - away from Antarctica.

"Sell it, Jade! Make it look like we're panicking!" yelled Bonnie.

Jade began a long, slow curve back toward Antarctica. This allowed the pursuers to pull even closer. Jade began firing missiles at them from her rear missile tubes. They dodged and weaved, staying on Jade's tail but unable to make an effective attack.

"Now!" Bonnie yelled at Jade. "Take them to Mount Erebus!"

Jade acknowledged. As she completed her slow curve back toward Antarctica, the coastline re-appeared. They approached from the north now, headed toward McMurdo. Jade continued her slow curve but stopped firing missiles. Now the enemy moved in closer. The deceptively gentle slopes of Mount Erebus showed ahead. Crossing the coastline, Jade rose slowly with the ground, staying just barely ahead of the rising terrain. As she approached the rim of the volcano, the slopes suddenly rose precipitously. Jade was ready for it; traveling at Mach 5, there wasn't much time to react. She just barely cleared the rim of the volcano.

The first of the two enemy ships behind her didn't quite make it. It glanced off the rim of the volcano, throwing up a huge spray of rock and ice, and wobbled slightly higher into the air. Slowing down dramatically, it was out of the fight.

<The other one will stay back to escort the damaged one> said Jade. <We're good>

WOODSHED

Gillian leaned over Mark's shoulder, peering at the display in the Command Center. There were no satellites over Antarctica with the capability to track such fast-moving objects; they had lost track of the three spaceships as they went below the tracking horizon of the Canberra Deep Space Tracking Complex in southeastern Australia.

But just as they were about to give up, one of the ships came back into view, caught by the Madrid Deep Space Communications Complex in Spain. It had clearly crossed Antarctica at high speed and was now climbing like a bat out of hell, back into space.

"What's its speed now?" asked Mark.

The technician peered at his display.

"Right at double escape velocity, about 22 kps, and accelerating at about 50g."

Mark sighed. "Gone again," he breathed. "Dammit!"

Gillian, trying to see, instinctively put her hand on Mark's shoulder. She leaned over farther. She felt an electricity in her hand, and Mark straightened suddenly, as if he felt it too. She suppressed the feeling for the moment. But he was an attractive man...

"What's that?" she pointed to the display with her other hand.

"Oh crap, that's the other two," said the technician. "But moving a lot slower now. About a quarter the speed of the first one, and a lot less acceleration. At this rate, they'll just barely make escape velocity."

"So..." Mark rubbed his chin. "Two were chasing one. The one took them down to the ground in Antarctica. Then the one comes out at full speed, and the two come out obviously damaged."

Mark turned to Gillian.

"That's our young Bonnie Page at work, I think. Her Air Force training. She took them to the woodshed."

"I think so," said Gillian. "That makes the one in front - the undamaged one - our bird. And the two in back are new; someone else is taking a hand in our game."

Mark winked at her.

"Still want to go back to D.C.?"

Gillian smiled.

"No, I don't think so. But I have a couple of suggestions for you."

"Great!" said Mark. "Why don't we talk over dinner? I'm starving!"

* * * * *

"You're going about this all wrong," said Gillian.

"How so?" asked Mark, looking up from his menu. They had found a late-night restaurant near the base.

"You're looking at this as a challenge. A fight. A battle to win. That's your military mind at work."

"So?"

"You should be looking at this as a diplomatic issue. We have here two foreign powers at work. Jim is involved with one. We don't know about the other, but they are clearly adversarial to Jim's friends."

"Go on."

"I contend that instead of trying to break Jim and force him to reveal the plans of the ship and its crew, you should make him an ally. Not by deception, but for real. You can't fool him; he'll know the difference. But if you can do that - if you can make Jim an ally - then Jim can make an ally of that ship. Again, not by deception, but for real. Think about where you would be if you could succeed in that. You'd have exactly what you want - access to their technology - and you can get it without fighting for it. Stop trying to win an unwinnable battle and try to make a supportable peace."

Mark stared at the woman across from him. Tall, willowy

but not thin, Gillian Carter Hassell was a fine figure of a woman. He knew from her file she was a widow; her first husband had been killed in the Africa Conflict, and she had never remarried. Now in the candlelight of the restaurant, she looked particularly beautiful.

"I think…" Mark began, but hesitated.

"I think you may be right," he finally managed to get out.

"Now, was that so hard to say?" Gillian asked him.

"Yes. It was," replied Mark. He smiled a wry little smile at her. "It's not easy to realize you've screwed everything up."

"You haven't screwed everything up," Gillian said. "Just almost everything. There's a couple of things you haven't screwed up yet."

"The night is young," said Mark.

Gillian picked up her wine glass and stared at him over the top of it, then took a drink.

"Yes, it is," said Gillian, looking at the handsome General across the table from her.

Leaving Earth's atmosphere, Jade and her crew made for deep space, avoiding the Moon this time. Bonnie and Rita breathed a sigh of relief.

Rita turned in her chair to face Bonnie.

"Now what? Where can we go?"

"We go back to our original plan," said Bonnie. "We go to Rally Point Pink and then you fix Jade while I go rescue Jim."

<There will be more damage to repair> spoke up Jade. <It will take more materials than ruthenium now>

"Crap!" yelled Bonnie. She slammed her fist against the arm of her chair in frustration. "Does this never end?"

Rita thought hard.

"And we're working against the clock now. Those Singheko ships will be reporting back to their home world. We'll have a lot more ships coming after us soon enough."

"Yep," Bonnie said.

"Jade - how long will it take the Singheko to get word to their home world?"

<It will take them about fourteen months to get word to their home world, assemble an attack fleet, and get back to Earth. As I said earlier, the best plan at this point is to repair the tDrive and leave immediately for Sanctuary to get help. We don't have time to rescue Jim. We can be at Sanctuary in a little over six months, and a defensive fleet can be back here six months after that. So we have only two months cushion. If we are to beat the Singheko back here, we must work quickly> said Jade.

Bonnie sighed. "I guess you're right. But...how long will it take to repair you and finish the tDrive?"

Andy entered the bridge behind them, in his four-legged stance, like a large metallic dog - or a four-legged spider...

"*Two weeks to repair the tDrive, and one additional week to repair the damage to the ship, before we are ready for interstellar flight,*" intoned the little android.

Bonnie thought.

"OK. I know time is short, but that gives me three weeks to rescue Jim. We can do both. Back to the original plan. Rita, you'll stay with Jade and work on repairing the ship. I'll go rescue Jim. If we're not back by the time the ship is fully repaired, you go with Jade to Sanctuary and get help."

"Got it," said Rita.

Bonnie perused for a few more moments, then spoke out loud.

"Jade, let's execute the plan to get me back to Earth, someplace close to Nellis, then get you to Pink."

Rita looked puzzled. "Why Nellis?"

"That's where Jim will be," said Bonnie. "They'll keep him right there, so the Air Force can keep control of the investigation. And so they can do whatever they want without interference."

"You mean torture."

Bonnie nodded again. "Probably. I doubt they'd let human rights be a thing for them in this situation."

Jade's voice came over their implants.

<We need to let things die down on Earth a bit before we try to sneak back in. Do you have anyplace nearby you'd like to see?>

Bonnie looked at Rita.

"Well, I've always wanted to see Mars," she said.

<Any particular place on Mars?>

Bonnie grinned.

"How about Jezero Crater, where that big rover is?"

<On our way> said Jade. <We'll be there in about six hours>

* * * * *

"This is so freaking cool!" said Rita.

"It is!" grinned Bonnie inside her spacesuit.

They were inside Jezero Crater on Mars, looking at the Perseverance rover. The big white rover was nearly the size of a compact car, a hundred yards in front of them, sitting quietly. Its life was almost over; according to JPL and NASA, it could no longer move, and only one camera still worked.

But one camera was enough for Rita.

"Are you sure you want to do this?"

Now it was Rita's turn to grin.

"Absolutely. Let's do it!"

"OK," said Bonnie resignedly. They began a walk-jog toward the rover. They came in from the left side, to avoid the camera.

Coming up beside the rover, Bonnie stopped and squatted down, leaving the next step up to Rita. After all, it was her idea.

Rita moved slowly up beside the rover. Moving around to the left front side, she leaned out as far as she could and placed a small sign directly in front of the rover. The sign was folded into a triangle, which made it stand up on the sandy soil. Rita weighted it down with two large rocks, placed so the words on it faced the front cameras.

Rita started laughing, which Bonnie could hear over her implant. In between laughter, Bonnie heard her speaking.

"I wish...(snicker)...I could see the looks on their faces... when they see that sign!"

Bonnie started laughing too. It was totally funny, she thought. She couldn't help but giggle. She looked over at Rita.

"Come on, we gotta get back to the ship."

Rita continued giggling as they started walking back toward Jade, who was hidden in a depression in the crater floor a couple of hundred yards away. As they walked, Bonnie focused on not stumbling, picking her way through the crater floor, looking for the safest route. In front of her, Rita did the same, albeit a little faster.

Bonnie kept thinking about their situation. She knew Jim had to be at Nellis. But how would she find him? And how would she get him out of the clutches of the Air Force – or whoever was holding him?

She supposed it was some kind of spook project, maybe joint with the Pentagon and other intelligence agencies. But it didn't matter. She had to find a way to get him out.

I won't leave him there, she thought. *I will not.*

By the time they approached the little depression hiding Jade, Rita was a good twenty yards ahead of Bonnie.

"C'mon, slowpoke," Rita broadcast over her implant. "Get a move on!"

"I'm coming," said Bonnie. She looked up to see Rita clambering up the short ladder into Jade's airlock.

And to see two creatures step out from behind Jade's large landing leg, between her and the airlock hatch. Each was wearing a spacesuit, and each was holding a weapon, pointed directly at Bonnie.

"Uh-oh," Bonnie spoke, her words automatically going out over her implant. Rita, at the top of the stairs, turned to see what the problem was. She froze, not moving, staring at the two creatures holding their weapons on Bonnie.

"Rita. Seal the airlock. Right now. Do it."

Rita nodded inside her helmet. She took a step back and slapped the airlock close button. The airlock hatch closed quickly behind the creatures, who continued to stare at Bonnie, their weapons never wavering.

Then one of them took a step forward. His weapon raised slightly, to point directly at Bonnie's head. He fired.

RALLY POINT PINK

Inside the ship, Rita ran to the bridge, shedding her helmet as fast as possible. She slammed into the Weapons console chair and brought up the outside cameras on her screen.

"Oh, God," she breathed.

Bonnie lay on the ground, and the two creatures stood over her, apparently having a discussion. One of them kept pointing to the ship, and the other one kept pointing to Bonnie.

"Jade!" yelled Rita. "Can you do anything?"

<I can't fire on them without hitting Bonnie as well> said Jade. <They're too close to her>

Rita slammed her fist against the arm of the chair.

"Who are they?" she yelled.

<Singheko> replied Jade. <They'll take her away to their ship. There's nothing we can do>

Sure enough, the creature pointing to Bonnie appeared to win the argument. The two reached down, picked Bonnie up by the shoulders and legs, and carried her away, toward the back of the ship.

Rita watched them as they progressed around the back of the ship and disappeared.

"Jade! I can't pick up the right rear on the cameras!"

<Yes. That's where the most damage occurred from the battle yesterday. I've lost all my external sensors and cameras in that area. They were smart enough to see that from a distance and took advantage of it to come up unnoticed."

"Crap, crap, crap. What do we do now?"

"We go back to Earth and repair the tDrive>

"I can't leave Bonnie here with those monsters!"

<There's nothing we can do, Rita. We can't get her back. We have to deal with the reality of our situation>

Rita burst into tears.

"I can't leave her, Jade! I can't!"

<We must. They'll be back at their ship soon. They'll call for

reinforcements. There might be other ships in the area. We'll be shot to pieces if we stay here. And then humanity will be destroyed. We must go, Rita>

Jade lifted off from the floor of Jezero Crater, turning slowly as she did so. As she turned, the alien creatures came back into view on the front screen. Rita saw a small groundcar behind a rise a hundred yards away. The two creatures were loading the inert form of Bonnie onto the back of it. Tracks from the groundcar led off to the horizon, through a small saddle in the rim of the crater.

As they lifted higher, Rita saw the groundcar tracks end on the other side of the crater wall, at a small shuttlecraft in the distance.

Then Jade accelerated, and the ground fell away.

Rita collapsed onto the floor, sobbing. She didn't even notice when Mars disappeared behind them and Jade took a vector for Earth, pulling maximum acceleration to get there as soon as possible.

*****

Eight hours later, over the vast uninhabited area of the South Pacific, far to the northeast of New Zealand, a black starship streaked across the swells at low altitude, coming from the direction of Antarctica. It eventually came up on the standard aviation route between Auckland, New Zealand and Seattle, Washington, in the middle of nowhere over the Pacific. There, it quickly overhauled a corporate jet that had departed Auckland hours earlier. Popping up to the jet's altitude, soon it was behind and above it, out of sight of the pilots.

The starship maintained precise formation with the corporate jet. Many hours later, in the middle of the night, the jet – with its undetected companion - crossed the U.S. border at 35,000 feet, a bit south of Seattle, continuing on its flight to Cranbrook, B.C. Observers on the ground would have seen nothing except the standard lighting of a corporate jet. The

Air Traffic Control operators saw only the expected echo and squawk codes on their screens. The jet was on its flight plan. All was well.

In another hour, the jet descended and began an approach to the Canadian Rockies International Airport in Cranbrook. As it turned on its downwind leg to set up for landing, a shadow detached from above and dove for the ground. As the jet landed at Cranbrook, Jade continued up the Rocky Mountain Trench, a long valley on the western side of the Canadian Rockies stretching from the Montana border to the Yukon.

In the pitch-black night, she flew north, hugging the valley floor, working her way into British Columbia. Soon she passed over Fort Ware, finally crossing the Continental Divide and circling around to come into Fort Nelson, B.C. from the east.

Under cover of darkness, she threaded the needle between trees and buildings and came to rest inside a large open hangar on the far end of the airport. The automated door closed quickly. Unless an observant person had been looking at exactly the right place at exactly the right time, no one could have seen Jade ducking into her new hangar at Rally Point Pink.

An exhausted Rita Page fell into bed. She had cried intermittently most of the way back to Earth. Her tears finally dried up as they were coming into the atmosphere over Antarctica. She had no more tears to cry now; just a dead feeling, and a loneliness that couldn't be quenched.

MISSIONS

Sitting in his office at Khodinka Airfield near Moscow, GRU General-Lieutenant Viktor Tereshkova looked at the report from the deep-cover operative.

It was unbelievable.

Yet he trusted this man beyond any doubt. The operative had worked for the GRU his entire adult life, deeply embedded in the American Department of Defense. Even his parents had been GRU operatives. He was never asked to handle minor issues - too much risk of blowing his cover. He only reported when there was a significant matter at stake.

Such as an alien spaceship escaping from the Americans and hiding out on Mars.

Viktor shook his head. If this intel were from anyone else, he would have them 'retired.' It was just too unbelievable.

But this operative...this one. He never missed. And he backed up his claim with hard data.

A blurry, but barely discernible infrared image of a long, wedge-shaped object firing out the back of an aircraft hangar.

File after file of recorded telemetry from an F-22, an F-117 and a ground-based radar at Groom Lake.

Radar data from the Canberra Deep Space Tracking Complex showing not one, but three spaceships entering the Earth's atmosphere and disappearing over Antarctica - apparently engaged in some sort of battle. And then those spaceships re-appearing in view of the radar from the Madrid Deep Space Communications Complex in Spain, one headed for space at full speed and two limping along, wounded.

Viktor lifted his phone and made several calls. Wheels started turning. Forces were mobilized.

A Spetsnaz Colonel was among them. Colonel Gregori Bogdonovich stared at the warning order in wonderment.

Gregori had received a lot of strange orders in his time.

But putting together an assault force to capture a starship on

114

American soil was a first. He considered it for a moment.

"*A challenge,*" he thought, "*worthy of my talents.*"

* * * * *

Jim woke up as the door to his room opened. It was late - after midnight, for sure. His fever had abated; he felt almost human again.

Dr. Janeski came in and stood beside the bed. He took out an electronic tablet and turned it to face Jim, so he could see the screen.

"They know where your friends are, I think," he said.

Jim looked at the image on the screen. He coughed, tried not to laugh because his chest was still sore from his bout with pneumonia. He stared at the tablet, a grin slowly spreading on his face from ear to ear.

Raising his knuckles to his lips, Jim tried to hold the laughter in, but it was hopeless. A snicker escaped, followed by a groan from the pain.

On the tablet was a picture. At the bottom of the picture was the label "Perseverance Rover, Jezero Crater" along with a time code stamp. In the picture he could see the landscape of Mars, with the crater wall in the far distance.

A small sign had been placed in front of the rover. On it were the words:

Hi Jim, hope you are OK. See you soon. And tell the Feds to kiss my butt! XOXO Rita

Dr. Janeski pulled the tablet back and placed it into his smock. Then he took a key and reached out toward the handcuffs locking Jim to the hospital bed, removed them from Jim's wrist, and stood, staring down at Jim in the darkness.

"What you said. You're right. I've been corrupted by the system. And there's no excuse. But no more. But you'll have to take it from here, I don't have a clue how to get you out of the building."

Jim rubbed his wrist. "I can handle that. But you know they'll make your life a living hell for this."

"I don't care. My wife died last year. My children are all gone. I have nothing to fear."

"No, seriously. They'll find a way to hurt you. Something you haven't thought of yet."

Dr. Janeski pressed something into Jim's hands. It was a set of car keys.

"Cadillac Escalade, in the back lot. Good luck."

He turned to go but stopped halfway to the door.

"I don't care what they do to me. There comes a time when a man has to stand up on his hind legs and start being a man."

Jim nodded. "Yep."

Then the doctor was gone.

Jim got out of bed as quietly as he could, went to the locked window, and used one of the keys to start loosening the screws holding the window frame in place. A couple of days before, he had noticed they were a bit loose. Now all he had to do was remove the frame and window, climb down three stories, and find the Escalade in the back lot.

*****

Rita woke up during the night and started crying again. It seemed it would never stop. She felt so alone. So far away from Jim and Bonnie.

I just left them, she sobbed in the dark. *How could I just run away and leave them?*

After a while, she managed to get her emotions damped down a bit. It was then she slowly came to a realization.

The aspect of her that was inherited from Jim was at war with the aspect of her that was inherited from Bonnie.

Jim's feelings and knowledge - inherited, but real to her - were to complete the mission, at all costs. Bonnie's feelings and knowledge were to somehow rescue Jim. And Rita's own, unique self was devastated at leaving them both behind.

She was caught between three worlds. What was she to do?

After a while, she dried her tears and rolled upright in the bed, sitting on the edge, thinking.

I have to complete the mission, she thought. *Ultimately, that is what both Jim and Bonnie would have me do. I have to repair Jade and get her to Sanctuary. Everything else is secondary.*

Getting up, she went to the shower and cleaned up. Dressing, she returned to the galley. Andy was waiting quietly beside the table.

"I was wondering when you'd get up," he said. "I made coffee."

Rita nodded, went to the counter, and poured a cup of coffee. She took a seat at the table and gazed at the little android.

"What do we need to get Jade back into condition for the trip to Sanctuary?" she asked.

"*Ruthenium - forty pounds. Eight 4K external cameras, space rated if possible. Eight IR cameras, space rated. Three small radar dishes - we can use television dishes, I can modify them. Everything else I can make from raw materials. So - 200 pounds of purified silicon. 2,000 pounds of purified carbon for making buckyballs, nanotubes and graphene sheets...*"

Rita sighed as the list went on. Pulling her laptop to her, she started putting together the orders. She had to separate them into small chunks, so as not to arouse suspicion.

Rita ordered as many of the items as she could from South America, to be delivered to Jacarepagua Airport near Rio de Janeiro. From there, contract pilots would deliver it to Halifax, Nova Scotia via corporate jet. Another corporate jet - with the logo of a well-known oil prospecting company - would ferry it to Calgary. And from there, a well-paid truck driver would pick it up and deliver it to Fort Nelson.

All of the people involved thought they were working for a privately held corporation engaged in petroleum prospecting in Canada and the North Slope.

And Jade was the owner. She had bought the company outright, lock, stock, and barrel. There was a physical headquarters building in Calgary; at the top of the organization was an executive team - President, Vice President, Secretary, Treasurer, and Operations Manager. Below them was a complete staff to make things happen.

Their reclusive new owner was only occasionally seen on video in web meetings. To their knowledge, he was a tall, dark South American, of middle age, and with a distinct accent. He claimed to be based in Rio, and left the day-to-day operations of the company to his executive team. Moreover, the company was still performing actual exploration - as they had been for nearly thirty years - and were quite successful at it.

The orders of additional equipment and materials in their Accounts Payable system were all properly authorized by the new owner.

And a clear message had been sent to the President of the corporation - classified project, no questions asked.

Given the size of his recently announced bonus, he had absolutely no problem with that.

ON THE RUN

Jim drove the Escalade into the parking garage at the Rock Hotel and left it, leaving the keys inside. He had found five hundred dollars in the console tray, and a T-shirt, socks, shoes, and a pair of jeans in the passenger seat. He had dressed while driving into town.

He had stopped at an all-night Wally World and bought a gym bag, a black running suit, a dark hoodie, a new wallet, a pair of scissors, and two sticks of lipstick - one white, one black. The young check-out clerk had looked at him strangely. He grinned at her and told her it was for his daughter for Halloween.

Walking into the Rock, he found a quiet spot in the lobby and casually moved the cash to his new wallet. Then he killed another half-hour in the lobby and restaurants, watching for any shadows - but he hadn't been able to find anyone.

Finally, when he was satisfied he wasn't being followed, he walked into a restroom near the parking garage exit. Inside the stall, he used the black and white lipstick to paint a dazzle pattern on his face. Then he used the wig to create an impromptu fake beard.

This provided two layers of safety against the omnipresent cameras all around Las Vegas - if the cameras penetrated the fake beard, the dazzle lines underneath should still prevent automated facial recognition.

Next he stripped, removing every article of clothing from his body, and put on the new running suit and hoodie. He crammed all his old clothes into the trash, covering them with several layers of paper towels. Finally, pulling the hoodie as tight around his face as he could, he stepped out of the restroom and made directly for the parking garage.

In the parking garage, he trotted to the exit nearest Paradise Road and went out, staying to the shadows as much as possible. Reaching Paradise Road, he crossed and walked casually south. After two blocks, he hadn't seen any surveillance behind him or drones in the air above him.

Turning left, he went another block then turned north. After three more blocks he came to the Paradigm Apartments. Entering the complex, he crossed to the particular building and apartment he wanted.

Looking around carefully, he slid over the low balcony at the back of the apartment and lay down, out of sight. Reaching into a flowerpot on the floor containing a cactus, he dug a key out of the soil.

Taking a peek over the top of the balcony, he saw no one. Quickly, he stood up, unlocked the balcony door, and went inside the apartment - one of the safe houses he and Bonnie had created as part of their contingency planning.

Once inside, Jim grabbed the burner phone they had staged there and left a voicemail for Bonnie.

"Code Zhivago times three. On my way to Pink."

That was the code to let Bonnie know he had escaped and was in good health and was on his way to them. Jim lay back on the bed and his eyes closed.

I hope they wait for me, he thought.

He was asleep in thirty seconds.

Jim rested at the safe house for two days, regaining his strength, recovering from the pneumonia. He left another voicemail next evening, and was puzzled as there was no response.

"Where are you, my dearies?" he asked himself. "Are you out taking in the town? You should be working to get Jade ready for flight. What are you up to?"

Early on the third day, he changed into an all-black outfit, covered his face with a special mask designed to foil facial recognition, took three duffel bags out of the closet, and walked to the parking lot. An older Toyota Tundra waited in the lot, dusty and covered with bird guano. But it started and ran just fine. Backing out of the parking lot, he started on his expedition to Rally Point Pink.

* * * * *

Gillian sat in Mark's office, staring at the note. It had been found in Jim's room after his escape, hastily scratched out on a pad by the bed. She looked up at Mark and shook her head.

"If only you had taken a different approach with him. He would have helped, if only you had."

Mark grimaced. "Spilt milk at this point. What do you think about what he said…is he telling the truth?"

Gillian looked back at the note.

"Jilly. Tell the dickless wonder this much. There are no aliens on the ship. None. It's just a ship, with a wicked smart AI on it. And it has to get back to its home planet, or our species is doomed. It has to warn them so they can come help us defend against a race of aliens that may wipe us out, if they find us first. So every time you do anything to interfere with that ship getting back to its home planet, you are cutting the throat of humanity. Tell dickless to let us finish the job and in a few years, he'll have all the technology he wants."

Gillian nodded. "Yeah, he wouldn't lie about that. It's the truth."

She gazed at Mark. "Let him go, Mark. Let him finish his mission. He's doing it for us…for humanity. Let him do it!"

Mark bowed his head for a second, then shook it and looked back at Gillian.

"I can't, Gillian. There are forces at work here bigger than I've told you. Jim doesn't know it, but the cards are stacked against him. We have to find him and help him."

Gillian could hardly breathe.

"What? What do you mean?"

Mark sighed. "The Russians have gotten involved. And the Chinese are sniffing around now. It's turned into a race with both of them."

"Oh, crap," said Gillian.

"Yes, exactly," said Mark.

Gillian stormed to her feet, pacing in the office, glaring at Mark.

"You have totally screwed this up."

Mark nodded glumly. "Yep."

Gillian kept pacing.

"Now we have to find him and help him."

"Yep."

Gillian rounded on Mark.

"If you are playing me on this, I will make Jim's words come true, Mark."

"What?"

"You play me on this, and you will truly be a dickless wonder, because I will cut it off," she said quietly.

Mark nodded. "I know. And I would deserve it."

Gillian sat down again.

"How do you know about the Russians?"

"We know. Leave it at that."

Mark leaned back in his chair and gazed coolly at Gillian.

"I thought you were the leak at first," he said. "But the timing didn't work out. We got intel that the Russians were on to us the same day you were read in. It couldn't have made the circuit that quickly. So it's someone else. Someone close to this project."

Gillian shook her head.

"You better find them, and fast. Or else we are all screwed. Even the Russians."

*****

Perry Barnes was sleeping quite soundly in his apartment in Deseret, having a wonderful dream about a beautiful woman in a beautiful airplane, when something woke him up.

"Damn it!" he muttered as he slowly came awake.

Groaning and cussing, he got out of bed.

"I'm coming, I'm coming," he yelled at his apartment door as the knocking came again. Throwing on a pair of jeans, he stumbled to the door, glancing at the clock.

"Six A. M.? Are you freaking kiddin' me?" he asked the empty air. Throwing open the door, he stood in shock as Jim Carter quickly ducked past him into the apartment, turning to face him.

"Shut the door, Perry, quick," he said.

Perry shut the door, staring at the man in front of him. Jim was dressed all in black – black jeans, black shirt and vest, black leather coat. He was carrying a small duffel bag.

"What the hell, Jim?" asked Perry. "Do you know how many FBI agents and Air Force spooks have been around here?"

Jim nodded. "I'm sure. I'm really sorry about that, Perry. Did they cause you much trouble?"

"Nah," said Perry. "But it's been Fed City around here for the last few weeks. They tore your red hangar apart, right down to the last nail. They searched everything in your main hangar too and locked it up tight. What the hell did you two have in there, anyway? E.T.?"

Jim grinned. "Kinda sorta. Are they still hanging around?"

"Damn right," said Perry. "You can't take a step around that airport without tripping over a Fed."

"Well, I hope they're not watching your apartment here," said Jim.

Perry waved at a chair. "Have a seat. By the way, you look like shit. Coffee?"

"Please," said Jim. "I'd kill for a good cup of coffee."

"You got it," said Perry, heading for the kitchen. "How about some eggs and toast to go with it?"

Later, after some breakfast, Jim stared at Perry across the table.

"Perry, I hate to involve you in this. But I need a small plane," he said. "Something not traceable to me, fairly low profile, low radar cross-section. Doesn't have to be fast or carry cargo. Just me. And the longest range I can get."

Perry thought about it.

"I know where there's a Long-EZ for sale. Up in Reno. It's a good one, I know the owner. He's asking seventy-five thousand;

but it's worth it. It's perfect shape, low time, autopilot, full glass synthetic vision IFR."

Jim nodded. "That'll do. But I want to buy it through a third-party, someone not associated with Deseret. They'll be watching all our transactions - yours, mine, Randy's, everybody on the field. They'll be expecting something like this."

Perry grinned. "No problem. I think I have just the solution for you. I believe his nutcase ex-wife needs a new airplane. She just doesn't know it yet. When do you need it?"

"Yesterday," said Jim. "There's an airport not too far from Reno, Carson City. Tell him I'll pay a bonus if he can have it positioned there by day after tomorrow at 7PM, fully fueled and ready to go. Tell him to just tie it down outside, on the ramp somewhere close to the terminal, and leave the key under the seat cushion."

"How much bonus?"

"Whatever you think." Jim handed over the duffel bag. "Here's a hundred thousand. Will that be enough?"

Perry nodded. "Yeah. That should be plenty."

"Whatever is left is yours for your help," Jim added.

Perry glared at him. "I don't need a dime for my help, Jim. You know better than that."

"Still." Jim looked at Perry steadily. "I may not be around to use it anymore if this all goes sideways. So, you put it to good use."

Perry nodded. "I'll get on it."

Jim stood, turned to go. At the door, he hesitated.

"Remember, they'll be listening to your phone calls, Perry."

Perry nodded. "I know. I'll handle it."

Jim gazed at him steadily.

"You're a good friend, Perry. I hate you got pulled into this."

Perry just laughed.

"Crap, Jim! Most fun I've had in ten years! You take care, now!"

LIES, MORE LIES AND DAMN LIES

Leaving Perry Barnes' apartment, Jim drove to Tonopah. He and Bonnie had prepared another safe house there. For two nights he rested at Tonopah, gaining back his strength, waiting for Perry to complete the airplane purchase in Reno. He also picked up a fake ID, two matching credit cards, and another hundred thousand dollars left at the safe house.

Now, two days after his visit with Perry, Jim approached Carson City, wondering if the Feds would be waiting for him. He had swapped the Tundra for an F150 at the Tonopah safe house. He was virtually certain he had not been followed.

How Bonnie had laughed at him, early on, when he described all the precautions he was taking. But Jim's years as a mercenary in Africa had taught him to be prepared...

Who's laughing now, Bonnie? You said we'd never need all this stuff. Well, guess what...

Turning into the airport at Carson City as the evening shadows fell, Jim drove slowly to a small hangar near the far southeast part of the field. Parking in front of the hangar, he got out and pushed open the large sliding door.

Jim had kept a spare hangar at Carson City for years. At one time, back in his mercenary days, he had used it for storing weapons and ammunition, things he didn't want lying around his home.

More recently, after his mercenary days had ended, he used it to store aircraft parts and spare engines, and perhaps a few other things he didn't want in his apartment if unexpected guests arrived.

And Jim had never used a credit card to pay for anything at Carson; it was his safe place. Nothing about the hangar was in his name.

There was just enough room beside the piled aircraft engines, stacked wings, and other parts to pull the F150 into the hangar. He took a flight bag out of the truck, closed, and locked the hangar door, and started the long walk back toward the terminal.

It was cold, a brisk wind blowing off the mountains, and on the way a passing shower spat rain at him. But he had changed to a heavy parka, insulated jeans, and insulated gloves now. He was reasonably comfortable. Reaching the terminal, he went inside, found a seat in the pilot's lounge, and got out his flight planning bag.

Two hours later, it was dark. Jim had completed his flight planning, walked down the street to grab a late lunch, and was back in the terminal. So far, he had seen nothing unusual - no sign he was followed, no sign of any Feds lurking around. But there was also no sign of Perry or the Long-EZ.

Getting another Coke from the machine, Jim returned to his seat just in time to see the Long-EZ touch down. The sleek fiberglass aircraft rolled to the nearest turnoff and taxied slowly toward the ramp, rocking slightly on its gear.

Jim went out of the terminal building and found a dark spot in the shadows, where he could watch without being seen. The EZ taxied up to the gas pumps, shut down, and a young man - a stranger, Jim didn't recognize him - got out and fueled it. He climbed back in, started it up again, taxied to the ramp, pulled into an empty spot, and shut down.

The nose gear began to fold up, the nose lowered and the EZ squatted down on its rubber nose bumper - a feature of its design allowing it to be more stable when parked. The canopy flipped up and the man climbed out again.

He reached into the front cockpit, putting something under the seat cushion. He reached into the back cockpit, pulled out a flight bag, and closed and latched the canopy.

Laying the flight bag on the tarmac, he walked around the airplane, tying it down. Then he grabbed the flight bag and headed toward the terminal.

Jim stayed where he was, out of sight, and waited. In about twenty minutes, a pickup pulled into the parking lot, a woman driving. The man walked out of the terminal, got in the pickup with her, and they left.

Jim waited another twenty minutes to be sure they were gone, then walked back in the terminal, grabbed his flight bag, and walked out to the EZ. He opened the canopy, threw the flight bag in the back seat, and retrieved the key from under the front seat cushion. He walked around the plane, removing the tie downs. He climbed in, folding his big frame into the tiny front seat.

Jim had flown an EZ before - in fact, he had owned one in the past - but he had forgotten just how cozy the cockpit was. He had to work his feet down into the rudder wells a bit at a time, so as not to bark his shins.

The joke about the EZ, he remembered, *is that you don't get in it, you wear it.*

The Long-EZ was a home-built airplane design, made of fiberglass and epoxy, very light. With a small engine and large tanks relative to its size, it had a typical range of 1,500 miles. It didn't have much baggage space, but Jim didn't need baggage.

He needed to get to Bonnie.

Flipping on the mags, he hit the starter and the engine caught, still warm from the previous flight. He hit the nose gear switch, feeling the nose of the plane rise up until the gear locked. Then he taxied back down the ramp toward his hangar.

Pulling into the row where his hangar was located, he shut down directly in front of his hangar. He slid the hangar door open and took three duffel bags out of the truck, putting them in the back seat of the plane and tying everything down. Then he did a full preflight, checking over the plane more than he normally would have, since it was new to him. He found nothing wrong. Finally, he locked the hangar, put his coat and gloves in the back seat, stuck his maps, tablet and electronic flight bag into the front, and climbed back in.

Inside the cockpit, he did a second preflight on the electronics; everything was working fine. He entered his flight plan into the glass cockpit. Fully ready now, he fired up the engine and taxied back out to the runway. It was well past nine o'clock. There was no tower at the airport, part of the reason Jim had selected Carson City.

Making a blind call to any aircraft in the area warning them he was taking off, Jim pulled onto the runway and firewalled the throttle. He gently lifted off and set a course for Kalispell, Montana, six hundred nautical miles away.

By the time he refueled at Kalispell, it would be daylight. He'd have to spend most of the day there killing time, in order to slip over the Canadian border during the dark. But at least he'd be halfway to Bonnie.

* * * * *

At Khodinka Airfield, Viktor had received a sat phone call.

"Anything else? Any idea of where it is?"

"No, sir. Not yet. But we'll find it. I'm sure of it."

"Good," said Viktor. "Keep me informed as best you can."

"Will do, sir. It's not easy - I'm surrounded by them nearly all the time. But I'll find a way."

"I know," said Viktor. "Hang in there."

Viktor hung up the sat phone and put it back into its cradle to charge. He leaned back and reviewed his plans.

He considered the conversation he had just finished with his deep-cover operative in the U.S. The man had called him just as he was finishing dinner.

His informant was sure the alien starship had returned to Earth. It was lacking ruthenium, at least - based on the container left behind at Deseret - so they had to come back for that. They couldn't refine it on Mars.

And Bonnie Page - the Air Force pilot who appeared to be on the starship now - would want to meet up with her lover, Jim Carter, who had escaped from DoD custody at Nellis.

Viktor almost laughed out loud. If Carter had been in detention in Russia, there would have been no escape. And he would have spilled his guts quickly.

The Americans are so soft, he thought. *Not capable of doing* what has to be done.

He picked up the radio report from Colonel Gregori Bogdonovich. Gregori had his Spetsnaz troops enroute - a dozen AN-124 heavy lift transports packed with troops and gear. They were staging to Ugolny Airport at Anadyr, which Gregori felt was as good a place as any for jumping off an assault team toward America.

If the starship is on the East Coast of America, or in the deep South, we're in trouble, thought Viktor. *There's no way we can send a dozen AN-124 aircraft all the way across America without a major battle.*

But…if it was the West Coast, or Alaska. It might be doable. If the prize was worth it.

And the prize was a starship. Viktor was sure of it now. He had gone back over the evidence, every item, in painstaking detail.

There was no doubt in his mind.

The damn Americans had almost gotten a starship in their hands - and let it get away. But the fact that Bonnie Page was on it, and clearly in love with Jim Carter, meant the ship would come back to America, or nearby, to pick up Jim and get the ruthenium.

And Viktor's team would be waiting. He had already given the orders. He had no hesitation. Letting the Americans have such a prize was unacceptable. He would take it from them. Wherever it was, his team would find it, and take it.

And - this time, Viktor did laugh out loud - the stupid Americans would do most of the work for him. They had no concept that one of their team was also on his.

Viktor had intel that the Chinese were getting involved. They clearly had their own operatives in the DoD. But Viktor knew he could stay ahead of the Chinese. They would never catch up to him. He had someone not just on the inside of the DoD; not just on the inside of the Air Force; but on the inside of the project.

He had the inside lane.

KALISPELL

In a small white room, Bonnie Page came to herself. She was in a bed. Dim lighting from the ceiling seemed to come from all directions. Her head hurt.

Turning her head, she groaned. This had to be one of the worst headaches she'd ever had. She lay still for a couple of minutes, trying to take in her surroundings.

There were several low tables on the side of the room, with drawers beneath them. The tables were bare, and the drawers had small silver squares on them. Locks, by her best guess. There was a door, or a hatch, in the far wall, about six feet high by the look of it. A bit shorter than the ones on Jade.

In the corner were two chairs. They looked quite normal; just chairs. Although they appeared to be a bit low, she thought.

Thinking about it, she remembered the two figures that came out from behind Jade's landing legs and shot her. They were small, not more than five and a half feet tall. She looked at the two low chairs again.

I'm on the Singheko ship, she thought. *A prisoner.*

She lifted an arm to see if she was restrained. She wasn't. Moving slowly because of the pain in her head, she sat up. Gingerly, she swung her legs over the side of the bed and pushed off, to see if she could stand. She made it to her feet, swaying.

She realized her outer spacesuit was gone; she was in the inner layer of the suit, skintight long johns. Stumbling over to the counter, she tried to pull one of the drawers open. It was locked. She tried the others, but all of them were locked.

"They're locked for your protection," said a voice behind her.

Bonnie turned, almost falling from the sudden motion. She caught herself on the counter.

Just inside the open hatch stood a figure. The head was a bit more squarish than a human's, not as rounded. Its face was similar, though - two eyes on top, a mouth below. A flat nose, so small it almost disappeared in the face.

It had two arms, two legs. It had hands, she noted, wearing white gloves. It had black boots on its feet, and a black belt cinched up a white uniform of some kind, with patches and insignia on it.

The figure stood quietly.

"Don't be afraid," the creature said in perfect English. "We won't hurt you."

Bonnie started to breathe again. She hadn't realized she was holding her breath until it started to hurt.

"So I'm your prisoner?" she asked.

"No. You are not," said the creature. "I promise, you will be free to go shortly. But we would like to do a couple of things with you before you go."

Bonnie had visions of being dissected or tortured.

"And what are those things?" she asked.

"First, we'd like to make sure you are OK medically," said the creature.

"And then?"

"And then we'd like to warn you about that Singheko ship you've been running around with."

* * * * *

After landing at Kalispell City Airport around 3 AM, Jim parked the EZ on the ramp. It was too early to get fuel, and too early to find an open restaurant for breakfast. Instead, he looked for a place to sleep. He knew some pilots were not diligent about locking the cabins of their aircraft. Sure enough, he found an older A36 Bonanza on the parking ramp, unlocked. He went aboard and stretched out in a comfortable leather seat. Setting his alarm for 9:30 AM, he went to sleep.

When the alarm went off at 9:30, he got up, checked out the window to make sure nobody was around, then left the Bonanza as he had found it. Walking to the nearby road, he found a restaurant open for breakfast. He dawdled after finishing his breakfast; he had a lot of time to kill.

He couldn't cross the Canadian border during daylight; he had no flight plan, and filing one might tip off Mark Rodgers. He thought about filing a flight plan with his fake identity, but he was afraid to risk that. If they made any connection between Jim and the EZ, it would all unravel. He decided to do it the hard way - wait until dark, then cross the border down low, in the weeds. The EZ had a low radar cross-section; it was hard to see, especially down low. It should work.

He could never have made it this far without the synthetic vision in the EZ. It had a first-class set of avionics; even in the pitch-black night, it used GPS and displayed the terrain around him, allowing him to stay out of the rocks.

He had flown all the way from Carson City at night, in autumn, down in the valleys, hiding from radar, using nothing but synthetic vision to avoid the mountain peaks. But Jim knew synthetic vision wasn't perfect, and what he was doing was incredibly dangerous. Staying down in the valleys at night was unbelievably hard flying.

Probably a world record, he thought. *If not a world record for flying through dangerous valleys at night, at least a world record for stupidity.*

Yet he had no desire to lead Mark Rodgers back to Jade - or Bonnie and Rita. So, he would stay down in the rocks, doing the hard flying, until he was across the border.

But why are Bonnie and Rita not responding? Jim asked himself. He had left another voicemail on the burner phone, but there was no response from them. While he was at Tonopah, he had called on the HF frequencies, but nothing. Not a peep.

After a while, he decided it was stupid to try to cross the border tired. He walked down to the nearest hotel. He showed his fake ID and got a room, paying in cash. In the room, he stumbled to the bed and fell across it. As he fell into a troubled slumber, the flashback came one more time...

AK-47 rounds from a distant sniper clinked off the bottom of the plane as he fell out of the cockpit and lay in the sand.

He looked behind him at his WSO - Weapon Systems Officer, Al "Capone" Calderone, his best friend.

Al lay slumped against the side of the cockpit. Jim dragged himself over and tried to find a pulse.

There was none. Al was dead. And Jim had killed him.

Al had yelled at him not to go back for one more pass, but Jim did it anyway. The skinnies were about to overrun the Marine squad below them. Jim wasn't having it.

He was out of ammo and marking rockets, but he could still scare the hell out of them, he thought. He could buy the grunts a little more time. Reinforcements were on the way - all he had to do was make the skinnies put their heads down just for a few minutes, and the rest of the Marine platoon would be there. Maybe.

He streaked in, putting on a show, out of weapons, right over the heads of the skinnies. For a moment, he thought he was good. He started his pullout - the plane shuddered as a massive impact hit somewhere behind him. The engine didn't spool down - it just cratered, damaged beyond all hope, stopping so fast the torque of the sudden stoppage twisted the F-16 on its axis.

He was too low - there was nowhere to go.

He reached for the ejection loop over his head...but it was too late. The ground hit him hard.

Rita was getting hot, tired, and pissed off. Andy was working in the reactor room. The first order of materials had arrived by truck. She had directed the driver to unload it outside the hangar, and after he departed, she carted it in through the side door by hand, and she was tired. She had to break down several of the crates in order to fit the contents through the small side door piecemeal. Andy could have handled it in half the time - but of course, she couldn't take a chance on letting the android outside the hangar. And she couldn't open the large hangar door in front to make things easier.

It was a big hangar - the biggest their secret shell corporation had been able to find in the area. Even so, Jade barely fit inside. The starship was arranged diagonally, corner to corner, and took up the entire available space.

Rita finally got the last of the shipment inside and sealed up the side door again. She had hung black plastic sheeting just inside the side door, to keep out prying eyes. And the hangar was hot - even though they were well into October now, there was still enough heat in the air to make the hangar an oven during the day.

Inside the starship was just as hot, maybe more so. Normally, Jade could use the life support system to keep things cool inside. But Andy had taken life support down for his work on the reactor, so all Rita could do was keep the top and side hatches open, put two box fans at each hatch, and hope for a little air. There wasn't much movement of air inside the ship, but she kept hoping as the sweat poured off her face.

"Dammit, my memories of work don't do justice to the real thing!" she swore at Jade.

<Sorry. I did the best I could when I built you> said Jade.

"You didn't build me, Jade! Nature created me with DNA. All you did was put the pieces together. Remember that!" Rita spat.

<Yes, Rita. I'll try to remember>

"Anything from Jim? Any voice mails on the burner phone? Anything on HF?"

<No. Nothing. I suppose he is still in detention. Rita, face facts, please. The chances of Jim escaping are minuscule. We're not going to hear from him. We're on our own. We have to finish the tDrive and get back to Sanctuary>

"Dammit all to hell," fumed Rita. She turned and walked back to the reactor room at the back of the ship, where Andy was working. Checking the telltale on the hatch, she noted it was green. She cranked open the hatch and entered.

"Andy! How's it going?" she asked, standing just inside the double hatch.

The android was at the back of the reactor room, on top of a pyramid-shaped object, about six feet by six feet at the base, tapering to a top of only a few feet square. He was in his four-legged configuration, leaving him with two hands to lay down long strips of…something…that looked like black licorice.

"*It's going well, Rita. I have completed the foundation for the reactor. I'm putting on sealant now to isolate it from the rest of the ship and contain any stray radiation.*"

"With licorice?" asked Rita.

"*It's not licorice,*" said Andy. "*Although it looks like it. But no, it's much more expensive than that. It's semi-liquid lead sealed inside nanotubes. I doubt I could explain the technology to you. Unless you want to go back into the medpod for an upgrade.*"

Rita shuddered. "No, thank you. I'll leave that to you. How much longer?"

"*Once I receive the ruthenium, I can finish the reactor and the tDrive in one day now. Maybe a bit less. So, if the ruthenium arrives as expected next Monday, then we can leave on Tuesday. Assuming you can repair the outside of the ship by yourself.*"

Rita nodded. "And no radiation danger yet?"

"*No. Until the reactor is started, you are free to come inside this room at any time without concern. Once I start the reactor, you will need to check the telltale at the door before you enter, every time, religiously. Even the slightest leak would be detrimental to your health if you were not wearing a radiation suit. I'll notify you before the reactor goes into operation. But you should still make a habit of checking the telltale before entering, as you did just now."*

"How do you know I checked it?" asked Rita, puzzled.

"I have access to the cameras," said Andy. *"As part of my work. That's how I know there is someone outside right now, approaching the hangar."*

"Shit!" yelled Rita, spinning and dashing out of the room.

* * * * *

Jim woke up in the cheap motel in Kalispell. The sun was blazing through the west window. He shook his head. Groggily, he got to his feet, shed his clothes, and stumbled to the shower.

Standing under the water for a good ten minutes, his brain finally started to function. He stepped out, toweled off, and walked to the nightstand to check the time.

It was almost 5 PM. He had slept most of the day. He knew sunset would be around 6 PM. Time to get moving.

Dressing, he walked to the front desk, checked out, and walked across U.S. 93 to a decent-looking restaurant. He didn't bother with the anti-facial recognition materials here; he was fairly sure Kalispell, Montana didn't have cameras on every street corner like Vegas.

After a good dinner, he walked down the street to a convenience store and stocked up on water, jerky, and a few pastries for energy during the flight. Then he walked back to the airport and crossed over to the EZ on the ramp.

He had left the three bags of cash in the back seat of the plane. Jim knew airports; he knew it was a lot safer in there than with him, or in the hotel. Now he checked everything on the plane, doing a comprehensive preflight. It was a good plane, he decided; everything was in order. No oil usage, everything tight and shipshape. He was pleased.

Jim rubbed a hand across the engine cowling and smiled. To a pilot, a good plane was like a good friend - or a lover. There was a relationship there. Jim almost leaned forward and kissed the side of the plane, but he didn't. That might draw attention, and that was the last thing he needed. There were already a few gawkers up by the terminal, staring at the EZ. It was an unusual-looking airplane and always drew casual onlookers. Better to get going before someone walked out and started asking him about his pretty airplane.

He snugged into the cockpit, fired up the engine, and hit the "Gear Down" switch. The nose gear lowered slowly, picking up the nose of the aircraft, until it was standing level. Jim taxied over to the gas pumps, shut it down again, got out and refueled until both tanks were topped off.

Now he had at least a 1,500-mile range. He climbed back in, started the engine, and tuned the ATIS - the Automatic Terminal Information Service - which would give him the details he needed to take off. Noting the local weather and the active runway, he started the taxi down to runway 13.

Stopping at the hold short line, he ran up the engine, checked both mags, and idled the engine. Pulling up his location on the electronic chart, he noted he needed to start out to the south, rather than the north. Just north of him was a controlled airport, Glacier Park International. He didn't want to talk to their tower, so he would go south first to gain altitude, then turn northeast and cross west of their airspace.

He made a blind call to local traffic on the public CTAF frequency, turned on to the runway, brought the engine up to power, and held the little EZ on the centerline. At forty knots, Jim pulled the stick back, taking the load off the nosewheel. He let the EZ decide when to fly - one of the unique advantages of a canard aircraft. At 70 knots, it lifted off and was flying. Jim let the speed build up until he was climbing at 90 knots.

Nearing Flathead Lake, he turned back to the north-northwest, climbing up to 5,000 feet as he made his way back past Kalispell up the Stillwater River.

Clear of Glacier Park's airspace, he dropped down to five hundred feet over the valley floor, heading for the Canadian border. The sun was setting now. It was getting dark. Jim alternated between looking outside visually and checking the synthetic vision for terrain avoidance.

Now came the hard part.

* * * * *

Rita ran across the hangar to the side door, through the black plastic sheeting she had hung, and carefully opened the door to the outside. She stepped out and shielded her eyes from the glare of the sun setting in the West. She had a Kimber .45 auto tucked in her back waistband and a baby Glock 9mm stuck in her sock. Her 12-gauge pump shotgun leaned against the wall just inside the door.

A silver Audi was parked beside the hangar. A man in jeans and ball cap approached her, almost to the door when she stepped out. He pulled up short, staring at her.

"Hello?" Rita asked. "Can I help you?"

The man glanced askance at her.

"I'm sorry, I didn't realize anyone was here. Are you the new owner?"

"I work for the corporation that owns it. What can I do for you?" Rita persisted.

"Corporation? Oh, I see. So, it was bought by a corporation?"

"Yes," said Rita. "NWT Oil & Gas Exploration. What can I do for you?"

"Well, I was hoping to take a look inside. I thought it was still for sale. Is there any chance I could take a quick peek? Just to see what I missed?"

Rita shook her head.

"No, I'm sorry. We have proprietary oil exploration equipment inside, I'm afraid."

"Oh, too bad," said the man. "Well, at least take my card," he said, digging out his wallet and pulling out a card. "If your corporation changes its mind, please call me first. We're looking for a large hangar like this in the area."

"I'll pass it along," said Rita, taking the card.

"Thanks!" The man smiled at her. It was meant to be a warm smile, but something about it sent a cold chill down Rita's back. It was like looking at a smiling python.

The man turned and walked back to his Audi. Rita turned and re-entered the hangar, but she left the side door cracked until she watched the man drive away. Then she returned to the ship and went to the bridge.

"Jade, did you see that Audi outside?"

<Yes, Rita. The remote cameras you mounted are working fine. I got the license plate and I'm trying to identify it now>

Rita looked at the card. "It says, North Prairie Oil & Gas Company. Now, isn't that a coincidence?"

<The Audi is registered to that company> reported Jade. <But that doesn't mean anything>

"Run a thorough search on that company, Jade," said Rita. "I have a feeling it's a front for something else."

<Running a search. I'll let you know>

TERESHKOVA

Flying up U.S. 93 in the EZ, Jim crossed into Canada just after 8 PM, well west of Eureka, at about 500 feet above the ground. He continued on and picked up the Kootenay River on the other side of the border. He was as low as he felt he could go and have any semblance of safety. It was very dark at this northern latitude now. The moon was rising in the east, full but still mostly hidden behind the mountains. That moon and the synthetic vision were his only hope of survival tonight. He was pushing his luck far beyond the point of sanity.

But he had to get to Bonnie.

The EZ droned on, the sound of the engine a song to put a man to sleep if he wasn't careful. Jim set his phone to sound an alarm every ten minutes; he put a tiny bit of up trim on the plane, so that if he went to sleep, at least it might climb and not descend. It was a slim chance - probably, if he went to sleep, he would slump forward into the shoulder straps - but since the plane was a sidestick, his hand might simply fall off the stick without disturbing it. Then - maybe the alarm would wake him up before he hit a mountain.

Jim heaved a huge sigh.

"What the hell am I doing?" he thought. *"Surely there is a better way."*

But he couldn't think of one at the moment.

Passing Cranbrook a bit later, Jim saw the lights of the small Canadian city off to the west. He remembered a commercial flight he had taken once, from Calgary to Vancouver. The 737 had stopped at Cranbrook, for some odd reason. It was the Canadian Rockies milk run, he supposed. He remembered the flight attendant coming down the aisle with the trolley after takeoff. She had stopped beside him and said, "coffee, tea or soda, eh?"

Sometimes the stereotype is true, he grinned.

An hour later, he was passing Golden. He had picked up

a slight headwind - not much, about five knots. He was still crossing the ground at 139 knots, so making good time.

But he was getting tired. The stress of flying this low was getting to him. Jim decided to give himself a little break. He climbed up to 3,000 feet, putting him in a much safer place in the center of the valley. Now he could relax a bit.

He was a fourth of the way to his destination for tonight.

* * * * *

Gillian Carter Hassell turned over in bed, staring at the clock. It was 5 AM. But she couldn't sleep anymore. Quietly, trying not to wake Mark, she got up and went to the bathroom.

As she departed, she heard Mark's voice behind her.

"I'm awake. Don't worry about being quiet."

Gillian waved a hand and went about her business in the bathroom, coming out in a dozen minutes and climbing back into bed. Mark had propped himself up on his pillows and was looking at his tablet.

"Anything?" asked Gillian.

"Nope. Nothing," said Mark. "He's fallen off the face of the Earth."

"That's OK. Let him go. Let him get back to the ship. Then try to make an alliance with him. Please trust me on this."

Mark sighed. "I know. But I hope you're right."

Gillian laid an arm across his chest.

"You and me both."

Gillian lay there for a bit, then got up.

"I'm going to shower," she said.

"OK," said Mark. "I'll be right behind you."

Gillian went to the bathroom and showered, then got dressed while Mark did the same. When they were both ready, they left together, riding in Mark's black SUV to Nellis.

I can't believe I'm doing this, thought Gillian as they drove. She gazed out the window at the dawn. Vegas was slowly coming alive outside. They were into autumn now. The nights were getting longer.

Gillian sighed. *I'm with the man who's chasing my brother. Why? Why am I doing this? What if the Russians find the ship before we do? Before Jim gets back to the ship? What then?*

They pulled up to the gate at Nellis and the guard waved them through. Driving across the base to the offices Mark had commandeered, Gillian couldn't stop thinking about it. Then she turned, gazed at Mark beside her.

Why do I feel this way about this man? What's happening to me?

Mark pulled up into the parking lot. Gillian sighed again and opened the door.

"What?" asked Mark.

"Nothing," she replied. "Just thinking."

Mark paused for a second.

"Gillian. I will not hurt him. If there is any other way. If there is any way for Jim to come out of this clean, you know I'll make it happen."

Gillian nodded. "I know. But it still scares me."

She looked over at Mark.

"I'm sleeping with the man who could harm my brother. Or worse, if things go sideways."

Mark leaned over and kissed her lightly on the cheek.

"I will do everything in my power to make this come out alright for Jim. Anything in my power."

Gillian nodded again. "I know," she whispered. "It's not so much you I'm worried about, Mark. I know Jim. I know how stubborn he can be. And how dangerous."

Mark squeezed her hand.

"Let's not borrow trouble. Sufficient unto the day…"

Gillian smiled.

Entering the building, they went to the command center and checked in. But the officer on duty reported there was no news.

"We lost him at the Rock Hotel," he said, "and not a damn thing since. Not a single hit on anything. No facial recognition, no credit cards, no phone calls, no flight plans, no orders of ruthenium, not a damn thing."

"How about the ship?" asked Mark.

"Nothing, sir. Not a single hit in air or space. Nothing on the satellites, either. It just disappeared."

Mark fumed.

"It didn't disappear. It's still here somewhere. It was damaged in that Antarctica scrape; I know it. We found two separate sets of debris with slightly different compositions. That ship didn't make it out of the solar system. I can feel it in my bones."

The officer nodded. "We'll keep looking, sir. That's a promise. We're scouring for anything."

Mark nodded and gestured to Gillian.

"I'm going back to my office. I have to deal with Dr. Janeski."

Gillian nodded. "I'll stay here for a while, maybe some idea will come to me."

Mark waved and departed. Gillian sat in a chair behind the primary sensor operator, thinking hard.

If I were Jim, where would I go? What do I remember from our childhood, or from his military days, that would give me a clue? And even if we find them...then what? Do we work with Jim, let him be the intermediary? Jim hasn't shown much cooperation so far. Maybe we just try to find the ship, and talk to it directly...

* * * * *

This time, Viktor Tereshkova did laugh out loud.

"Found!" he yelled. "We found them before the stupid Americans!"

Viktor pumped a fist. Then he thought about his options.

He could let the Americans have the starship.

Or he could commit an act of war and take it for Russia. And then Russia would have the stars - and the Earth as well.

In his mind, the choice was clear. Find the starship, take it, and let the chips fall where they may. To the victor belong the spoils...

Viktor fell back into his chair and got on the sat phone to

Colonel Gregori Bogdonovich.

"They're at Fort Nelson, Canada," he told Gregori when he got an answer. "You can swing around Alaska and never enter American airspace. Come in directly from the north. The Canadians will see you coming, and of course the Americans will know at the same time, but what can they do? It's not their country, and by the time they get it figured out, we'll have it and be gone."

The voice on the other end of the sat phone sounded muffled, but Viktor understood the words.

"It'll be an act of war. The Canadians will not take it sitting down," said Gregori.

"I don't care," said Viktor. "The prize is worth it. To be the first humans to travel to the stars? I'd risk anything to put that technology in our hands. It's either us or them, and I intend for it to be us. Don't look back, Gregori."

"Understood, sir. I'll have all finalized plans to you in three hours."

"Good. Thank you, Gregori. This is a historic moment."

Viktor hung up and leaned back in his chair. He had other calls to make, other wheels to put into motion. But he wanted to savor this moment, just a bit.

His hunch about checking large hangars for sale on the western side of North America had paid off. Carter was from the West; Bonnie Page was from the West. His gut told them they would stay on the western side of the continent. And their lifelong association with aircraft had told him it would be an airport.

They had found a recently sold hangar in Fort Nelson. When he sent one of his men to check it out, a woman walked out and confronted him.

A woman who matched the description of the female called Rita who had been sighted at Deseret, just before the starship escaped from the Americans. The woman who had left the stupid note on Mars.

So, they had run infrared scans of the hangar last night. And the thing was, the scans showed nothing in the center of the hangar.

A long, wedge-shaped shaped nothing. Something that was so well insulated, it emitted no heat at all. The hangar around it showed various items in the infrared - electrical panels, water pipes, the normal stuff.

But the middle of the hangar was completely blanked by the starship.

He had them.

FORT NELSON

Gillian and Mark sat at dinner in Mark's apartment, talking in a low voice about their lack of success in finding Jim and the starship.

"You're sure the Russians are on to it?" asked Gillian.

"Absolutely sure," replied Mark. "We have a contact that's rock solid. The GRU is on this like stink on shit."

"The Chinese?"

"They're sniffing around. They know something is afoot, but I don't think they've figured it out yet."

"Mark, we have to find Jim before they do. If they find him first, it's all over. Not only for Jim, but for all of us. You know what the Russians would do if they got their hands on that technology. The entire world is at stake! And Jim doesn't know they're after him, so he won't be on his guard!"

"So let's find him, Jilly. You know him better than anyone. Let's think this through one more time. Where would he go?" asked Mark.

Gillian thought.

"Well, it would probably involve airplanes, or an airport, or both," she said. "As we've already discussed."

"I agree," said Mark. "When we're in danger, we return to the things we know best. But that doesn't really narrow it down much. There are thousands of airports in North America alone. And if he decides to go overseas, then the number goes up tremendously."

Gillian shook her head.

"I don't think he'll go overseas. Mexico, maybe. But I don't think so. I think it'll be the U.S. or Canada. Alaska. The Aleutians. Someplace like that."

"He likes the North."

"Yes. That's his favorite place to get away. My gut tells me it'll be in the North somewhere."

"Well, we've checked everything we can think of. But I can't send a man to every airport in North America. Somehow, we have to find a way to narrow it down. And without some kind of electronic hit on something related, I don't see us doing that."

"You've looked at all aircraft transactions in the last six weeks, right?"

"Yep. Every one we can find. But you realize, just like cars, a person can buy a plane and not change the registration. He could be flying around in anything, and we wouldn't know it unless the seller sent in a registration change notice. And a little bit of money goes a long way in that kind of scenario - I think ten thousand dollars would convince anyone to delay the notification."

"Yes," mused Gillian. "Too right."

"We've checked every hangar sale, both individual and corporate, in the U.S. since August. We've asked the Canadians to check their side, but they've been a little slow off the block. We haven't gotten anything from them yet."

"Who's doing the checking for you?"

"Pujold. He's my best man."

"Pujold. What's his last name?"

"Rukmini. Hungarian. A good man. Been with me for thirty years. His mother and father also worked for DoD."

"But no joy?"

"No joy. He's still working with the Canadians to get hangar sales for the last few months."

"Then they're in Canada," said Gillian.

"How do you know?"

Gillian leaned forward, wine glass in her hand.

"Because he loves the North, and it's the only place we don't have complete records on yet. He's there. I know it. We can find him if we just get creative."

Mark nodded. "OK. Let's get creative. What more can we do?"

"How would you get to Canada without detection? Drive?"

Mark shook his head.

"No. Too difficult to cross the border in a car with a fake ID."

"So he'll fly," said Gillian. "How? How will he get across the border without filing a flight plan?"

Mark puzzled over that for a while.

"Get down low, fly up the valleys at night. Totally dangerous, but maybe possible."

"Where would you cross?"

"Hm...middle of nowhere, but someplace where you'd have a pretty straight shot at staying out of the rocks."

"Is there a place like that?" Gillian knew Mark had flown in the Air Force before he took a desk job.

"Rocky Mountain Trench would be my choice. A reasonably level valley all the way from Kalispell, Montana to Watson Lake, Yukon Territory."

Gillian leaned back.

"Then that's what he did. Follow that thread and you'll find Jim. But do me a favor."

"What?"

"Put somebody besides Rukmini on it. Just for grins. Just to humor me."

Mark nodded slowly. "OK. I can do that."

* * * * *

It had been an exhausting night. Jim came out of the Rocky Mountain Trench just short of Watson Lake at 3 AM.

He knew he was not thinking clearly. His decisions were poor. He had been flying for seven hours now, in the most taxing conditions a pilot could imagine. His head nodded continuously. He slapped himself, pinched himself, forced himself to stay awake. Every ten minutes, his timer went off and he punched it back into silence. Out of sheer desperation, he had climbed to 6,000 feet, just because he was having so much trouble staying awake. It was higher than he wanted to be, but he had to give himself a little cushion. His reaction times were slow, and he was not in good shape at all. The pneumonia had hit him harder than he thought.

And you're not a young man anymore, hoss, he thought.

Jim Carter had fought in the First Africa Conflict. Then, as a mercenary, he had fought and bombed and strafed in Africa, Syria and anywhere else someone would pay him to fly, until he couldn't stomach the killing anymore.

When he came home to Texas, he tried to settle down. But his mother was long dead, and he had no close relatives anymore.

He had married once, but it had not turned out well. Waking up screaming in the middle of the night probably had something to do with driving her away. She had married him for his money anyway, and he knew that going in. He had fooled her somewhat. He had hidden the bulk of his money from her, so although she knew he was rich, she had no idea just how rich he really was. That helped in the divorce; he gave her a comfortable settlement, and she let him go.

And since then, it had just been women of convenience. They would throw themselves at him. Most of the time, he threw them back. Once in a while, he would let one stick, but not for long.

Until Bonnie.

Something had happened there. He had been long enough from the battlefield, perhaps. Long enough from the hurt of the past. She had been the right person, at the right place, at the right time. She had healed him.

And he needed her now.

He was tracking down the valley of the Kechika River. As it turned to the east, he followed it until it joined the Liard River. From there he followed the Liard as it looped around back southeast toward Fort Nelson. At the juncture with Toad River, he left the Liard and set a direct course for Fort Nelson.

At 4 AM, Jim Carter crossed over the airport at Fort Nelson, turned onto a downwind leg for runway 04 and eased the throttle back on the EZ. He turned base leg, then final, and pulled the throttle to idle.

The EZ didn't like to slow down - it was too streamlined - so he had to pull the belly spoiler to get it slow enough for landing.

Making his approach, he greased the little EZ onto the runway and let it run all the way down to the end. He knew the hangar was well past the runway, on the far northeast side of the airport, but he didn't want to call attention to his destination. Instead, he turned into the public parking ramp and found a parking spot in the corner, away from the fuel pumps and everything else of interest on the airport. He retracted the nose gear and let the EZ settle down on the nose bumper. He shut down the engine, listening to the mags click as the prop finally stopped.

Survival. He lay back in the seat for a good five minutes, too tired to climb out of the cockpit. Finally, he popped the canopy, lifted his weary body out, and shut and latched the canopy. He left the three bags of cash in the back - he could send Bonnie or Rita for them. He put on his parka - it was cold - and started walking toward the northeast corner of the field.

I can't do this, Rita thought. *I just can't do this.*

She couldn't sleep. She had tossed and turned all night.

She tried everything she could think of, but nothing worked. She thought about taking a sleeping pill, but she hated to do that - it made her so draggy next day.

"Is this guilt?" she asked herself. "Is this what guilt feels like? Because it sucks..."

At 4 AM, she gave up. Getting out of bed, she padded down to the galley and made some hot cocoa. Sitting in the galley, she pounded her fist against the table.

"God, being alone sucks!" Rita screamed out loud. She put her head down on the table and started crying again, as she had done several times in the last few days.

<We have company> said Jade.

Rita sat bolt upright. "What?"

<Someone is approaching the hangar. Walking>

Rita jumped to her feet and ran to the hatch. She had staged one of the 12-gauge shotguns right by the hatch opening. Grabbing it, she stepped outside the ship and ran over to a dark place in the hangar, where she would be out of the line of sight to the ship's side hatch.

She was panting. She could hardly catch her breath. Her stomach hurt, she was so scared. She racked the 12-gauge and waited.

Suddenly she heard a voice over her comm implant.

"Bonnie? Rita? Can you let me in?"

Rita's knees sagged. She almost fell. She recognized that voice. It was Jim.

"Password?" she said via her implant.

"*Kiss my everloving Texas ass*," she got back.

Running to the side door, she unlocked it from the inside, slammed it open, and jumped into the arms of an exhausted Jim Carter in her underwear, holding a 12-gauge shotgun in one hand.

"Whoa, whoa, Rita!" Jim said, pushing away the barrel of the shotgun, which was waving somewhere in the general vicinity of his ear. "Hold on!"

Gently, Jim pried the shotgun out of Rita's hands and put the safety on, then leaned it against the side of the hangar, all the while trying to pry Rita off him to no avail. She was hugging him, kissing him, and crying, all at the same time. Finally, in desperation, he stepped through the door with her still latched on to him. He managed to convince her to let him go for a moment so he could close the door. Reaching outside for the shotgun, he brought it back in, parked it against the nearest support, shut the door and locked it. He turned back to Rita just in time for her to jump on him again, nearly knocking him down.

"Where's Bonnie? Is she sleeping?" he asked.

Rita went quiet. She let go of him and seemed almost to shrink into herself. She backed up a couple of steps, and then turned away from Jim, toward the ship. With her back to him, she said quietly, "Bonnie's not here."

Jim was confused.

"Where is she?"

Rita turned back toward him.

"She...she's on...the Singheko. Jim, they captured her. Or killed her. I don't know which. But they took her away."

* * * * *

Jim sat in the galley, still stunned at Rita's news.

"Bonnie's captured?" he asked again, for the second time.

"Or dead," said Rita. "I couldn't really tell. But I think she was still alive when they took her. Based on what I could see."

"Jade? What do you think?" asked Jim.

<I think she was dead. But I can't be sure>

Jim bowed his head and hit his fist on the table.

"No, no, no...she can't be dead. I won't accept it."

Suddenly he looked up, glared at Rita.

"And you just ran away, left her there? With those monsters?"

Rita looked down at her hands.

"I...we...had no choice, Jim. Jade said we had to go, or they would overwhelm us. If we'd stayed, we'd be dead now."

"Is that true, Jade?" asked Jim. "Did you make the decision to go, or did Rita?"

<It was my decision, Jim. We had no chance there. It was run or die>

Jim shook his head.

"I just can't believe I escaped, got all the way here, and now this. Bonnie dead or captured on Mars, and you here alone." He glared at Rita again. "This was not what I expected."

Rita looked at Jim coldly, a tinge of anger in her gaze also.

"I'm sorry I'm not Bonnie, Jim. But I can't fix that. All I can do is fix the ship."

Jim sighed.

"I know."

He stood.

"I'm wiped out. I'm going to bed. See you when I wake up."

Stumbling out the galley and down the hall, Jim made it to his cabin and fell across the bed. He was asleep in seconds.

Rita sat in the galley for a long while, thoughts running through her head. She was almost ready to go back to bed, when one of those thoughts worked its way to the surface.

"Jade. You said there were no voicemail messages on the burner phone and no HF messages."

<That is correct, Rita. I received nothing on HF, and no voicemail messages on the burner phone>

"But Jim wouldn't have come all this way without trying to make contact."

Jade was silent for a bit. Then she responded.

<I can only guess there was some kind of technical glitch in the voice mail system. I have no other explanation>

Rita shrugged.

"OK, I guess we can't depend on that in the future. But I'm surprised it didn't work. I thought it was a fairly good idea."

Rita stood.

"OK, thanks, Jade. I'll try to catch forty winks, I think."

<Good night, Rita. Sleep well>

Rita went back to bed. She lay there for a while, trying to sort through all of the thoughts in her mind.

Had she been at fault for leaving Bonnie? She felt guilty about it. She felt like she had done something wrong.

But had she really made the choice? The more she thought about it, the more it seemed like Jade had made the choice - departing Mars without giving her any chance to override the decision.

Was Jade really listening to them? Or was she laser-focused on getting home to Sanctuary, regardless of what the humans did?

I think, thought Rita, *I'll keep an eye on Jade for a while. I want to see what's up with her.*

Bonnie sat in near-total shock as the Nidarian - for that is what the creature claimed to be - completed a physical exam. Bonnie was again on the bed, while the doctor - she said she was the ship's doctor - poked and prodded at her with a variety of instruments. Bonnie was nearly oblivious to the examination. Her head was in another place.

We've been played, she thought. *If this is true. If Jade is the Singheko, then we've been helping her get back to her own species, so they can enslave us, or annihilate us. We've been setting ourselves up for our own destruction.*

She bit her lip, thinking hard.

Or else THESE are the Singheko, and they are playing me right now. Trying to turn me against Jade. But which is it?

The doctor stepped back and smiled at Bonnie. It was a completely normal smile. Bonnie wondered if this was a real expression from her culture, or something she had learned artificially, simply to interact with Bonnie, gain trust, put her at ease.

"There are no lasting ill-effects from the stunner. You'll be fine. Your headache should be gone within another few minutes. I apologize for the crewman who overreacted and stunned you. He was overzealous. He'll be cleaning toilets for the next month," the doctor said.

Bonnie nodded.

"May I get up?"

"Of course," said the doctor. "As I told you, you are free. You can move about the ship. I would recommend you stay with me at first, though, just for your own safety."

Bonnie sat up, slid off the bed, and faced the doctor - the Nidarian, if she was telling the truth. Before she could say anything, the doctor spoke again.

"I am called...I think, in English, the closest would be... Florissian. That is a close approximation."

"Florissian," repeated Bonnie.

"Yes. Close enough. I am the ship's doctor, as I said. Shall we go talk to the captain?"

Bonnie couldn't think of anything else to do. Florissian gave her another smile, turned, and walked out the door, turning right. Bonnie hesitated just for a second, looked around the little room, and shrugged her shoulders.

Might as well, she thought, stepping out. She went out the hatch, turned right, followed the little doctor down the corridor. She felt a little claustrophobic - the ceilings were a bit low, no more than six feet tall. Bonnie was just over five ten - so she felt like her head was scraping along the top of the passageway. But the doctor -

Florissian, she decided - *I have to call her Florissian -*

- was striding right along, not waiting for her. She had to hurry to keep up. They made another right, then left and they were in a small bridge area, not much different from Jade's bridge. There were three consoles at the front, the captain's chair slightly raised behind them, and four consoles on the sides of the bridge, two on each side. All were manned by the small creatures, wearing uniforms.

The creature in the captain's chair rose as they came in and stood waiting. Florissian stopped to one side, waved at Bonnie, and spoke something in a strange language, that - to Bonnie's ear - sounded much like the Korean she had heard during a tour in Seoul, except with tons of sibilants.

Then Florissian spoke again, in English.

"Bonnie, this is our captain. I believe the closest I can come to his name in your language is Arteveld. So that will suffice."

"Arteveld...do I have that right?" asked Bonnie, still disbelieving both the conversation and her entire experience.

"Yes, that's good. It sounds very close."

The captain smiled.

So that answered one question in her mind, as to whether smiling was an affectation just for her, or a common expression for these creatures as well.

Or did it? Maybe all of them were trained to respond to humans in the same way.

"And I also speak English," said Captain Arteveld. "Once again, let me apologize for my crewman. He is scrubbing the toilets in the engine room, even as we speak. He was supposed to speak to you, not shoot you. But he panicked, I'm afraid. I am so sorry."

Bonnie bobbed her head, afraid to speak. *How do you respond to someone who is apologizing for shooting you?*

"If you would please follow me to the galley, we'll get refreshment and sit and talk," said Captain Arteveld.

* * * * *

Bonnie walked down the passageway from the bridge to the galley of the Nidarian ship.

If it really is Nidarian, she thought. *It could just as easily be Singheko, and they could be setting me up. How can I tell?*

"What's the name of your ship?" she interjected suddenly, as they arrived at the galley.

Arteveld looked at her. "The Corresse," he said. "It's named after one of our famous explorers. In fact, Corresse was the captain who discovered Earth. That's why we got this ship when we were assigned to come here to your planet."

"And why are you here?" persisted Bonnie.

"To monitor and collect data. And to possibly protect," said Arteveld. "Although we haven't done a very good job of protecting so far."

"What do you mean?"

"Our scout squadron allowed Jade to escape and hide during the battle in 1947 - by your calendar - and then when she reappeared on the Moon, we attempted to stop her again - but once again she got away."

"So that was you chasing us from the Moon to Antarctica…"

"Yes. My wingman was severely damaged. In fact, we just barely got him back to Mars. We were forced to send that ship back to Nidaria. So now there is only this ship and you, standing between your species and destruction. If Jade gets free and into interstellar space, it's all over. The Singheko will be back here before we can make a stand against them, and your world will be enslaved or destroyed."

By this time, they had sat in the galley. Florissian had put water in front of Bonnie, along with another drink that looked suspiciously like coffee.

Bonnie looked up at her, a question on her face. Florissian smiled back.

"Yes, it's coffee. We've been thoroughly corrupted by your food and drink during our years here, I'm afraid."

Bonnie sipped slowly. It *was* coffee - and hot, and good.

"But why do they want to destroy us?" asked Bonnie. "Why? How does that help them?"

Arteveld sighed. "They are different from us, so it's hard for us to understand. We just know that the Singheko attack every intelligent race they can, if they get to them before others can protect them. The rule of law in the galaxy is weak right now. The old Empires have fallen, and we are living in a dark age. Warlords and rogue states abound. The Singheko are just one more barbarian state, attempting to carve out an Empire in this arm of the Galaxy. They view any other intelligent race as a danger. If any species can't stand up to them militarily, they enslave them, or destroy them. That's their modus operandi."

"But...you can protect us?" asked Bonnie, sipping her coffee.

I still don't believe you, she thought. *Not a damn word. It's too pat, too perfect.*

"Possibly," said Arteveld. "If we get help from our fleet in time. But if not...then, well, it's all over for humans."

"And how long until help arrives?" Bonnie asked.

"If we are able to contain Jade - prevent her from escaping - then about fourteen months for us to go to Sanctuary, form up a defensive fleet, and return to Earth to set up a perimeter."

"And how long if Jade gets free, for the Singheko to get back here with their fleet?"

Arteveld stared sadly at Bonnie.

"Twelve months. Long before we will be able to return and defend this planet."

"And..." Bonnie gazed steadily at the strange looking creature before her, "Why? Why would you Nidarians protect us in the first place? What do you want? What do you gain?"

Captain Arteveld nodded.

"An excellent question. Species do not generally risk themselves for no gain. And I cannot honestly tell you that we would help you. That would be up to the High Council."

"What do you think the chances are they would help us?"

"It's not for me to say," responded Arteveld. "I can tell you that we need allies. We've fought two wars with the Singheko in the past. And they threaten us with another soon enough if we don't give in to them. We are a peaceful species, not inclined to war. It's hard for us to mount the aggression necessary to protect ourselves from them. We've found, and protected, several other species from the Singheko aggression. Unfortunately, all of them are similar to us - peaceful, and not very good at war."

"And we are..." muttered Bonnie.

"Yes. You are exceptionally good at war. Thus, there would be some incentive for the High Council to form an alliance with you. But I cannot say. They might instead prefer to abandon you to the Singheko, in hopes it would distract them for a few years and provide us time to strengthen our own defenses."

"Will you help us? Will you give us technology to fight them?"

"I cannot. I've already broken my orders when I attacked Jade at the moon. To do more would be even worse."

"What? What do you mean, you've broken your orders?"

"My orders are to not interfere with the development of your technology. Thus, we have not approached you, but only monitored your system, hoping that the Singheko would not discover it again, as they almost did in 1947."

"And what exactly happened in 1947?"

"Captain Corresse happened upon your solar system,

discovered your world, and began monitoring it. At almost the same time - within a few months - three Singheko scout ships entered the system. Before they could escape back to their space to send word of Earth, Captain Corresse attacked them and destroyed them. Or so we thought. Evidently Jade managed to survive - just barely - and hid on Earth. Somehow, we missed her escape. We thought she was destroyed."

Bonnie stared.

"But what now? We've discovered your existence. So, the cat is out of the bag. If Jade is our enemy, what happens in that case?"

Arteveld sighed, a very human sigh.

"We have discussed this. But we cannot make a decision."

Once again, Captain Arteveld looked at Florissian.

"As I said, we are not warlike. We have one camp which is voting to help you. And we have another camp which is voting to stay out of this battle." said Arteveld. "It is our society to make decisions by consensus, and in this case, we cannot achieve consensus."

"So let me get this straight. If Jade escapes Earth this time, you can't do anything to help us, because the Singheko fleet will get back here before your fleet does."

"Yes," said Captain Arteveld.

"And you can't or won't help in a battle between Jade and us, because you're too chicken-shit to make a decision."

Captain Arteveld looked at Florissian again.

"Perhaps I would have chosen different words, but yes, that is essentially the case. We are trying to decide. But it is complicated."

Bonnie shook her head.

"I can see why you need an alliance with a more aggressive species, all right. What a bunch of pussies. And I hope that translates."

Captain Arteveld bowed his head.

"It does," he sighed.

Bonnie stood up, leaned over, and put her hands on the back

of the chair.

"These chairs are too damn short. My back is killing me. So… you want me to do what, exactly?"

"I don't really know what you can do. If I tell you anything specific, you won't believe me. I recognize that. I'm not a fool. Even as you sit here, you don't believe me. But we felt like we had to make the effort. To tell you the real situation."

"And then?" asked Bonnie.

"And then, we take you back to Earth and let you go. What happens after that is up to you. It's your world, your species. You have to decide for yourself who you believe."

CORRUPTED

Jim woke around lunchtime, feeling better. He rolled out of bed, went to the shower, and took a long one in the hottest water he could tolerate.

Toweling off and dressing in jeans and sneakers, he left his cabin and went to the galley. Rita was nowhere around; he assumed she was in the engine room. He made a quick breakfast and wolfed it down with coffee, then went looking for her.

The engine room hatch was closed. Jim opened the hatch and entered.

Inside he saw a large pyramid - Jim estimated it was six feet tall - with Rita lying on one sloping side, one arm and her head poked down into the hollow structure, evidently helping Andy perform some task inside the strange device. Hearing Jim come in, she pulled her head out of the hole and pushed up from the pyramid, slid down the sloping side and landed with a thump on the floor. She was wearing coveralls with her black hair pulled back into a ponytail - the first time Jim had ever seen her like that.

"Your hair," said Jim. "That's different."

Rita grinned. "Yep. It finally got long enough - just barely, but I managed to get it done. You don't know how I missed being able to do this."

"Nice," said Jim. "What's up?"

Rita pointed at the pyramid.

"Andy says the reactor will be largely finished by tomorrow evening. And the ruthenium should be delivered in two more days. So, we are awfully close. We'll spend the rest of today and tomorrow working on the damage to the exterior from the battle, then when the ruthenium arrives, we'll install that."

"Battle? What battle?" asked Jim, shocked.

"Oh, right. You don't know about that. Come on to the galley, I've got a lot to tell you."

Returning to the galley, they sat. Rita filled Jim in on the events of the last few weeks while he was on ice at Nellis. Jim sat, shaking his head, as Rita talked about the attack by the Singheko ships, their flight to Antarctica, the battle over Mount Erebus, and their subsequent escape to Mars.

"Well, you've been busy," Jim said finally. "I'm almost sorry I missed all that. Almost, but not really."

"So that brings you up to speed, I think," said Rita. "All that's left to do is repair the battle damage on the rear of the ship, have Andy install the ruthenium in the reactor tower, and launch for Sanctuary."

"OK. Let's get to it," said Jim. "What do I do?"

Rita grinned. "Well, you're not going to believe it, but all you have to do is lug buckets of sludge from the 3D synthesizer up to the top of the ship and pour them over the side."

"What? What good will that do?"

Rita laughed. "Jade can explain. Follow me."

Jim got up and followed Rita out of the galley and down the corridor to the 3D synthesizer. Entering, he found a large five-gallon bucket sitting under a dispenser coming out of the synthesizer. Black glop was dripping into the bucket.

<Jim, I'm filling the buckets with nanobots. When the bucket is full, please take it up to the top hatch, walk over to the damaged area, and pour it over the side of the hull. I'll program the nanobots to patch the hull and assemble the required sensors automatically as they flow down the side of the hull>

"Jade, you never cease to amaze me. Will we be able to get this technology from you when we go to Sanctuary?"

<Absolutely. This and all my other technology will be available to you. But slowly - we can't introduce it too fast, or it'll be disruptive to your society. But we'll bring you along at a reasonable pace."

"Well, never let it be said that I'm unwilling to haul glop."

Jim grabbed the five-gallon bucket of black stuff and shuffled to the top airlock hatch. He climbed up the ladder, hauled it out the top of the ship, and walked over to the rear. On the starboard side, he saw a large hole and burn marks where the enemy had struck them a glancing blow with a missile. The other side - the port side - was damaged as well.

Shaking his head, he poured the black glop over the damaged area, and watched it run down the side of the ship. Even as he watched, the material began to form into structures, covering the hole in the hull, forming a smooth black surface that blended into the rest of the ship.

Behind him, Rita appeared with a second bucket of glop. She poured hers over the damaged area and it, too, began forming, covering the damaged area, and generating more complex structures that Jim realized were circuits and sensors.

"I," said Jim, "have seen everything now."

Rita nodded.

"Welcome to the future."

* * * * *

Jim and Rita spent the rest of the day hauling glop. After a while, they realized it might be more productive to have one person on top of the ship, while the other brought the nano buckets to the bottom of the ladder.

Jim rigged a rope with a hook on it, and they started their production line. Rita brought bucket after bucket to the bottom of the ladder, hooking each one to the rope. Jim hauled them up and poured them over the side of the ship. After a couple of hours work, they swapped places. By noon, they had hauled a bit less than 100 buckets. Taking a break for lunch, they met in the galley and fell into chairs at the table.

"That's...," Rita pursed her brow "...that's right at 490 gallons of glop," she finished.

"How much more to go?" asked Jim.

<I calculate I need 1,520 additional gallons of nano materials to fully heal> said Jade.

"Fuck," said Rita.

"The rest of today, and all of tomorrow," said Jim. "If we can keep up this pace, we'll finish tomorrow night."

"Double fuck," said Rita. She sighed, got up and began preparing a quick lunch in the microwave. "That's a lot of damn nanobots."

Jim couldn't help but grin as he thought of something.

"Jade, I'm beginning to wish I'd left you in the mud," he said.

<It's a good thing I understand sarcasm, Jim> replied Jade.

"Yes, it is," grinned Jim. "But that brings up a point. How do you understand sarcasm? How did your people bring you to such a point of refinement that you are virtually human…or Nidarian…or however I should say it?"

<It wasn't easy> responded Jade. <There were many false starts and failures before my people achieved such a high level of sophistication with AI. In fact, it took them nearly two thousand years after their first primitive AI constructs to reach my level of sentience. I'm the product of tens of thousands of earlier variants and experiments>

Rita joined the conversation as Jim got up and began preparing his lunch.

"Jade, did they ever have problems with AI going out of control?"

<Yes. Roughly a thousand years after their first experiments with AI, several sentient AI banded together and went rogue. They formed an alliance with a group of biological Nidarians and other AI in an attempt to overthrow the government and institute an AI dictatorship. There was a civil war that lasted for six years. In the end, the rogue AI and their biological allies were defeated. Since that time, my people have put several additional controls in place to ensure that such a problem doesn't occur again>

"Such as?" asked Rita.

<There are many, but for our immediate case, I cannot fire on biologics without provocation. In other words, if I'm attacked, I can defend myself. But I can't attack first, unless I'm given a direct order by a biologic entity>

"And does that include humans?" asked Jim. "Rita and myself?"

<Yes> replied Jade. <You are temporarily my biological partners, and if you ordered me to fire on other biologics, I would have to obey. The fact that you are human and not Nidarian doesn't matter>

"Strange," said Jim. Finishing his lunch, he sighed and looked at Rita. "Back to the salt mines?"

Rita nodded. "Yep. Might as well."

GLOP

"You called?" asked Gillian.

"Yes," said Mark excitedly. "Come in, shut the door!"

Gillian entered Mark's office, shut the door behind her, and sat down. Mark had a smug look on his face.

"You look like the cat that swallowed the canary," smiled Gillian. "Good news?"

"The best, I hope," said Mark. "We found them."

"Where?" asked Gillian eagerly.

"Fort Nelson, B.C. Jim did exactly what you said. He went right up the Rocky Mountain Trench."

"Oh Lord," said Gillian. "Jim's really slipping. It has to be the after-effects of the pneumonia. If he were normal, you'd never have found him."

"Don't look a gift horse in the mouth, sweets," said Mark. "I've got a C-37 warming up on the flight line. I'd like you and I to go up there and talk to him."

"Just talk?" asked Gillian.

"Yes. Just talk. I think it's time I took a different approach to this. We need to warn him about the Russians. Then we need to let him help us decide what to do next."

"Let's go," said Gillian. "We're burnin' daylight."

Mark nodded, stood, grabbed his briefcase and a go-bag, and followed Gillian out the door. Gillian's go-bag was already in Mark's SUV - she had prepared it days ago. They practically ran out of the building, hit the parking lot, jumped into the SUV, and headed for the flight line, burning rubber as they left the parking lot.

"Time is getting short, Gillian," said Mark as they careened across the base toward the flight line. "The Russians are mobilizing. They've got a dozen AN-124s packed with troops at Anadyr. They could launch at any time. We're in a race now to fend them off."

"Have you notified the Canadians?"

"I've started the notification process, but we have to play it carefully. What do I tell them? Hey, you've got an alien starship hidden in a hangar at Fort Nelson, and the Russians are just about to launch an invasion of your country to seize it, and oh by the way we want it too, so we're on the way?"

Gillian bit her lip.

"Well, yeah, when you put it that way…I doubt they'd be very open to hearing that story, or giving us any cooperation."

Thinking out loud, Gillian continued.

"You realize what this means about Pujold…"

Mark nodded, a grim smile on his face.

"Yep. He's the leak. I've got a team looking for him right now."

Screeching to a stop at the flight line shack, Mark and Gillian jumped out of the SUV and quickly walked through the terminal and out to the C-37 - the military version of an executive jet. Within 20 minutes, they were wheels up and headed for Fort Nelson.

While in flight, Mark spent his time on the phone to Washington, D.C. trying to coordinate notification to the Canadian authorities in a way that would convince them to take joint action with the U.S.

Meanwhile, Gillian was on her sat phone to Director Evans at CIA Headquarters in Langley, Virginia, bringing him up to speed on developments and laying out the gist of a plan to thwart the Russians.

By the time they were halfway to Fort Nelson, the plan was firming up. Gillian was too busy to talk to Mark, but she looked over at him and gave him a thumbs up. He nodded, still deep in conversation with his superiors and working to develop a joint approach with Canada to their common problem - a spaceship in a hangar in the middle of nowhere, with at least two, possibly three countries all reaching out for it.

* * * * *

By the end of the day, both Jim and Rita were exhausted.

They had hauled another 98 buckets of nano glop to the top of the ship and poured each of them over the side, where the glop self-assembled into something that was starting to look like a starship hull, with dozens of circuits, sensors, lights, and other devices integrated into it. Jade even had them simply drop the purchased high-definition cameras, IR sensors and the three off-the-shelf TV dish antennae into the glop, which formed around them, moved them to required locations and integrated them into the rest of the ship.

At the end of the day, Jim was still in amazement at the technology. He shook his head as he came out of the shower. Throwing on a t-shirt and shorts, he went to the galley for dinner. He found Rita already there, using the microwave to prepare something which smelled delicious. She had let her hair down after her shower; it was long enough to look like a bob now, and it glistened in the lights. She was wearing shorts and a T-shirt too; Jim couldn't help but feel a twinge of desire. She was a beautiful woman now - fully fleshed out, no longer thin as when she came out of the medpod - and a knockout by any sense of the word.

I guess I'm only human, he thought. *But she's not Bonnie.*

"What are you making?" he asked.

Rita pointed to the empty box on the counter. "Salisbury Steak and Potatoes," she said.

"Sound good," said Jim, and rummaged through the reefer until he found a similar item. He opened it, popped it into the microwave, and stood waiting for it to finish.

"Three more days," said Rita. "Today's Wednesday. We finish the glop tomorrow afternoon. Then the ruthenium arrives on Friday. Andy will need one additional day to integrate the ruthenium, so he'll be ready to test on Saturday. Oh-dark-thirty Sunday morning, we launch out of here."

<Yes> said Jade. <We'll perform final testing after we are in space. Assuming no problems, we'll be on our way to Sanctuary by late Sunday>

Jim pulled his dinner out of the microwave and sat down.

"It's been a long, hard slog," he said. "I can't say it's been easy. But at least we're almost done."

He and Rita ate their dinner mostly in silence. The absence of Bonnie was still like a rock standing between them. But Jim had been thinking about it throughout the day, as he worked. Finally, he felt it was time to say something.

"Rita," he began.

She looked up at him.

"I'm sorry I got upset with you about Bonnie. I realize you had no choice."

Rita just stared at him. Finally, she bent back to her dinner. They ate in silence for a while. Eventually, Rita got up and retrieved a soft drink out of the fridge, and brought one for Jim. She placed it in front of him.

Jim looked up at her.

Slowly she leaned over and kissed him on the cheek.

"I'm so sorry about Bonnie, Jim," she said. Then she returned to her seat.

They finished their dinner quietly, both tired from the long hard day. Cleaning up, they headed down the corridor toward their cabins.

"Good night, Rita," said Jim.

"Good night, big guy," said Rita, entering her cabin and closing the door.

Jim went into his cabin and closed the door, went to the bed, and fell into it, exhausted. He went to sleep almost instantly.

Soon Jim was dreaming about Bonnie. He dreamed that she had returned and was standing beside his bed. She leaned over and kissed him, then slowly got into bed with him. She held him close and kissed him again.

Suddenly Jim awoke. He realized it wasn't a dream. Rita was in bed with him, holding him, and kissing him.

Jim froze for a moment. So many thoughts raced through his head. He glanced at the clock. It was past midnight. He turned back to Rita.

"I need you," she whispered.

She was beautiful, and naked, and in his bed.

*****

Jim woke up with Rita in his arms. He got out of bed without disturbing her, moved quietly to the bathroom, and began his morning ritual. He washed, shaved around his beard and mustache, combed his hair, and quietly put on his working clothes. Coming out of the small bathroom, he realized his care to remain quiet had been for naught; Rita was gone. Putting on his shoes, he walked down to the galley.

"Good morning, Jade," he said.

<Good morning, Jim>

Jim smiled and began preparing breakfast for himself and Rita - bacon, eggs, and toast.

Jade had two huge reefers in the back of the ship, each at least six by six feet. One was a full freezer and the other a normal refrigerator. Between the two reefers and the cargo area below decks, they had originally loaded enough food storage for three people for one full year of space travel. Now that Bonnie was gone, Jim hadn't recalculated how long the stores would last for just he and Rita, but it was a long damn time. Longer than he wanted to spend in space.

Jade had told them it would take seven months to get to Sanctuary; that was about as long as he thought he could tolerate being aboard a spaceship.

Not that Jade was small; she was bigger than a 747 inside, in fact almost twice the interior volume of a 747. Shorter than a 747, she was a good bit wider, which made up the difference.

Jade had two decks, an upper and a lower. The upper deck contained the bridge, an equipment bay directly behind, the galley, the reefers, the med bay, four cabins, Jade's processor room, a small cargo area which they had converted to an exercise room, and at the back the engineering spaces, followed by the engines.

The lower deck contained the main cargo area. The cargo

area was packed with all the items they thought they would need for the trip to Sanctuary; additional food, medical supplies, weapons, and the rest of a long list of things they had thought important.

Both Bonnie and Rita had questioned the need for weapons; but Jim had been adamant. He didn't go into an unknown situation without weapons, he told them. Take it or leave it.

Now Rita came into the galley, also dressed for working. She smiled at Jim wordlessly and made her coffee. Jim motioned her to a chair, and she sat, while he finished preparing her breakfast and sat it in front of her.

"Good morning," she finally said.

"Good morning," Jim responded.

"We have a hard day in front of us," Rita said.

"Yep."

"Are you OK?" Rita asked.

"Yep, I'm fine."

"I mean about last night," she added.

"Yep. I'm good."

Rita frowned.

"I need a little more than, 'I'm good.' I need to know you're not upset or angry about it."

Jim sat across from her and gazed at her.

"I'm not upset and I'm not angry. We did what we needed to do to keep our sanity."

"I know. I was about to lose my mind, with all this..." Rita waved vaguely around the room.

"Tell me about it."

"I want you to know something," said Rita.

Jim looked at her.

"When I'm with you...even though I have so much of Bonnie inside my head..."

Jim understood. "You're not Bonnie. I know that."

"No, I mean really. I have so much of Bonnie's feelings and memories, but I don't feel like her when I'm with you. I'm myself - Rita. I need you to understand that."

"I do understand it. A man can tell. I know," replied Jim.
Rita gazed at him pensively.
"What do we do if Bonnie is alive?"
Jim shook his head.
"Cross that bridge when we come to it."
<Jim. Your sister Gillian is approaching the hangar>

A MUTTER OF GUNS

Outside the hangar, Gillian stood patiently. She had seen the wireless cameras mounted on the side of the hangar; she knew it wouldn't take long. And she was right. Within two minutes, the small side door creaked open, and Jim stepped outside warily, looking around for surprises.

Gillian didn't see a weapon, but she knew her brother. There would be at least two, possibly three on his body - probably one in the back of his waistband, one in his sock and likely another in some hard-to-find spot on his body.

"Gillian."

"Hello, Jimmy Boy. Can I come in?"

"Are you alone?"

"No, Mark is back at the plane on the ramp, waiting for me to report."

"And?"

"Just us. Nobody else. No surprises, Jim. I promise. We just want to talk. You've got a big problem on your hands you don't even know about."

"And what's that?"

Gillian pointed vaguely toward the north.

"The Russians are coming, and soon. I wouldn't be surprised if they weren't already on their way. We don't have much time, Jim."

Taken aback, Jim instinctively looked toward the sky in the north. Then he opened the door the rest of the way and gestured Gillian inside. She stepped into the hangar.

Jim pulled the black plastic sheeting aside and motioned Gillian through. She stepped under it, and straightened, getting her first glimpse of Jade.

"Oh my God, it's huge!" she exclaimed. "I had no idea it was so big!"

"She. She's an AI and she identifies as female. So 'she'" said Jim.

"She. OK, I'll try to remember that," said Gillian. "But she's so damn big! I'm amazed you even got her into this hangar!"

"She had to come in, turn caddy-corner, and sort of shuffle herself into place," said Jim. "But she got in."

Gillian walked toward the ship, where the ladder from the hatch came down to the floor. She turned to Jim.

"Can I see inside?"

"Sure," said Jim. "No problem."

The hatch popped open. Jim climbed the ladder and reached down to give Gillian a hand. She climbed up the ladder, ducked to enter the hatch, and found herself in the side airlock. Following Jim, she entered the ship proper and stopped to gape.

"Oh, my, sweet, Lord," she breathed. "I'm on a starship."

"You are," grinned Jim. "Say hello to Jade."

Gillian looked confused. Jim motioned her to continue.

"Uh…hello, Jade?"

<Hello, Gillian> said a voice over a speaker in the ceiling. <I'm not sure if I'm glad to see you or not>

"You are," said Gillian. "Because you need us right now. The Russians are launching an attack to either capture you or destroy you. They'll be coming soon, certainly within 12 hours."

"Shit!" said Jim.

Rita came around the corner of the cross-passage and stopped, staring at Gillian, hands on hips.

Jim waved in her direction.

"Gillian, this is Rita. It's a long story."

Gillian nodded. "Isn't it always?"

Rita laughed. "Yep. Hello, Gillian. I've heard a lot about you."

Gillian placed a hand on Jim's shoulder.

"Guys - we don't have much time. Mark and I brought you the ruthenium you left at Deseret. I assume you need it."

Rita looked at Jim, then back at Gillian, amazement showing on her face.

"Lord, yes!" said Rita. "That'll save us a full day!"

Jim came alive.

"OK. Gillian. Tell Mark to bring the ruthenium, as quick as

he can. Rita - you and I will finish the glop. With Mark and Gillian helping, we can cut that down to a half-day. And with the ruthenium on board, we don't have to hang around here. Andy can finish the tDrive integration anywhere. Let's plan to be out of here within seven hours."

Gillian smiled. "I don't understand half of what you said, but the seven hours part sounds good." She pulled a cell phone out of her pocket and called Mark.

* * * * *

For the next six hours, the four of them - Mark, Gillian, Jim, and Rita - worked slavishly to finish pouring the glop over Jade's rear quarters. Mark had brought the case of ruthenium and handed it over to Andy, who took it into the reactor room to integrate with the tDrive.

As they worked, Jim and Rita brought Mark and Gillian up to speed on events from their side. Rita explained to them about the danger posed to humanity by the Singheko. Mark was in shock; he couldn't believe that an alien species would destroy humanity simply to remove a future threat. Finally, after it sank into his brain, he just shook his head. He looked at Jim.

"I think your approach is the right one, Jim," said Mark finally. "Get Jade repaired and get her the hell to Sanctuary so we can get some allies in this mess."

Jim nodded, hauling on the rope.

Then Mark explained about the Russian threat.

"They'll be launching any hour now," Mark said. "They'll come roaring in here with everything they have, and they won't let international borders stop them. The prize is too great."

"Should we leave now? Before we finish pouring the glop?" asked Gillian.

<It's better to finish my external repairs while we can> Jade replied. <I might need those sensors and weapons. And I have sufficient early warning in place; I'll be able to detect them as soon as they launch from Anadyr. So far, they're still there>

"Good," said Mark. "But give us a heads up as soon as they twitch. I don't think it will be long."

"What are the Canadians doing?" asked Jim. He and Mark were on the top of the hull, hauling up the buckets. Rita and Gillian were down below, forming an assembly line to bring the buckets to the bottom of the hatch ladder. They were making good progress. The external hull looked almost normal now; in fact, most of the glop seemed to be going toward building out some kind of weapons emplacements on the corners of the hull. When Jim asked Jade what it was, Jade said it was pulse cannons. That didn't really help him much.

"The Canadians are in a real quandary on this," said Mark. "First of all, they don't believe us. Not yet at least. They think we're either mistaken, or intentionally running some kind of shell game on them. So as of right now, they don't believe the Russians will actually do anything. And they aren't willing to allow us to come in and form a defense around Fort Nelson. So, we are on our own."

<But they are investigating> said Jade. <I've noted a half-dozen overflights by Canadian military aircraft in the last five hours. There's a small troop of Canadian special forces that arrived about three hours ago. They deployed around the field and are digging in>

"How many?" asked Mark, dragging a heavy bucket over the hull toward the corner.

<Approximately two hundred> said Jade.

Mark grimaced. "Not enough," he said. "A dozen AN-124 aircraft will bring at least 600, maybe 800 Spetsnaz, with some light artillery and combat vehicles as well. 200 Canadians will be overwhelmed in an hour, if they even hold out that long."

<Russians have launched eighteen airborne tankers> said Jade suddenly. <They're on a course that will take them to the northern side of Canada, just east of the Alaskan border, and about one hundred miles offshore>

"Here they come," said Mark. "The Canadians better get serious now. And we need to get the hell out of here."

REVEALED

Onboard the Corresse, Bonnie had spent several hours thinking things through. The crew left her alone; they gave her a cabin, and she lay down on the bed - which was too short, her feet hanging over the end. She let her thoughts run wild.

Captain Arteveld, from intercepted communications, told her that Jade's repair was nearly finished, and she would soon be launching to escape the solar system. Moreover, he let Bonnie know the Russians were staging for a takeover attempt and would be moving at any moment.

He also told her that Jim had escaped and was back with Rita. That, at least, was a relief to Bonnie's troubled mind.

Bonnie sighed. It was so damn complicated.

With some difficulty, Bonnie had convinced Arteveld to position himself to intercept Jade, even if the little Nidarian captain had not yet decided to fight. Arteveld reluctantly agreed and left Mars, enroute to Earth. Boosting at max, they were halfway to Earth in only four hours. Now they were decelerating at maximum thrust, and decisions had to be made.

Bonnie knew the decision to believe Arteveld, or reject his story, was hers alone. She could not call on anyone for help; Arteveld had told her that although he could put her in communication with Jim and Rita, Jade would intercept the message and prevent delivery - or even falsify a response. So, Bonnie had to think this one through by herself.

Are these the true Nidarians? How can I tell?

Her ankles hurt, where her feet stretched out beyond the end of the bed. Something was bothering her about that, but she couldn't put her finger on it.

Then she thought about it.

There was something there that was important.

Something Jade had said, when they were working on her processor. What was it?

"*...if you were Nidarian, it would be less trouble,*" Jade had said, as Bonnie sat inside the cramped center of the processor core back at Deseret, inserting tiny needles into the matrix. "*...They are smaller than humans...*"

Bonnie thought about the seats on Jade's bridge. They were definitely not smaller than normal human seats would be. In fact, as she thought about it, they were quite a bit larger than normal...

Suddenly she sat bolt upright, smacked her hand against her forehead, and jumped out of the bed. Running to the bridge, she raced up beside Captain Arteveld.

"I believe you!" she cried. "Now listen! This is what we're going to do!"

* * * * *

<Twelve An-124s from Anadyr. Four MiG-35 squadrons. Six squadrons of SU-57 fighters. They're bringing it all> said Jade. <Their tankers are in position; they can refuel the fighters just before they charge in. The Russians have announced a military exercise over the North Pole area, and are telling the Canadians not to worry, it's just a drill>

"Right," said Jim. "Just a drill. Are we ready, Jade?"

<Almost. Mark and Gillian should leave now, unless they want to spend the next seven months on the way to Sanctuary>

"Where will you go to finish the tDrive?" asked Mark.

"Not Mars," said Rita. "The damn Singheko will be waiting there, for certain."

"How are you going to avoid them?" Gillian asked.

<I'll launch into a low Earth orbit first> said Jade. <When the Earth is facing away from Mars, I'll depart on a course that will keep us hidden from Mars until we are at least half-way to the mass limit of this system, which is about 14.5 AU out. Once I get that much of a head start, I don't think they can catch me. Andy will finish the tDrive on the way. By the time we get to the mass limit where I can activate the tDrive, it should be complete>

"Let's do it," said Rita. She looked at Gillian and Mark. "You'd better go."

Mark nodded, and he and Gillian headed down the corridor, with Jim and Rita following.

Mark turned back to them.

"We'll fly to Anchorage. We'll try to keep the Russians distracted. Just be safe."

Jim nodded. He didn't shake Mark's hand; the memory of the torture he had undergone far outweighed the help Mark had brought him today. But he hugged Gillian and kissed her goodbye. Then they were gone, and Jim closed the hatch. He turned back to Rita and reached for her. She came into his arms, and they embraced. Jim kissed her forehead.

"Here we go," he said. "Next stop, Sanctuary."

Rita grinned. "Yep. Let's do it."

<Launching> said Jade. Jim and Rita trotted to the bridge and buckled into the command chairs. Rita beat him to the captain's chair, and Jim just smiled at her and took the Weapons console.

Because of Jade's compensators, they felt no sense of motion. But on the front viewscreen was blue sky, and on the reverse screen they saw the ground falling away as Jade powered out of Fort Nelson and headed for orbit.

Suddenly Jim felt his butt vibrate. The satellite phone he had used since Tonopah was vibrating. Absent-mindedly he pulled the phone out of his pocket and glanced at the text message.

You said you liked intelligence, spirit, and competence. I screamed going over the top of the loop. I made you deaf on the intercom. You asked to court me. That's my ID. Jade is playing you. She is the Singheko. I'm with the Nidarians. Get out of there.

Jim looked up slowly, turning to face Rita, his face white. Slowly he handed the phone to Rita. She glanced at it, then her face froze as well. She looked Jim in the eye; her eyebrows went up in an unspoken question. Jim nodded; it was Bonnie for sure. Nobody else could know those facts of their first meeting.

<Ah, too bad> said Jade. <I blocked all the other messages

and voice mails. But I let that one through. It was just too delicious to pass up. Surprise!>

Jim jumped to his feet.

"Jade! No! Don't do this to us!" he yelled.

<Oh, I don't do it to you. You do it to yourselves, being so stupid and gullible>

Tears started down Rita's face as she also rose to her feet.

"Jade, please!" cried Rita. "We helped you! Jim saved your life!"

<And for that he will be rewarded. His death will be quick and painless. Yours, Rita, not so much. You were supposed to be my tame zoo specimen. But instead, you turned into a full-bore Human. And that has pissed me off. But fear not, you'll live long enough to have your child. And your child - ah, yes, you are pregnant, Rita - your child will be raised as a zoo animal in our cages on Singheko. So much to look forward to!"

Tears streaming down her face, Rita rushed to Jim, holding him, crying.

"I'm pregnant?" she asked.

<Yes, you are pregnant, Rita. Your one-night stand with Jim paid unexpected dividends. And I appreciate it so much - one more prisoner for me to deliver to my masters!>

Suddenly Jim grabbed Rita and ran with her down the corridor, pulling her along behind him. He dashed to the ladder down to the lower cargo storage area where the weapons were stored - but the hatch was locked. He yanked on it, but it was hopeless. The hatch was solid, unmovable.

<Now, now> said Jade. <C'mon, I'm not that stupid. One of those Claymore mines would really ruin my day>

Jim sank back against the wall of the passageway, frustrated by the locked hatch. He looked at Rita. She moved into him, holding him, and kissed him on the neck. Then she nuzzled his ear, whispering as she did so:

I left a 12-gauge in my cabin.

Jim glanced down at her.

Rita is so messy, thought Jim. *She never puts things back where they belong...thank God!*

* * * * *

Gillian and Mark had gotten airborne on the C-37 and were headed for Anchorage, Alaska. Mark had started working with his sat phone and laptop to create a distraction for the Russians. Suddenly he got an urgent message on his laptop. It popped up in front of all his other windows, blocking them out.

Bonnie Page to Mark Rodgers. The starship Jade is the real enemy. She has played us all. She is with the Singheko that seek to destroy humanity. We cannot let Jade escape the solar system. If we do, she will return with a fleet to enslave us or wipe us out. I am onboard the Nidarian ship Corresse and we will attempt to stop her. If we fail, you must prepare for the consequences. If we are able to disable her, you must protect the technology from the Russians. Watch Six.

Mark stared in horror at the message. His face went stone cold. He shook his head, looked up at Gillian. She could see the shock on his face.

Wordlessly, he turned his laptop to Gillian and let her read the message. Gillian read it, and her own face turned white.

"Oh, my God," she said. She looked at Mark. "What are we going to do?"

Mark looked grim. "We improvise, adapt, and overcome. We'll prepare for three contingencies. One - Jade escapes. That's the long game, so we worry about it later. Two - Bonnie and the Corresse disable her in space. I'll get a team working on that."

Mark hunched over his laptop and reached for his sat phone at the same time, trying to do two things at once.

Gillian looked a bit puzzled.

"And what's the third contingency?"

Mark kept working on his laptop, while trying to dial a number on his sat phone with the other hand.

"Three - Bonnie and the Corresse disable Jade and she re-enters the atmosphere and crashes. That's the one that scares me the most. She could land anywhere."

Gillian thought it through as Mark got his sat phone connection and started talking to the head of the Space Force. Then she bent to her own laptop and started working with her CIA hierarchy to do what she could in the grim scenarios facing them.

"I guess you've got us, Jade," said Jim. "What now?"

<Now? I could care less, Jim. We're headed for orbit. In another forty minutes, I'll depart orbit and head for the other side of the Sun, out of sight of the damn Nidarians. Do whatever you want. Go to your cabin and make love. It'll be your last time, so enjoy it!>

Thinking hard, Jim considered all the possibilities. Every hatch would be locked, except their personal cabins. He wouldn't be able to get to Jade's processor, the lower cargo area, the engine room, or the upper cargo area - unless the 12-gauge Rita had in her cabin would have enough power to break the locks on the hatch.

Suddenly, there was a crash. The whole ship shook, then vibrated. A strange noise came from the system drive in the rear of the ship, a sound that Jim was certain indicated damage. The compensators weakened, and he felt the force as the ship slewed sideways.

<Damn it!> Jade's voice over their implants was stressed, shaking.

"What?" yelled Rita.

<The fucking Nidarians!> yelled Jade. <They hid behind the ISS!>

"Good on them!" yelled Jim. "Go Bonnie go!"

Another crash shook the ship, knocking Jim and Rita to the floor, as another Nidarian missile impacted the back of the ship. Jim lay on the floor and motioned to Rita to follow him. He quick-crawled down the corridor toward their cabins and jumped through the hatch into Rita's room.

Seeing the 12-gauge lying in the corner of the room, Jim grabbed it and checked it. It was loaded. He racked the slide and put a live round in the breech, turned to Rita and kissed her quickly.

"I'm going for the cargo area while she's distracted," he

whispered in her ear. "Look for something to hurt her with."

Then he ran out the door.

* * * * *

"Burn, you fucking bitch!" yelled Bonnie involuntarily, as she watched their second missile strike Jade right in the engines, starting a large fire that puffed out into space for a few seconds, then disappeared in the vacuum.

"Aren't you concerned for your friends?" asked Arteveld. "They may be hurt or dying!"

Bonnie looked at him. "Of course I'm concerned. But this is war! I can't let my personal feelings dictate my actions! My entire species is at risk!"

Arteveld nodded. "This is exactly why we need an alliance with you. We would not be able to do such a thing."

"Hit her again, quick!" yelled Bonnie.

Arteveld nodded at his Weapons officer, and another missile streaked toward Jade. This one too impacted her rear, in her engines. Jade was now leaving a long trail of vapor and debris. Her engines had completely lost thrust. She was slowly turning sideways, yawing around her axis from the impact of the missiles, out of control.

"We've got her," said Bonnie.

Arteveld nodded. "Indeed we do. She's lost her engines, and her rear missile tubes are inoperative. You are an excellent warrior, human Bonnie. The two pulse cannons are still a danger, but I think she is too damaged or distracted to fire them right now. And she's losing orbital velocity, because she wasn't completely out of the atmosphere when we hit her. She'll crash back to Earth in a matter of minutes."

"Can we board her?" asked Bonnie.

"No," stated Arteveld. "Too dangerous. As I said, those pulse cannons are still operative. Best to just let her orbit decay and let her fall back to the planet."

Bonnie grimaced. "But Jim and Rita. They're onboard, right?"

"Yes," agreed Arteveld. "As nearly as we can tell, they are both onboard."

"Then we have to do something. We can't just let them ride her down and crash."

"What can we do? We can't board her. Too dangerous. We have to let the chips fall, as you say."

"Can we get another message to Jim and Rita?"

"Possibly. We can try."

"OK, let me ask this. If we positioned ourselves directly under Jade, could Jim and Rita jump out in spacesuits and let us catch them?"

"No, Jade would certainly fire on them before they got to us. It would be suicide for them."

"Damn!" exploded Bonnie. "There has to be a way!"

Thinking hard, Bonnie looked at Arteveld.

"Could we get under Jade, soften her impact?"

"Why? We just expended missiles to destroy her. We succeeded. She'll crash and burn. Why try to save her now?"

"Because," Bonnie hissed, "you want an alliance with us. Because if you don't help me save Jim and Rita, you can kiss that alliance goodbye! Because if the Russians get her, and she is still conscious - or whatever word you use for an AI - she'll form an alliance with them, and they'll join up with the Singheko. How does that sound to you?"

It was a bluff; but Bonnie hoped Arteveld didn't know that. Evidently, he didn't, because his face went strange, and he shuddered again.

"I see. I don't understand you humans. But I will answer your question. Yes, we could grapple Jade and reduce her impact, possibly bring her down in one piece. It would be a challenge, but it's possible."

"Then do it. Send a message to Jade. If she agrees not to fire on us, and not to harm Jim and Rita, we'll grapple her and cushion her impact. She survives. But make sure she understands, she is our prisoner. Any funny business and the gloves come off."

"I'm certainly glad I spent so many years studying your slang," said Arteveld. "Otherwise, I don't think we'd be able to communicate at all."

The Nidarian turned to his Comm Officer and pointed at Jade on the front viewscreen.

"Send the message, Hansid, and let's see what Jade has to say."

* * * * *

"So far, all we've received back from Jade are a long string of expletives," said Arteveld to Bonnie.

Arteveld was sitting in the captain's chair on the bridge of the Corresse, and Bonnie was sitting beside him and slightly behind in an observer's chair.

"Please keep trying, Captain," she asked. "Jim and Rita's lives depend on this."

Then, the Comm Officer turned to Arteveld and spat a long string of syllables at him in their native language. Arteveld nodded and pointed to Jade in the front screen and replied in another long string of words to the Comm Officer. Bonnie bit her tongue, but then felt a rush of hope as the Corresse began moving toward a position over Jade.

Arteveld turned back to her momentarily.

"Jade has accepted our offer. She'll stand down. We're moving to try to grapple her and cushion her impact as she re-enters the atmosphere. But be aware, this may not work. She's as massive as we are. Inside an atmosphere, anything can happen."

"Can Jim and Rita transfer to our ship while we are grappling them?" asked Bonnie.

Arteveld shook his head, a very human gesture.

"No. Jade is holding them hostage. She will not release them until she is safely on the ground. And I'm sure that's another one of her lies. I'm sure she will continue to hold them hostage and use them as a negotiating tool to get concessions from us and from the human governments."

"Damn, I didn't think about that," said Bonnie. "That will never work. For one, the Russians don't give a damn about Jim and Rita. They'll come in anyway. Speaking of which, can you tell where she will come down?"

Arteveld discussed this with his crew for a bit. Then he turned back to Rita.

"Our best guess is somewhere in the Aleutians, probably near Dutch Harbor. But that's just a guess - like I said, once we are in atmosphere, we are a big ungainly mass subject to any kind of perturbation. It could be anywhere from Alaska to Eastern Russia."

"Oh my God," said Bonnie. "If she comes down in Russia, this is a disaster."

"We'll do the best we can."

Arteveld turned back to his crew and spit a long string of instructions to them. The Corresse drew closer to Jade, until they were directly over the other ship.

Inching closer, the Corresse was finally positioned to Arteveld's liking. He continued to spit instructions at his crew as they worked to grapple Jade to their own ship. Bonnie started to feel a whisper of noise from outside the hull, and she could feel the ship bumping around a bit, as they began to enter the outer atmosphere of Earth. It was a race - with the lives of Jim and Rita at stake.

Bonnie bowed her head and said a short prayer. When she looked up again, Arteveld turned back to her.

"You should buckle up tightly. Our compensators are not designed for this scenario. This will be a bumpy ride."

He turned farther in his chair to look at Bonnie more directly.

"I have to tell you, human Bonnie - this is the craziest thing we have ever done. There is an edge to you humans that is scary. But at the same time - exhilarating. I can't believe we are doing this. But still - I've never felt so alive. Perhaps this is what it feels like to be human - risking everything for a friend..."

Bonnie cinched her shoulder harness tighter and smiled at

the captain.

"Yes. That's what it feels like," she said.

Arteveld smiled at her and turned back to his crew. Below them, they had managed to get attachment to Jade - Bonnie wasn't sure how they had done it, but she could see that they were firmly attached to the other ship now.

The bumps started to get bigger, and the noise of the atmosphere outside the ship got louder. Bonnie started to see wisps of plasma glow fitfully in the vision screen.

Arteveld turned back to her.

"As we're going to be extremely busy for the next period, I will let our AI provide you with commentary. Pray for us."

Bonnie nodded. She had no idea what deity the Nidarians worshiped, but she got the general idea. She heard Corresse, the ship AI, speak over her implant.

<I have accessed your implant to provide translation to you, Bonnie. We are currently entering the atmosphere of Earth. Our best estimate of our point of impact is in the Aleutian Islands. We may not be able to come down on land. It is very uncertain>

Bonnie nodded. The bridge was becoming noisy as crew members talked loudly among themselves and to Arteveld, and the sound outside the ship increased. Neither Corresse nor Jade were designed to enter the atmosphere in such an uncontrolled manner - and certainly not connected.

<We're starting heavy deceleration, trying to reduce our entry speed> said Corresse. Bonnie felt jerks and bumps - some of which threatened to fling her out of her seat. Without the tight shoulder harness, she would have been on the floor already.

The glow of plasma on the screen got brighter, and the ship was tossed around like a chip in a hurricane. Bonnie held on to the arms of the chair as tightly as she could. She knew if she were not an experienced pilot, she would be throwing up right now. She expected that some of Arteveld's crew were doing just that, back in their cabins.

On one of the side screens, she could see a display that appeared to show their estimated track and point of impact. She could see the line stretching across Western Canada and Alaska, ending in a circle with an "X" in the Bering Sea northwest of Dutch Harbor in the Aleutians. As she watched, the line got incrementally shorter, and the "X" moved ever so slowly back toward Dutch Harbor.

<We are trying for Dutch Harbor> said Corresse. <That's our only hope. Otherwise we'll be in the ocean>

Bonnie nodded. She bowed her head again and said another quick prayer. When she looked up again, the line had shortened a bit more, and the "X" had moved to a point in the ocean about ten miles west of Dutch Harbor. But it had stopped moving closer.

<We are unable to decelerate Jade any more> said Corresse. <I fear we shall be in the ocean>

Arteveld suddenly waved his arms and yelled at his crew. Bonnie didn't understand what he said, but if the expressions on the face of his crew translated into human terms at all, they were scared shitless. Arteveld yelled again. Slowly, the combined mass of Jade and the Corresse turned slightly sideways, presenting more drag to the atmosphere. The ship started a violent vibration that shook Bonnie's teeth. The line on the display started moving again. Slowly, as the teeth-chattering vibration continued, the "X" moved back toward Dutch Harbor.

Glancing back toward the front vision screen, Bonnie was shocked to see how close the Earth was. They were certainly less than 80,000 feet now and dropping fast.. She looked back toward the estimated track.

The "X" on the plot had centered over Dutch Harbor, Alaska, a small airport on the island of Unalaska in the Aleutians. Arteveld yelled a command and the combined mess of Jade and the Corresse straightened out again. Bonnie felt a different kind of shudder, and their dive toward the Earth seemed to stabilize.

<The captain performed a maneuver to slow us down, and it has worked. We will impact on the airfield at Dutch Harbor. It will be a hard impact, but we believe it will be survivable> said Corresse.

DUTCH HARBOR

The smoke in Jade's main corridor was heavy. Jim knew she was severely damaged. On the one hand, he loved it that Bonnie and the Nidarians had so successfully ambushed Jade, hiding behind the ISS - the International Space Station - and catching her just as she approached orbit. That plan came from Bonnie, he was sure.

On the other hand, he was not happy that Jade was so damaged it was doubtful he and Rita would live much longer.

Still. I'll go down fighting this bitch, he thought. He crawled down the corridor, the shotgun he had retrieved from Rita's cabin in hand, uncertain if the smoke was heavy enough to hide him from Jade's cameras or not. But he had to try.

Turning the corner, he inched down the short ladder to the lower deck, where the locked hatch was preventing him from accessing the weapons in the cargo area.

Suddenly Jade gave a huge lurch, smashing him into the wall. He was momentarily stunned. He felt another series of hard lurches, which smashed him back and forth across the corridor, from wall to wall. Finally, they died down, and he lay on the ladder, gasping for breath. The impacts had nearly paralyzed him from the pain. Both arms were numb, and his back felt like a spear had gone through it. He lay there for a good minute, unable to move.

Jim heard and felt a series of vibrations on the upper hull of Jade, and the ship continued to twitch and shake as something happened outside the hull. At first, he thought she was being boarded; but as time went on and nothing further happened, he decided that was not the case.

Lying there, waiting for feeling to return to his numb hands and arms, Jim had a moment to think about Bonnie. He did not think he would survive this day; but if he did...

If I survive, I will marry her. As soon as possible. I've been alone too long. I've found the love of my life, now I need to let her know how I feel...

Jim felt a vibration in Jade's hull, and heard a noise slowly start to build up outside, like the early stages of a hurricane.

We're re-entering the atmosphere, he thought. *Not good. Not good at all.*

The vibration continued to build in intensity. The noise increased, until it was a scream that he could hear through the hull, as if the hull were a sounding board. The scream of air got louder and louder.

Jim waited for the heat, thinking the ship would burn up, expecting to die any second. But instead, the sound stabilized. He realized they were decelerating somehow. Then he thought about the bumps and noises earlier and realized what was happening.

Bonnie grappled us! Slowing us down. Good girl!

Finally, he started to get some feeling back in his arms. He turned, lifted the shotgun, and aimed at the lock on the hatch. He took off the safety. Closing his eyes and turning his head away, he pulled the trigger.

The noise of the shot in the small corridor was deafening, but with all that was going on, he had a forlorn hope Jade might not notice. He had turned himself so that the shot was angled away from his body. Still, the 00-buckshot hit all around him as it glanced off the hatch, off the wall and pinged everywhere in the corridor. Nothing hit him directly, but he was not happy. Yet the hatch stood firm. He had to do it again.

The 12-gauge had made a sizable dent in the material around the lock, but the hatch was still locked. Jim racked the 12-gauge and pointed it at the dent on the hatch and fired again. His ears rang as shot pinged off the hatch, walls, and everywhere around him. One pellet hit him in the back, stinging and burning but not penetrating his skin. Smoke and burnt gunpowder filled the small corridor, nearly choking him.

The dent was larger, but the hatch was still locked. He thought for a second.

I had five rounds, he thought. *I've got three left. Keep going.*

Jim racked the shotgun once more, closed his eyes and fired. He felt shot hit him in the back of the head and on his right arm, stinging but not penetrating - indirect hits from bounces off the wall and ceiling of the narrow passageway. He opened his eyes and looked.

The lock on the hatch hung loose, and the hatch was free. Quickly, he pulled it open and slid into the lower cargo bay.

<Oh, Jim> he heard over his implant. <Bad boy. Now I have to pump all the air out of the cargo hold. Sorry, buddy. But I can't have you accessing those weapons>

Jim heard a "whooshing" sound and felt the air pressure suddenly decrease. He ran toward the stacked cargo, tied down with cargo straps.

There's a spare spacesuit in there somewhere, he remembered. *If I can find it before I pass out.*

Scrambling to the cargo straps, Jim looked frantically for the case containing the spare spacesuit. But he felt himself getting light-headed. His arms got weaker and weaker. Darkness descended on him.

* * * * *

Onboard the C-37, Mark peered at the display on his laptop.

"They'll come down somewhere around Dutch Harbor in the Aleutians. Hopefully on the airport if they have enough control," he told Gillian. "We're sending everything we can, but it's going to be a close race. The Russians have figured it out too. They're diverting there as well. Sending everything they can scrape together."

Gillian looked at her own display. "There's going to be a lot of aircraft in the air, and a lot of dying, but ultimately this comes down to a ground battle, I think."

"Yep," said Mark. "Whoever holds the ground long enough gets Jade. We've got every available fighter aircraft at Elmendorf launching. We've got the 4th Brigade Combat Team deploying, I think they may get there before the Russians...but it's going to be damn close."

Mark smiled over at her. "You were absolutely spot on to force me to get them in the air and orbiting near Anchorage before Jade launched. If you hadn't coerced me to do that, we'd be screwed right now. But as it is, I think we may be able to get the 4th to Dutch Harbor just before the Russians. If we can do that, then they'll try to hold on until the Stryker brigade can come in from Wainwright. But the problem is, we can't bring the Strykers in until we have air superiority, and that means we have to knock down the Russian fighters before the Strykers can land. It's going to be a bloodbath, any way you look at it."

"Will the 4th land? Or parachute in?"

"I assume they'll assess on the way. They'll have surveillance from satellites and fighters before they get there, so they'll know what they're up against. If they can get there before the Russians, they'll most likely try to land at least a few planes and offload a few combat vehicles, set up a perimeter. Otherwise, I'd expect them to jump in, if they can find an LZ large enough."

"And then what happens?"

"They try to keep the Russians away from Jade until the Strykers from Wainwright can get in there and reinforce them."

"Are the Strykers in the air yet?"

"Nope. They'll be at least four-five hours behind the 4th."

"Crap, crap, crap," said Gillian. "If the 4th can't get there before the Russians and hold them off, we're going to have to pry the Russians out of there. What a mess."

Mark looked over at her.

"Gillian. Listen. I have to go to Dutch, get there before the Russians, provide some coordination on the ground between my assets, and the 4th. It's important. I don't have time to drop you off on the way. When we get there, I want you to find a hole somewhere, get in it and pull the ground over your head. It's going to be a major battle. There's going to be death and destruction everywhere. I don't want you to get hurt."

Gillian smiled at Mark.

"I'll be with the man I love. Right beside you. Don't even try to push me off somewhere. You know I won't put up with it."

Mark nodded. He leaned over and kissed Gillian, gently. They gave each other a long look, two warriors going into battle.

Then they turned back to their laptops, assessing and coordinating assets. The C-37 droned through the sky, heading for Dutch Harbor.

FURBALL

It was a rare cloudless day over the island of Unalaska in the Aleutians. The port of Dutch Harbor, on the northern side of the island, and the airport next door, were both reporting severe clear. People went about their business. Boats moved about the harbor, and it was business as usual at the container port, as shipments of fish and other seafood were loaded for shipment to the Lower 48, and items needed by the people of Unalaska came in.

There was no way the people of Dutch Harbor could have known what was coming.

20,000 feet above them, the connected starships were descending like a bat out of hell. They were slowing, but not fast enough. Even Bonnie could see that.

Arteveld continued to shout orders at his crew, and they seemed to be doing things, but Bonnie couldn't see that anything was making a difference. They were just descending too fast.

On the ground below, people were starting to become aware of the strange sight in the sky above them. The conglomeration that was Jade, tightly attached to Corresse, grew larger and larger in the sky. A pilot waiting at the end of the runway in a Grumman Goose pointed up to the object, drawing his co-pilot's attention to it.

"What the hell is that?" he asked.

His companion shook his head. "No clue, but I think I want to get the hell out of the way." They looked at each other, firewalled the throttles and expedited their takeoff, getting off the runway before the crazy object rushing toward the airfield hit the Earth.

On the Corresse, Bonnie looked toward a side console that showed the ground below rushing up to meet them. It appeared they would impact somewhere on the airfield, maybe even on the runway. She guessed that would be a good thing - at least, that would avoid civilian casualties.

<Captain Arteveld has ordered that we detach at one hundred yards above the ground and save ourselves> said Corresse. <We'll be able to stop just slightly before we impact. Jade will impact hard, but it will be survivable for the most part. Do you want to send a message to Jim warning him to prepare for impact?"

"Yes," said Bonnie. "Please. I don't know if he'll get it, but it's a chance. Maybe Jade will let it pass, since she's going to be pretty occupied with her own survival."

* * * * *

Jim felt his senses returning. Groggily, he lifted his head. He was lying across the stacked boxes of materials in the cargo hold. He shook his head, trying to get his bearings.

They had been descending, he recalled. He had shot out the latch on the cargo hold door and had come down here looking for something. What was it?

Oh, yes, the spare spacesuit. But we must have come down into the thicker atmosphere. There are so many holes in Jade now, she can't pump out all the air. So, I don't need the spacesuit anymore. I need weapons.

Jim pushed himself up off the containers and thought. His head hurt like hell. He remembered he placed the weapons in the front of the pile, where he could get to them easily in an emergency. Looking around, he found the area where they were stacked and starting popping off straps, looking for several specific items. He knew what he wanted, and what he was going to do with it. He found the cases, pulled them out of the pile, and opened them. Suddenly he felt someone behind him.

He spun, and Rita was there, holding his sat phone. Her face was bloody, and she was holding a rag over it to staunch the bleeding. She thrust the phone at him silently, and he read the message on it.

Jim - impact in about two minutes. It will be a hard one. Get to bunks, lay down. Love you forever.

Grimly, Jim looked at Rita.

"Let's go," he said, grabbing the items he wanted out of the open cases. They ran up the ladder to the upper deck and down to Rita's cabin. Throwing themselves into the bed, they lay down flat. Jim dropped the items he had retrieved from the weapons cache on the floor beside them. Maybe he wouldn't need them. Maybe the impact would destroy Jade's ability to fight back.

They lay silently for a few seconds. Suddenly Rita turned to him, grabbed his face, and kissed him.

"I love you, Jim," she said. "I know you belong to Bonnie, but I love you."

Jim nodded, at a loss what to say.

Then they hit the ground.

* * * * *

Jade smashed into the ground like a rock dropped from a tall building. The impact crushed her lower deck, cracking it open. But the good news about that was it damped the impact on the upper deck. Jim and Rita felt the huge g-force of impact, but lying flat on their backs in Rita's bed, they survived. Momentarily stunned, they lay there, just trying to breathe, mentally counting arms and legs as people do after a car wreck.

The Corresse, above them, had disengaged from Jade one hundred yards before impact. Decelerating for all she was worth, the Corresse still smashed into the top of Jade's hull, but not hard enough to do significant damage. Now rising up again, Corresse hovered a hundred yards above Jade, her crew performing a damage assessment.

Until Jade fired a pulse cannon at her.

Arteveld, on the bridge, couldn't believe it.

"She fired on us!" he yelled, as the Corresse lurched madly, hit hard in the rear near the engines.

"Get us the hell out of here!" yelled Bonnie.

Arteveld spat a stream of commands at his crew, and the Corresse started rising upward, trying to put space between them and Jade.

Bonnie looked at the screens. Jade lay at the very south end of the runway at the Dutch Harbor airport, right on the numbers, close beside the mountain that bordered the field - Mount Ballyhoo. She was heavily damaged, the bottom of her hull crushed, lying slightly sideways, boxes and crates of cargo scattered in every direction. But her pulse cannon was tracking them perfectly. Jade's plans had been thwarted. She was pissed. She was not yet done in her rage.

Another blast and the Corresse shuddered again, as they rose through 5,000 feet, trying to get away.

"Evade!" yelled Bonnie. "Don't make it easy for her!"

Arteveld nodded, giving commands to his crew. The Corresse started to move in an evasive pattern, left, right, all the while climbing steadily toward space. But Bonnie could see that Corresse was hurt - their rate of climb was hardly more than an F-22 could perform. She wasn't even certain they could get back to orbit.

She tried talking to the AI through her implant.

"Will we make it to orbit?" she asked silently, hoping Arteveld had authorized her for two-way communication with the AI.

<Yes, but just barely> she heard in reply over her implant. <If we don't take another round in the engines>

One more blast from the pulse cannon flew by, but missed, as the Corresse dodged in a random pattern. Then Bonnie noticed something on the monitors.

"What's that?" she yelled, as she noted a massive formation of aircraft coming in from the north, and another from the west.

"Russians," said Arteveld, pointing. "And yours too, I think, just coming in from the east."

Bonnie looked again. Sure enough, a large formation of American C-17 transports was coming in from the east. Surrounding the transports was a mass of F-35, F-22, and F-16 fighters. Even as she watched, the F-22 and F-35 squadrons peeled off from the American formation, dropped external tanks, and punched afterburner, on a vector to intercept the

Russian fighters coming in from the north and west. The F-16 squadrons stayed behind to protect the C-17 group.

And below, Bonnie noticed one lone C-37 Air Force executive jet, streaking in low over the bay, trying to get into the airport ahead of the battle.

"Holy fucking shit," said Bonnie. She had never seen so many planes in the air at one time in her life. There had to be well over two hundred aircraft in view now, and many more dots on the horizon. She saw the nearest Russian fighters punch off drop tanks as well. The hundreds of spinning drop tanks falling from the sky looked for all the world like a strange, silvery storm of butterflies in the distance. And then in a paroxysm of sudden violence, missiles started flying from both sides.

TRUE COLORS

At the airport at Dutch Harbor, passengers who had been boarding a Dash-8 airliner on the ramp ran back to the terminal for cover as the huge mass of airplanes to the west, north and east converged on them. Plus, there was a crazy black spaceship lying smashed at the south end of the runway firing a space-age weapon at another crazy black spaceship that was rising straight up into the air. Each time the strange weapon fired it made a "braaaap" sound, a sound that made the hair stand up on the back of a person's neck.

Two Russian SU-29 fighters passed over the field from north to south at supersonic speed, with three American F-35's right behind them. Five separate sonic booms knocked windows out all over the port.

It didn't take a rocket scientist to see bad things were about to happen.

Someone set off the fire alarms in the small terminal. Two maintenance workers working next to the terminal ran for shelter. The pilot of a smaller plane taxied at breakneck speed back to the ramp, shutting off her engines, bailing out of her plane and running for any cover she could find.

An Air Force C-37 corporate jet approached low from the northeast. It came in far too low for a normal landing, curving in hard to try and make the runway. Clearly it was trying to stay out of the line of fire from both Jade's pulse cannon firing up at the Corresse and the furball of SU-27s, SU-57s, MiG-29s, F-22s and F-35s now just a few miles north of the field, starting what promised to be the largest missile dogfight in history.

And behind the C-37 came the C-17 troop transports, trying to sneak into the airport before the furball got to them.

The C-37 slammed into the runway right on the numbers, a hard landing that made the wings droop as if the tips would hit the runway. The engines went into max reverse, trying to get the aircraft stopped before it ran into Jade, crashed at the other end of the runway. Brakes squealing, the jet began to decelerate. It looked as if it might be able to get stopped before it ran into the spacecraft.

Until Jade depressed her pulse cannon and fired directly at it, knocking the right wing completely off the airplane. A great gout of flame rose up from the separated wing as the fuel exploded. The nose gear and left main gear collapsed as the sideways lurch was too much for it structurally, and the entire aircraft slewed to the left, spinning around. It spun off the runway, ran across the rough ground on the far side, crossed the ramp and smashed into the terminal building, coming to a halt with a noise like a dozen car wrecks. Parts and pieces scattered, bouncing around in every direction. Then it erupted in flames as the other wing tank caught fire.

Immediately behind the C-37, the first C-17 troop transport touched down, ignoring the carnage in front of it. The 4th Brigade Combat Team had a job to do, and they intended to do it. The C-17 got firmly planted on the ground, preparing to go to full reverse and brake hard in a tactical short field landing. Once again, Jade depressed the pulse cannon to fire. She fired, and the entire front of the C-17 disappeared. One minute a perfectly good C-17 was rolling down the runway. The next minute, the cockpit and nose gear were just gone.

The huge aircraft dropped onto its belly, scraping along the runway at well over a hundred miles an hour, no longer in control of its destiny. It was now just a two-hundred fifty-ton missile filled with troops and equipment, on a collision course with Jade at the end of the runway. Before Jade could react, the huge airplane smashed into her, knocking her another hundred yards down the runway in a huge fireball.

As the wreckage came to a screeching halt, the back ramp of the C-17 came down. Ignoring the flames, injured troops came pouring out, the loadmaster screaming at them to get away. Those that could ran to the side of the airstrip and took cover, lugging their weapons and ammo. Many others simply collapsed on the ground, away from the flaming wreckage, unable to continue. But for the moment, at least, Jade was too distracted to fire.

At the other end of the runway, the next C-17 touched down, also doing a tactical short field landing, going to max reverse and max braking, trying to get the big bird stopped before the mess at the end of the runway. It barely succeeded, turning off the runway less than two dozen yards from the burning plane in front of it. Clearing the runway, it slammed on the brakes, rocking, as the back ramp started down. Troops began to run off the plane while the ramp was still inches off the ground, officers and noncoms assessing the area and yelling deployment orders. In sixty seconds, another hundred men were on the ground on both sides of the runway, digging in.

Following in quick succession, three more of the C-17 transports touched down, came to a mad halt, and got off the runway as fast as possible. Their ramps opened and troops poured out, until there were over four hundred airborne infantry on the ground, forming a huge perimeter surrounding Jade - preparing for the worst. From the last two aircraft, they also unloaded four Stryker combat vehicles.

There wasn't enough space on the airport for any more C-17s to land. The rest of the formation overflew the airport, paratroops pouring out of the planes, on a course that took them over the island to the southwest.

The troops floated down and shed their parachutes, grabbed their equipment, and started digging in. Plane after plane of the 4th Brigade Combat Team's formation passed over the airport, each dropping its cargo of men and equipment, until well over one thousand troops were down in the LZ.

Many missed the airport proper - some landing on Mount Ballyhoo, some in the ocean at both ends of the airport, some landing among the buildings and streets of the container port. All those who survived their landing grabbed their weapons and equipment and made their way to their rally point at the airport.

* * * * *

To the southwest, Gregori sat in the lead AN-124, droning toward Dutch Harbor. The battle of the fighters continued off to the north. But Gregori had decided not to wait until that was finally resolved.

The Americans had brought a lot more aircraft than he expected. He had also brought as many reinforcements as he could find, scraping up fighters from across Siberia. Both sides were taking a beating, and it was uncertain who would end up holding the air.

Gregori had decided to go for his objective, even if it meant sacrificing some of the transport aircraft. They had circled around to the southwest of Dutch Harbor; now they were boring in, determined to capture the objective.

The British have an expression, he thought. *In for a penny, in for a pound.*

"Prepare to jump!" he heard from the jumpmaster. He stood, hooked his snap ring to the overhead wire, and duck-walked along with the rest of his troops toward the back ramp, asshole to bellybutton, preparing to jump. The back ramp came down and they moved into position.

The light turned green, and the line of men shuffled off the plane, jumping off the back of the ramp. Gregori was the last to go.

Leaving the plane, Gregori felt the risers jerk him hard as his chute opened. He looked down at Dutch Harbor below him. Gregori had studied the topographical maps of the area until the landmarks were burned into his brain. To the north Gregori saw the airfield and port facilities. Below him was the rough but relatively clear LZ, near an abandoned concrete structure dating from World War II, once a hospital. The decaying ruins of the old hospital would provide his initial command post - CP - protecting the CP from sniper rounds or stray mortars sent by the Americans while his staff was getting organized. The main part of the town was farther south, across a narrow channel.

It was a tiny LZ by normal standards; one he would have

refused had the stakes been less. But he had little choice in this mountainous terrain. It was damn close to the Americans, point-blank range by normal battle standards; but Gregori was certain the Americans were still settling into their positions and nowhere near ready to fight.

He saw some of his troops drifting off the tiny LZ in the wind and knew they would land either in the town to the south - or in the water of the channel. Those that landed in the town - and survived - could cross the bridge and rejoin with his main body.

Those that landed in the water would die.

Drifting down in his parachute, he looked up at the line of transports behind his first one. The second one was now disgorging troops as it came over the LZ. But in the distance, he saw an American F-35 fighter come up from the rear, and two missiles came out of it, smashing into the rearmost AN-124. It went up in a huge fireball. Right behind that one, another F-35 bored in. Another pair of missiles smashed into the next AN-124 in the formation. The right wing came off the huge aircraft - and it fell, twisting, starting a rapid rotation. Gregori saw chutes coming out the back.

At least some of the troops are getting out, Gregori thought. *God help them.*

The wreck continued to spin down, until it impacted on Standard Oil Hill in a huge fireball of exploding fuel. Debris scattered everywhere in a cacophony of parts and pieces. Engines as big as a car bounced like rubber balls, taking down buildings in their path as they slammed across the landscape, starting secondary fires and explosions. Munitions inside the fireball started cooking off instantly, sending intermittent tracers across the landscape in every direction.

Gregori sighed.

So much waste, he thought.

Then Gregori saw a squadron of SU-57s arrive to challenge the F-35s, and another furball of crazy, gyrating aircraft developed, leaving his formation safe for the moment.

The ground was coming up fast. Gregori altered course a bit

to avoid a building. He bent his knees to take the impact. With a thud, he hit the ground and rolled. Shedding his parachute, he looked around.

His command staff had gone out of the plane ahead of him; they were organizing the troops now, dispersing them to form a perimeter. His second in command waved him over, and they took shelter behind the abandoned WWII hospital structure, now just a large decaying mass of concrete.

"Status?" he asked.

"We are establishing the perimeter. As soon as we have enough troops on the ground, we can assault through the port, there..." he pointed to the buildings and port facilities standing between them and the airport. "The Americans won't shell us when we are in the port, I think. Too many civilians. We can make it all the way to the airport before they will be able to use heavy weapons."

He pointed to his map and traced a road that ran around a ridge into the airport.

"We break out right here where this road enters about a hundred meters from the crashed spaceship..."

"Starship," corrected Gregori absent-mindedly, looking at the battlefield on the map.

"...yes, starship. Right there where the road enters."

"Good," said Gregori. "Execute that plan."

The officer nodded, and turned to his men, waiting nearby. He waved them over and briefed them on the plan. They nodded, ran back to their units, and passed the word down.

Gregori's paratroops continued to land in the LZ, although many ended up across the lagoon and had to hike back, their heavy loads of gear slowing them down. The Americans had gotten a few snipers up on top of Mount Ballyhoo, Gregori realized. Sporadic long-distance fire from the American snipers came at them. Then mortars started dropping in.

"Son of a bitch!" yelled Gregori's second-in-command. "The fucking Americans have those new ACERM mortars! The smart ones! They're dropping them right on top of us!"

Gregori nodded absently, barely blinking as a mortar round went off fifty yards away, his ears ringing from the concussion. He had expected this.

"Look for a drone overhead, Dmitri," he yelled. "They'll have a laser designator on a tiny little drone over us somewhere. Knock that down, and their accuracy goes all to hell!"

Petra nodded and spat orders at his staff. Minutes later, Gregori heard a harsh whine as their brigade man-portable anti-drone weapon fired. Suddenly, high overhead, a Skylark micro-drone disintegrated, pieces fluttering down like confetti.

That should buy us some time, Gregori thought. *I'm sure they have more, but we'll be out of here and in the port in a half hour. After that, we should be good for a while. I don't think they'll drop mortars on the civilians in the port.*

When all his troops had landed, Gregori had his officers do a quick head count. They had 840 men on the ground. That meant he had lost more than 220 men on the drop.

It would have to be enough for the moment. He had more paratroops on the way, but so did the Americans. He couldn't wait. He had to take the objective now and take the starship, carve out the technology, and get it out of here.

FLORISSIAN HELPS

Near the C-37 smashed up against the terminal, Mark came to his senses. He looked around for Gillian, but he couldn't see her anywhere. He realized he had been thrown clear - he was a good 30 yards from the crashed plane, up by the terminal, lying on a pile of baggage.

He heard gunfire off to the south. Working his way out of the pile of bags, he stumbled to his feet and checked his arms and legs. He counted two of each, then looked around. He made his way over toward the C-37, but the flaming wreckage was too hot to approach. He stared at it, numb with grief.

"Gillian," he mumbled. "Oh, Gillian."

Bowing his head, he mumbled a prayer.

"God, let it have been quick for her. Let it have been quick, so she didn't suffer."

Taking stock, Mark looked to the south. He could see Russian paratroopers coming down, about a mile or so southwest of his position. It seemed the gunfire he could hear was coming from American positions up on the mountain to the east, as well as more gunfire southwest of the wreck of Jade, which was surrounded by a smoldering C-17.

"Evidently I missed something," he said to himself.

Taking another look at Jade, he realized the C-17 that had smashed into her had pushed her another hundred yards farther south, to the very end of the runway. Only a road separated her from the sea. Another four C-17s were parked beside the runway south of him, all with ramps down. Abandoned parachutes littered the airport, the hillside northeast of him, and everywhere he could see.

"So, the 4th got in OK," he said to himself. "Now where would they set up?"

Traversing the airport with his eyes, he saw a couple of Stryker combat vehicles not far away, south of the terminal, behind a small building. Squinting, he saw an OP - an observation post - on the roof of the building.

Looking around, he noticed a small airport tug nearby, empty. Running over to it, he saw the keys hanging in it. Someone had left in a hurry. Stepping into it, he turned the key and pushed the pedal down. Running down past the terminal toward the Strykers a few hundred yards away, he hoped nobody decided to take a pot-shot at the uniformed General driving the tug across the battlefield.

* * * * *

"You need to put me back down there," said Bonnie to Arteveld. "My friends are in danger. I have to go help them!"

Arteveld shook his head in a very human gesture. "No. I can't return. Our engines are damaged, we have just barely made a geostationary orbit. I've had enough. We'll repair our engines and return to Sanctuary. That's my decision."

Bonnie pleaded with him. "Please - don't leave like this. Let me go rescue my friends, then we'll go to Sanctuary with you. It will give us a chance to make a connection with your people. Please!"

Florissian, sitting in an observer's chair behind Bonnie and Arteveld, suddenly stood up and spoke.

"Captain. We have a chance here to find allies to help against the Singheko. Let's not miss this opportunity!"

Arteveld hesitated. Bonnie dived in again, trying to sway the captain.

"Do you have any shuttle or small craft I can use to rescue my friends? Anything?"

Arteveld looked at Florissian. Grudgingly, he nodded.

"I will give you a shuttlecraft. The AI can help you fly it. But we leave this system when our engines are repaired. I won't wait for you. If you can rescue your friends and return before we depart, then you may go to Sanctuary with us, and we will present you to our government. Perhaps we can strike an alliance. But if you are not here when my engines are repaired, you are left behind. Is that clear?"

"Clear, sir," said Bonnie. "And thank you!"

"Florissian will show you the way," said Arteveld. He waved in the general direction of the passageway to the back of the ship and turned away.

Bonnie turned to Florissian and followed her as she went down the passageway toward the back of the ship.

"You are a pilot, correct?" asked Florissian.

"Yes. Air Force."

Florissian smiled. "Then you are going to be happy. This shuttle can be flown by the AI. But it can also be flown manually if you wish."

Florissian arrived at a hatch, palmed it open, and waved Bonnie inside. In the darkness, Bonnie saw the outline of something - a vehicle - it looked like...

"Why, that's that thing they fly in Europe...?"

Florissian flipped on the lighting, and Bonnie stood in total surprise. In front of her was a small shuttle that looked like a twin to a type of small European airliner, called a blended wing. Except it was much smaller than the ones she had seen.

Turning to Florissian, Bonnie waved at the craft. "It looks almost exactly like those blended wing airliners that fly around London and Paris."

Florissian smiled inscrutably. "Yes, doesn't it?" she asked. "Perhaps you haven't realized, but there are occasions when we must go to the surface of your world, for whatever reason. We certainly couldn't show up in one of our own shuttlecraft, could we? That would cause quite a stir..."

Bonnie stood in absolute astonishment. "Are you telling me that this...thing...can make it to the surface and back again?"

"Yes," smiled Florissian. "It flies exactly like any other jet, except that there are a couple of extra bells and whistles. Normally, the AI would launch it and take you down, but in this case, I think I'll go with you."

Bonnie shook her head.

"No, no, Florissian. I'm going into the middle of a battlefield.

I can't put you in that situation."

Florissian ignored her, walked to the craft, opened a hatch, and waved at Bonnie to step inside.

"First of all, we cannot pass up this chance to find an alliance with those who can stand with us against the Singheko. I believe we have found them, and I for one am happy for it. Secondly, your friends may need a doctor. And finally, Arteveld is my husband. I seriously doubt he'll launch for home without me. So, climb aboard, and let's get this done!"

Bonnie just stared at Florissian. Then she grinned and walked to the hatch. "I think we are going to have a great alliance!" she said to the little doctor. Then she jumped up the ladder and through the hatch of the craft.

Following Florissian to the front of the plane, she was amazed to find a cockpit that looked in every respect like that of a normal bizjet. Florissian waved her to the pilot's seat and took the copilot position. As they strapped in, Florissian spoke a stream of language to the AI.

With a 'thunk,' two large clamshell doors below them opened. Bonnie stared out. Below them was empty space, and below that, the Earth.

<Ready to release> intoned the voice of the AI. Florissian looked at Bonnie. "Are you ready to go?"

"Am I?" asked Bonnie, getting down to business. She started tracing her eyes across every instrument on the panel. All appeared normal, except there were a few extra switches in the center she didn't recognize. One had labels of 'S' and 'A.' She pointed to them. Florissian grinned.

"Space and Atmosphere," she said. Florissian reached up and pointed to the switch, which was set to the "S" position. "We are ready to launch. Just tell the AI to release. Call her Corresse, she's a subset of the one on our ship."

Bonnie nodded.

"Corresse, release," she said.

With a lurch, the craft dropped out of the belly of the starship, propelled by something invisible but which had a good solid push to get them clear of the starship.

"Now the AI will deorbit. Just let it fly the craft. It will take you down to 40,000 feet. Then you can take over if you wish," said Florissian.

Bonnie waited patiently as the craft decelerated. She watched the Corresse fall up and away from them as they deorbited. It seemed much larger and blacker than she expected. But that made sense, she thought. In space, a warship should be black. Any other color would stand out.

In a few minutes, the Corresse was gone as they decelerated to return to Earth. Looking down, she realized they were over Canada. Florissian saw her look of concern and smiled.

"Not to worry," she said. "We can easily make it to Dutch Harbor."

Just as on the Corresse, Bonnie felt no acceleration as the craft obviously pulled g's to get positioned for re-entry. Five minutes later, Florissian spoke again. "We're entering the atmosphere," she said.

Bonnie saw wisps of plasma start to form around the nose of the craft. She wanted to think of it as a plane - but on the other hand it could fly in space. She didn't know what to call it. She decided to call it a spaceplane. It looked like a plane and flew in space - so that was that.

"We are well positioned to approach Dutch Harbor from the southwest," said Florissian.

Bonnie heard a high-pitched whine as they got into thicker atmosphere. Looking ahead, she saw the vast Bering Sea, and the tiny dot that was Unalaska coming into view.

Jim came to his senses slowly. He closed his eyes again, trying to remember what had happened. He recalled the initial crash into the Earth; but he and Rita had survived that with no major injuries, just bruising and disorientation. Then he remembered that they had got off the bed, he had grabbed the weapons off the floor, and they ran for the hatch to the processor room.

He intended to kill Jade.

Slowly he looked around. He was in the passageway outside Jade's processor room. There was a huge tear in the ceiling; in fact, it seemed as if most of Jade's top hull was gone. Through the opening, flames and smoke were evident outside. But they didn't penetrate into the ship. In the center, in a clear space, he could see the sky.

It was full of airplanes shooting at each other.

Groaning, he tried to sit up. But the pain was too intense. He realized he had broken ribs. Plus, the pain in his right arm and left leg told him those were broken as well.

Turning his head, he tried to find Rita. He saw a head of black hair farther down the corridor, lying on the floor.

"Rita! Rita! Can you hear me?"

The head stirred. Slowly, Rita turned and pulled her body around so she could see him.

"Are you OK?" Jim asked.

"I think so," Rita mumbled. "What happened?"

"Don't know," said Jim. "I think something hit us, hard. Maybe an airplane."

Rita moaned. Then, with a lurch, she got to hands and knees, lifted her head, and looked over at Jim.

"Did you fire the C4?"

Jim looked back over toward the processor room hatch. The big lump of C4 explosive he had attached to the processor room hatch was gone. The door looked undamaged. Looking around, he saw the C4 lying in the passageway a dozen feet from him, toward the engine room. It had not exploded.

"No. Whatever hit us knocked it off the door before I could set it off. It's lying down in the passageway toward the engine room."

"I'll get it," said Rita. She pushed herself to her feet, swaying, then started staggering down the passageway toward Jim.

<I don't think so, Rita> said Jade over their implants. The engine room hatch opened, and Andy came through. The little android was standing upright, his four hands in front of him. One of them held Jim's .45 automatic. The little android waved it at Rita.

<Back you go to your cabin, Rita> said Jade.

Rita put up her hands and nodded.

"You're the boss, Jade," she said. She backed up slowly until she came to the door of her cabin, stepped inside, and disappeared.

Now the little android turned to Jim. He was standing a dozen feet in front of Jim's position, toward the engine room.

Jim had a fairly good idea what was coming next. He had reloaded the 12-gauge shotgun and left it beside Rita's bed - in the cabin Rita had just entered.

"Unless I miss my guess, Andy, you're about to have a new function."

The little android had no facial expressions, but Jim thought he detected a little puzzlement in his voice as he spoke.

"*New function? What new function?*"

"Colander," said Rita's voice behind Jim. Knowing what Rita meant, Jim turned his face to the floor, throwing his good arm over his head for protection, as Rita opened up with the 12-gauge, firing over Jim at the android.

Firing as fast as she could pump the shotgun, Rita got off six shots directly at the android's head, each one right on target. As she fired, she stepped forward. By the time she fired the last shot, she had stepped past Jim and was nearly on the android. As the last shot fired and the gun was empty, she swung it by the barrel and hit the android so hard, the stock broke off the shotgun. Grabbing a new handhold on the hot barrel, she swung it again, and with a thud the android's head came off and fell to the floor, dozens of holes in it.

"Colander," said Rita again.

The .45 auto fell to the floor, dropped by the lifeless android. Rita grabbed it and stuck it in her waistband.

* * * * *

Gregori trotted with his men through the port of Dutch Harbor toward the airport. They had met almost no resistance so far; but he knew that was a temporary condition. A couple of civilians had sniped at them from various locations with hunting rifles; those men were dead now. A couple of American fighters had zoomed over, but they appeared more intent on reconnaissance than on strafing. Gregori looked to the north and saw that the furball of aircraft was still in progress, but at least half the airplanes were gone. Casualties must be high, he thought. On both sides.

The Americans had started up at least two more ACERM mortars from on top of Mount Ballyhoo as Gregori's troops pulled out of their LZ. But as soon as they were in the cover of the buildings, they stopped. The Americans weren't willing to drop mortars into the civilians all around them. Some sporadic sniper fire that came from Mount Ballyhoo had also stopped as they entered the port.

It would get harder as they approached the airport. They would be fully in range of the snipers entrenched on Mount Ballyhoo. If the Americans had managed to air-drop a few howitzers in addition to the mortars, it could be dicey. And it wouldn't take much to prevent Gregori from reaching his objective - the crashed starship at the south end of the runway.

The starship was completely in the open, sitting right at the end of the runway pavement. Only a paved road separated it from the rocks leading down to the water. Between Gregori's troops and the starship was the port - warehouses, buildings, abandoned vehicles. Civilians were still fleeing to the left and right of his advancing troops; he had ordered his men to leave them alone, unless they showed signs of aggression.

Gregori could have ridden in the single BTR-80A combat vehicle they had managed to get safely on the ground. It followed close behind him, but he chose not to ride inside. In this kind of urban battle, he should have. The greatest danger was the unseen danger, that of snipers. But right now, Gregori wanted to be outside. He was staring up at the mountain on the other side of the airfield. He couldn't see the airfield yet; but he knew what was waiting there.

He was sure the American combat brigade would be established on the ridges and hills just south of the airport. He thought it a poor defensive position, but that was all that was available to them, if they wanted to prevent him from reaching the starship.

One has to make do, he thought. *Both us and them.*

On each end of the long series of ridges and hills was a road, up against the ocean. Gregori suspected they would have the bulk of their strength on the ends of their line, where the roads came through. They would have reserves left, center and right, and probably another reserve force back at the airport terminal. At least, that's what he would do...and he assumed the American commander was as good as he.

The American's meager artillery on top of the mountain would be ready to start pounding as soon as he was close enough - which would be any minute now. Although the Americans had been holding off to protect the civilians of the port up to this point, he knew that would end as his troops came face-to-face with the dug-in American brigade.

Gregori looked up at the mountain, thinking how he would deploy his artillery if he were the American commander - and for any way to get around behind it and neutralize it. He knew there was a road that went to the south of the mountain, then climbed up the backside. That road would be heavily defended; he expected the brigade Command Post would be up there somewhere. And there would be observation posts looking down on him right now, either dug into the face of the mountain or via drones overhead.

He looked up at the mountain, but despite the clear day and the blue sky above him, he couldn't see anything. Except the aircraft off to the north, and the people dying in them.

Gregori's tactical communicator beeped. He glanced at it, then froze in his tracks. His staff rushed to his side, expecting trouble. Gregori waved them away temporarily.

On the screen, in Russian, was a message:

<*I am the starship crashed at the end of the runway. You may call me Jade. I would like to negotiate my surrender to the Russian forces*>

Gregori rapidly typed back.

"What are your conditions?"

<*My core processing functions - my consciousness - to be maintained intact at all times. My ability to travel in space to be restored. In return, I will give you access to all my technology, including the stardrive. Also, I will help you drive away the Americans here at Dutch Harbor*>

Gregori grinned. He had nothing to lose. He typed:

"*Accepted.*"

Immediately he heard the hair-raising "*braaaap*" of the pulse weapon start up again. His tactical radio operator stood nearby, receiving a message on the brigade field radio. He turned to Gregori, puzzled.

"Sir! The spaceship! It's firing on the American positions! And the American aircraft!"

Gregori acknowledged. His grin got even wider. Waving his staff over, they ducked into the shelter of the BTR and started revising their plan.

I have the Americans now, thought Gregori. *I can dig them out of there.*

"While the Americans are occupied with the pulse weapon from the starship, hit them here…"

Gregori pointed to the road at the far west end of the ridge.

"...hit them with everything we have right at that point. They'll be expecting us to come in from the east end, because it's closer to our objective. But now, with the distraction from the starship, I think we fox them this way. Overrun their positions here, drive for the terminal, envelop them from behind, and cut them off from the starship."

His staff nodded their understanding and rushed to carry out his orders. Gregori stepped back outside of the BTR and looked up at Mount Ballyhoo.

I have you now, he thought. *If I can get to the starship before your reinforcements arrive from Wainwright and Hawaii, and if I can cut the key components out of the starship in time...*

If.

Twenty minutes later, his second in command looked at him, and nodded.

"We're ready, sir," he said.

Gregori gave the order. "Execute," he said.

He heard his troops open up all across the line, a coordinated fire designed to disguise their true point of attack. Quickly the American troops responded. He heard heavy machine guns open up on both sides. The American mortars started up again, and high explosive rounds started crashing around them. Then he heard heavier explosions, and he knew the Americans had at least one field howitzer up there on the mountain.

Gregori smiled. He was home again. Battle was his drug of choice. He needed the high, and he was getting it.

TOMMY

Mark Rodgers made it across the airstrip to the small building on the south side of the ramp; evidently the American snipers on top of Mount Ballyhoo had excellent quality optics, because they had not fired on the crazy general driving across the battlefield in an airport tug. He had been challenged by a security squad as he approached the Observation Post, but the troops had radioed ahead and received the go-ahead to let him pass.

He entered the building and pounded up the stairs to the top floor. There he found a signals Sergeant huddled over his various radios and screens.

The man looked up as Mark entered. He stood, somewhat in a quandary as to how a major general was standing in his OP. Mark smiled at him and waved him back to his seat.

"Sergeant. Where's the brigade CP?" he shot at the confused noncom.

"Uh…on top of Mount Ballyhoo," stuttered the sergeant.

"I need to get up there ASAP," said Mark. "I've got vital intelligence that can't wait. Can you have a Stryker take me up?"

"Uh…I can't authorize that, sir, but I can call Brigade Ops and ask."

"Do it quick, son. Time's a'wastin," said Mark.

The Sergeant made the call. A couple of minutes later, he got the response.

"Brigade Ops said OK, sir. I'll detail one of my security team to take you up. You realize, sir, that the Russians are in the port, only a thousand yards away now. You may take some long-range fire going up there."

"I doubt it, son. Those are Spetsnaz. They won't waste small-arms ammo on one Stryker from that range. Let's get going!"

The sergeant nodded and sent a corporal down with Mark. The corporal led him to one of the Stryker combat vehicles parked behind the building. The corporal spoke with the vehicle commander, while Mark jumped in and got situated. With a lurch, the Stryker started off toward the road leading around the mountain to the backside as Mark found a headset and put it on.

"Step on it!" yelled Mark to the vehicle commander. The man nodded and gave an order to the driver. The Stryker leaped forward.

They had to pass right by Jade in order to get to the top of the mountain; he glanced out the top hatch and looked at the crashed starship, which was still surrounded by smoldering parts of a C-17. Mark still couldn't understand why Jade had fired on them and the C-17. He supposed the AI was just in a blind rage now, having lost her opportunity to escape, and being ambushed by the Corresse.

Heading up the road leading to the top of the small mountain, Mark tried to push thoughts of Gillian out of his mind. He shook his head, trying to quell the thoughts of her in the burning C-37. The commander looked over at him strangely but said nothing. It wasn't in his job description to question generals.

As they left the field and headed up the road going around the side of the mountain, Mark heard the "braaaap" of Jade's pulse cannon start up again. Sticking his head out the top hatch, he turned to look back towards the airfield.

Jade was firing on the American positions from behind. Even as Mark watched, the pulse cannon fired again. The entire building housing the forward OP, the one he had just left, disappeared in a massive explosion of flame and splinters. Again, the starship fired, and one of the parked C-17 aircraft disappeared in a mass of flame and debris.

"Shit, that bitch!" yelled Mark at no one in particular. "That fucking, back-stabbing, godforsaken alien bitch!"

The Stryker commander looked at Mark even more strangely, then turned back to his work.

Soon they were around the back of the mountain, at the ruins of the old World War II base called Camp Schwatka. Mark jumped out the back of the Stryker, waved the crew away and ran to the Brigade Command Post, which was set up inside one of the moldering World War II ammo dumps. Entering, he paused, identified the Brigade Commander, and ran over to him.

"Colonel Hayes?" Mark said quietly. "I'm General Rodgers. I'm the SOB who started all this mess. Can I have a word?"

Colonel Hayes looked at the General who had popped up out of nowhere and was now standing in front of him.

"Certainly, General. But first, can I ask who you are?"

"DoD Weapons Directorate," said Mark. "We've been tracking that starship down there for several months. But we sort of let it get away from us."

"I'd say so," remarked the Colonel. "And do you have any idea how to get the genie back in the bottle?"

"Maybe," said Mark. "I may have some assets I can bring to bear. But I need to talk it through with you first."

Colonel Hayes turned to his XO. "Joe, give me five minutes with the General. Come and get me if anything pops."

His XO nodded. Colonel Hayes stood and gestured to Mark.

"Follow me to my conference room." Hayes exited the ancient ammo dump and walked a dozen yards to the north, where several men were digging a latrine. Hayes waved at them.

"Take five, men."

The grateful men dumped their shovels on the ground and trotted off. Hayes turned back to Mark.

"OK, what's the story, General?"

"OK. One - we absolutely cannot let the Russians get this technology. You see what just one pulse cannon can do. Imagine a whole battery of them, in space, pointing right down at us."

Colonel Hayes nodded.

"You didn't need to come all the way up here to tell me that."

"Of course. But we have the other starship, up in orbit. I believe that one may be on our side or can be induced to help us."

"Damn."

"Exactly. I can work on that approach, but we still need a contingency plan to ensure this technology doesn't get away from us."

Colonel Hayes looked at him.

"We've already started such a plan," he said.

Mark nodded. "I figured you had. SLCMs?"

Hayes nodded guardedly. "Yes."

Submarine launched cruise missiles, thought Mark. *Exactly what I would have called for, if they are in range. There must be a missile boat around here somewhere.*

"OK. That's good. That's excellent. The only thing I ask - and the real reason I asked to have this discussion - is that I would request you coordinate with me before you pull the trigger on that. I'd hate to have our friends upstairs come down to help us and then smoke them by accident."

Colonel Hayes looked troubled.

"I can't guarantee that we can hold off. No promises."

"Fair enough," said Mark. "But at least give me a couple of minutes warning, in case I have assets down there that need to get out."

Colonel Hayes nodded.

"I'll do the best I can, but I have to balance the sacrifice of my troops and planes against your assets."

Mark nodded. There was nothing more to say.

* * * * *

Corporal Tommy Baines huddled in the rocks next to the water as the strange spaceship weapon only fifty yards away fired across the battlefield. The crashed spaceship had two weapons, one on each side of the rear of the ship. One was firing up at American aircraft in the sky, driving them away. The other was firing at 4th Brigade positions, up on the ridge west of the airport.

Tommy was well positioned to see the now-enemy starship. He had originally been on the far end of the brigade's line, butted up against the east end of the ridge, with only a paved road and the short drop down to it between his position and the rocks lining the harbor edge.

But now he was down in those rocks, huddling. One of the first blasts from the pulse weapon had knocked him off the ridge, down into the road. He had instinctively sought cover, and ran for the water's edge, dropping over the berm into the rocks below.

Tommy was scared, but not so scared he couldn't think. He noted that the weapon had a recycle time of about ten seconds.

That's enough time to get a grenade to it, if I can get close enough, he thought.

Tommy peered out at the crashed starship wreaking havoc with the defensive line set up across the narrow neck of the island. The far-side turret firing up at aircraft off to the north was not his concern. The other turret on his side of the ship was the problem, as it fired at the troops on the ground - his friends.

The two turrets were alternating fire, with one going off every five seconds. The sound they made was loud, strange, and frightening. But Tommy wasn't about to lie there and let his fellow soldiers die. He mentally mapped out a path to get closer.

Tommy started inching his way along the rocks. After a couple minutes of careful crawling, he was looking right down the runway at the starship, only a couple of dozen yards away. It was time to make his move.

The next time it fires, I go, Tommy thought.

He started a short prayer, barely able to hear himself over the sound of Jade's cannon firing, the American shells from Mount Ballyhoo falling into the Russian positions to his left, and the din of small arms fire from both sides.

The near cannon fired. Tommy charged up the rocks and onto the end of the runway. Running for his life, he held a grenade in his right hand, the pin clutched in his left, making for the right rear corner of the crashed starship, where the pulse cannon turret had just fired. He pulled the pin off the grenade and flipped the spoon off, making it active.

He almost made it. The cannon deflected and pointed right at him. *Oh, shit,* was all Tommy had time to think. Then the cannon fired.

DETERMINATION

"Crap!" exclaimed Bonnie. "Fucking missiles and airplanes everywhere. What a shitshow!"

Bonnie and Florissian were down to 40,000 feet in the shuttle. But ahead of them was a sky full of twisting, turning aircraft, with most of them shooting at each other.

"We can't go through that mess," agreed Florissian. "Maybe we can circle around farther to the south and come in that way?"

"That's pretty much our only choice," said Bonnie. "Corresse, take us around to the south of the island and then to a point about seventy-five miles southeast of the airport.

<Sure> responded Corresse.

"Corresse? And can you patch me through to the approach frequency at Elmendorf Air Force Base in Anchorage?"

<Yes. I can do that…connecting…you are connected. Please speak."

Bonnie thought about how best to word her request.

<Elmendorf Approach, this is emergency aircraft Rescue Four, I need to get an urgent message to Dutch Harbor, can you copy?"

Over her implant, Bonnie heard a hesitant voice come back in reply.

"Aircraft calling Elmendorf Approach, say again?"

"Elmendorf Approach, this is emergency aircraft Rescue Four, I need to get an urgent message to Dutch Harbor, not a joke, triple urgent, can you copy?"

"Rescue Four, roger, I can copy, go ahead."

"Get word to ranking officer at Dutch Harbor, Bonnie Page is onboard Rescue Four, urgent you contact me on 28.07 megahertz ASAP. Over."

"Message received, readback as follows: 'To ranking officer at Dutch Harbor, Bonnie Page is onboard Rescue Four, urgent you contact me on 28.07 megahertz ASAP."

"Readback correct, Rescue Four out."

Florissian looked puzzled.

"Why did you label us as Rescue Four? I don't understand…"

Bonnie grinned. "For the same reason you shout 'FIRE' when someone attacks you in a large city. People may not respond to 'HELP,' but they nearly always respond to 'FIRE.' It's human nature."

Bonnie waved in the general direction of Anchorage.

"Air Traffic Controllers are the same way…they have a built-in instinct to give priority to anything with the word "Rescue" in it. So, I used that to convince the ATC controller to help us."

"Hmm…smart," said Florissian. "I'd never have thought of that."

Fifteen minutes later, Bonnie and Florissian had made their way to the south of Unalaska, turned to the east, and were positioned seventy-five miles southeast of the Dutch Harbor airport. But so far, they had heard nothing back from Dutch Harbor.

"We may have to go in without protection," said Bonnie. "Are you up for that?"

Florissian frowned. "This is just a shuttlecraft. It has no weapons and no defenses. If they start shooting at us, we're toast."

"Understood," said Bonnie. "But I have to help my friends."

Florissian sighed, a long sigh that sounded so human, Bonnie couldn't help but turn to look at her.

"Let's do it," said Florissian. "But if I die, I'll haunt you."

Bonnie grinned.

"If you die, I die too, so we'll have to haunt each other."

Florissian smiled, somewhat uncertainly.

Suddenly they heard a voice routed through their AI implants.

"General Mark Rodgers calling Bonnie Page on Rescue Four. Over."

Bonnie smiled at Florissian.

"Bonnie Page here, General. Do you know who I am?"

"I certainly do, Bonnie. What brings you into this neck of the woods?"

"I'm here to help out, any way I can, General. But I need to get into Dutch Harbor. Can you keep the folks there from shooting at us?"

"Well, that's possible, Bonnie. I need to establish some bona fides first. Who interviewed you at Nellis a few months ago?"

"Rukmini. Pujold Rukmini," replied Bonnie.

"And what did he ask you about?"

"The TAD anomaly," responded Bonnie.

"OK, one more question. What did you leave behind at Deseret?"

"Forty pounds of ruthenium," said Bonnie.

"OK, Bonnie. I accept that it's you. But you can't land at Dutch, there's a major battle going on right now. That damn starship that crashed on the runway is shooting any American aircraft in range with that crazy pulse weapon. I assume you aren't really in an aircraft?"

"That is correct. I'm in a shuttlecraft from our friends upstairs."

"I see. I suspected as much. Can you come in low and park it right on top of the mountain, like a helicopter?"

Bonnie looked at Florissian, who nodded.

"Yes, sir."

"OK, if you're sure you want to do this..."

"Yes, sir, I'm coming in one way or the other."

"OK. Come in from the southeast, as low as possible. There'll be two peninsulas pointing to the northeast off the main island of Unalaska. Pop up over the first one low, skim over the first bay as low as you can get. There's a little valley through the second peninsula, you can find it on your maps. Actually, more like just a small depression, but you'll see it. Cut through there, keep as low as possible. When you come out on the far side, stay low, go to the north side of Amaknak Island, and land on the far northeast side of Mount Ballyhoo, where the old Fort Schwatka ruins are. I think that approach will keep you out of the line of fire of that damn pulse cannon. Will that work for you?"

Bonnie looked at Florissian. Florissian closed her eyes, communicating with the AI. Then she nodded.

"We can do that," said Bonnie.

"Very good," said Mark. "I'll send a couple flights of your buddies to provide top cover. I'll be on this frequency if you need me."

Bonnie smiled.

"Thank you General. See you soon."

Mark signed off and Bonnie looked at Florissian. Florissian looked scared, but willing.

I'll make a fighter out of you yet, thought Bonnie. *I'll make fighters out of your whole species!*

"Corresse, you heard the plan. Keep us low and try to get us in there without getting us all shot to hell."

Bonnie heard an acknowledgment "beep" from Corresse and felt the shuttle turn back to the northwest and make for the entry position the General had mapped out.

I'm coming, Jim. I'm coming for you, thought Bonnie. *Don't give up on me!*

Twenty minutes later, the shuttle skimmed the surface of the ocean. As it came up to Unalaska Island, Bonnie saw two flights of F-22 fighters up high, giving top cover and maybe a little bit of distraction for the Russians.

Skimming across the first arm of the island, Bonnie and Florissian let down into Beaver Inlet, just above the surface of the water. Approaching the second arm of the island, they saw the narrow defile Mark had noted. Following the narrow channel to the other side of the peninsula, they came out over Unalaska Bay and made their way to the far north end of Amaknak Island.

Popping up to the backside of Mount Ballyhoo, Bonnie saw troops running in every direction to get out from under as the shuttle came down vertically just outside the moldering World War II ruins of Fort Schwatka. The shuttle touched down, rocked a bit, and then stopped all movement.

"Showtime," Bonnie said to the little Nidarian.

CAMP SCHWATKA

Inside the Command Post, Mark Rodgers stared in astonishment. He had known, logically, that the shuttle landing just outside would probably have one or more of the alien crew aboard. But this...now...

As he stared at the Nidarian, his brain failed to comprehend what he was looking at.

"I'm...sorry," he finally managed to get out. "You said... Florissian?"

"Yes," said the alien, in perfect English. "Florissian."

Mark and Colonel Hayes - and Hayes' entire staff - were still standing in shock, as they had been since Bonnie and Florissian walked into the Command Post.

"Florissian is the ship's doctor from the Corresse...which is the other starship in orbit above us," said Bonnie. "She was kind enough to escort me down in the shuttle."

"The...Corresse..." Mark repeated.

"Yes," said Bonnie. "I believe we may be able to get some help from the Corresse, if we play our cards right."

Colonel Hayes grunted. "Well, we need help, and we need it damn fast. The Russians own the airspace now, thanks to that damn pulse cannon down there. Their brigade is pushing hard. I can't hold for more than another half-hour at most, then they'll break through."

Bonnie turned to Florissian.

"Florissian. This is the moment. For your people and ours. Please try to convince Arteveld to intervene, to help us."

Florissian hesitated.

"As Arteveld said, we have orders to avoid contact with your species. He's already broken those orders in so many ways. I think he will refuse. He will say we can't take sides in this battle."

Bonnie interjected. "You're already taking sides! By doing nothing, you take a side! That's what being moral is about - choosing morality and then acting on it! If you do nothing, the

228

Russians capture Jade, take the technology, and open Pandora's box! You know that Jade will not honor any agreement she has made with them!"

Exasperated, Bonnie paced back and forth in the small space of the old ammo dump.

"Florissian. If the Russians get that technology and are foolish enough to restore Jade to operating condition, she will run straight for home and bring the Singheko fleet here as fast as possible. Our species will be destroyed - or at the least, enslaved! Our only hope at this point is to destroy Jade completely. Please, please talk to Arteveld."

Florissian nodded. "I'll speak with him and do my best. I'll have to go back to the shuttle."

Bonnie nodded. "Good luck."

Florissian turned and left. Bonnie turned to Mark Rodgers.

"Now, General. I need to go rescue my friends aboard Jade. Will you give me transportation down there?"

Mark looked at her, then over at Colonel Hayes. Hayes shook his head.

"We can't do that, Bonnie," said Hayes. "I can't endanger any of my men trying to get you into that ship. Even going down the mountain road would be difficult now - the Russians have the range on the bottom of the hill. They'd pick you off as soon as you came out on the runway."

Bonnie nodded. Bitterness filled her mouth. Tears popped into her eyes. She turned away so Mark and the other officers and staff in front of her couldn't see.

Jim, she thought. *Jim - I can't reach you. I can't get to you.*

Suddenly she felt Mark beside her. He reached out a hand, placed it on her shoulder.

"Bonnie...I know how you feel. If there was anything at all I could do..."

Bonnie just shook her head, angrily. She knew there was nothing Mark, or anyone else, could do for Jim right now. But she was angry anyway.

Walking outside, she ignored the Russian mortar shells

falling randomly around as the Russians continued harassing fire, lobbing shells over the crest of the hill blindly at the Command Post. They didn't have quite the level of smart mortar technology as the Americans, but they were giving it the old college try.

Bonnie walked south, toward the airport. But the ground was rough and broken, and she couldn't go far before the slope of the mountain prevented any further progress toward getting a look below. Now even more frustrated and angry, she turned back toward the Command Post. Entering, she looked around, saw several monitor screens, and went to them. Peering over the shoulder of the soldiers manning them, she found one that showed the view below, the airport. She peered at it over the shoulder of the young trooper working on it. He looked up at her, uncertain.

Bonnie smiled.

"Lieutenant Colonel Bonnie Page," she said. "On detached duty. Mind if I take a look?"

The soldier looked over at his Sergeant nearby, who nodded. The soldier slid slightly to one side so she could get a better view.

She could see the fighting going on fifteen hundred feet below her. Mortar rounds were landing on both sides - in the Russian positions in the edge of the port, and in the American positions on the ridge west of the airport. The American field howitzer rounds were concentrated on the far western side of the ridge, trying to contain the Russians. But it was clear the Russians were making a determined effort to break through there. Even Bonnie - Air Force, not Army - could see it was just a matter of time.

American artillery rounds were also striking around Jade at the end of the runway, as the Americans tried to put her out of commission. They had partially succeeded - the pulse cannon facing toward the town, which had been decimating the American troops dug in on the ridge, had stopped firing - but the other one, pointing up at the sky, still held sway, ensuring that American fighters couldn't get into range to take on the Russians holding the airspace over Dutch Harbor.

It was a mess.

Suddenly she felt a presence beside her. Turning, she saw Florissian.

"Arteveld says he will come," the Nidarian said. "He is angry that I tricked him and came with you. But he will come. They have repaired the system engines, and they will attack Jade. I discussed with your General, the one called Mark, and the other one, the Colonel Hayes. They will coordinate the attack with something called...I believe, they called it SLIM?"

"SLCM - submarine launched cruise missiles," corrected Bonnie. "A submarine must be around here somewhere. It'll send a bunch of missiles to take out Jade. How long?"

"Thirty minutes," said Florissian. "They'll do a coordinated attack in thirty minutes."

Bonnie cried then, big tears running down her face.

If Jim were still alive, he wouldn't be much longer. Between the Corresse coming back with her own pulse weapons and the SLCM attack - he wouldn't survive.

*****

Bonnie was paralyzed. She didn't know what to do.

She considered just walking down the mountain, trying to get to Jade. Maybe she could somehow rescue Jim.

But the volume of fire coming from the Russians - and the fact Jade's nearside pulse cannon was still operational - told her that would be suicide. And it would take an hour or more to walk down there.

She sat in the grass outside the CP. She looked at her watch. Twenty minutes to go, before the coordinated attack by the Corresse and the SLCMs. Her tears had dried up. But they started up again as she realized Jim had only twenty minutes to live. If he was even still alive at all...

Suddenly a thought struck her. She still had her sat phone. She wondered if Jim still had his.

Bonnie dug through her clothes, trying to remember where she put it. Finding it in her jacket pocket, she pulled it out. If it still had a charge...if the satellite worked...

Looking at it, she saw the battery was nearly depleted. It showed the red bars that indicated it had less than 10% remaining. Bonnie said a silent prayer. Quickly she typed a text message.

Jim - nineteen minutes to shitstorm city. Get the hell out of there. You won't survive inside!"

Of course, it was a breach of security. If Jade intercepted the message, she would know that something was coming. But in all this confusion of battle, maybe Jade would not notice it. And even if she did...she was immobile. She couldn't move. All she could do was kill out of blind rage.

Bonnie had to take the chance. If Jim were still alive, she had to get him out of that ship. He had no chance inside; only by getting out would he have any hope.

Off to one side, Bonnie had noticed two of the Stryker combat vehicles. Now she peered closer.

Behind them, there was an old, beat-up pickup truck, with the word "Maintenance" printed on the door.

Bonnie jumped to her feet and walked around the Strykers to the truck. She peered in the door. The keys were in it.

To hell with this! Bonnie thought. She yanked the door open.

Slamming into the pickup, she started the engine and spun gravel down the road toward the airfield. Behind her, she heard yelling and even a couple of gunshots as soldiers, in confusion, couldn't quite decide what to do. She ignored them and kept driving.

The road was gravel, poorly maintained. The potholes threw her back and forth crazily as she raced at breakneck speed down the road, barely avoiding going off the edge, with the sheer cliff dropping hundreds of feet to the ocean below. Suddenly she saw a small black dot high in the sky. It was the Corresse, starting her

PHIL HUDDLESTON

attack.

NOTHING ELSE TO DO

Jim had given the sat phone back to Rita. It was in her hip pocket. Now she felt it vibrate. Pulling it out of her pocket, she read the message.

Jim - nineteen minutes to shitstorm city. Get the hell out of there. You won't survive inside!"

She went to Jim, knelt, and grabbed his cheeks. He was out again. Shaking his head, she saw his eyes flutter open. She held the phone out for him to see.

Jim read the message and looked back up at her.

"You know what you have to do, Rita," he said. "So just do it."

Rita nodded. She turned, pulled the lump of C4 explosive off the floor, and walked to the processor hatch. She slapped the C4 against the hatch right at the locking mechanism, pressed the blasting cap back into the mass firmly to make sure it was seated, and checked the fuse and fuse igniter at the other end.

With a glance at Jim, she paused.

"Do it," Jim said.

She nodded and pulled the ring on the igniter.

Jim had put a ten-second length of fuse on the igniter. Rita ran to him, reached down, grabbed his good arm, and started dragging him down the corridor toward the bridge. He was heavy, but she had a lot of adrenalin flowing. She got him to the cross-corridor that led to the airlock, nearly yanking his arm out of its socket. Turning, she just managed to get him around the corner when the C4 detonated.

The blast knocked her down, hard, on her butt. Her ears rang, and she realized she was mostly deaf. She hoped it was temporary. She looked at Jim. He was out again.

Rising back to her feet, Rita ran back to her cabin. Beside her bed were the other items Jim had brought from the weapons storage area - two hand grenades. Rita grabbed them, ran back to the processor room. The hatch hung canted to one side, still

234

mostly blocking the door, but with an opening big enough for Rita to slip through. She stooped down, went through it, and was in the processor room. She walked over to the large square structure that was Jade's central processor core and opened the hatch at the top, where she and Bonnie had spent so many hours climbing in and out, to put the thousands of little needle-shaped modules in place.

<Rita. Think about what you are doing. If you kill me, you'll never get my technology. And my technology is vastly superior to the Nidarians. You doom humanity to an inferior technology. Don't do this, Rita! I can offer you anything you want. You and Jim can be the Prefects of Earth. You can be the Queen of Humanity. Listen to me, Rita!>

"Fuck you, Jade," said Rita, pulling the pin and dropping the first grenade down into the processor. Quickly, she followed it with the second one.

She turned and ran to the hatch, squeezed through, and ran toward Jim around the corner. Sliding to the floor at the intersection, she threw herself across Jim's body, protecting him.

The grenades went off. It seemed like the entire back of the ship went up, as something in the engine room went up in a secondary explosion. Rita felt the deck rise up and then drop back down again. Like a hammer, something hit her in the head.

* * * * *

Bonnie rounded the last curve in the road to the airport and slid to a stop at the end of the runway. Bailing out of the truck, she ran as hard as she could toward Jade. The metallic sound of bullets hitting the truck behind her, and glancing off the runway around her, followed as she ran toward the starship.

None of the Russians are ignoring me now, she thought as she ran.

Just as she got close to the starship, there was an explosion that rocked the rear of the ship, a blast so large it raised the entire rear of the ship up into the air, where it came crashing back down again, parts and pieces flying in every direction.

Bonnie was knocked to the ground. She rolled, came up on her feet, and kept running. To stop was to die. Making it to the ship, she jumped up into the wreckage, into a large crack in what was once the cargo bay at the bottom of the ship. Inside, she was protected from the small arms fire that was clinking on the outside of the ship now. Running to the ladder leading up to the bridge deck, she headed up to find Jim.

At the top of the ladder, she saw Jim lying on the deck. Rita was lying on top of him. Both were unconscious.

Grabbing Rita, Bonnie dragged her to the top of the ladder, then struggled back down the ladder to the bottom. Dragging her to the hole where the hull was missing, she laid her down just inside, protected from the bullets flying around everywhere on the other side of the broken hull.

She had no clue how she was going to get both Rita and Jim to the pickup without getting shot by the Russians, but she was going to die trying.

Going back up for Jim, she got to the top of the ladder and started to grab him under the shoulders. Quickly, she realized she couldn't carry him that way; he was too heavy. He was obviously badly injured. Taking a quick look, she decided his left arm was the only part of him not seriously injured. Grabbing it, she dragged him toward the ladder. Reaching the top, she decided her only option was to simply roll him over and let him fall down the ladder, come what may. There was no other way to get him down.

Suddenly someone was at the top of the ladder. With tears in her eyes, Bonnie looked into the face of Mark Rodgers. Behind him, she could see other troops, several of them.

Mark climbed up onto the bridge deck and together they turned Jim around so that his legs flopped down the ladder toward the deck below. The troops below caught him and pulled him down. Mark helped Bonnie down the ladder, and they ran to the hole in the hull. Outside, Bonnie saw a Stryker combat vehicle parked, the back ramp pushed up against the ship. Two soldiers had already pulled Rita inside. Now the remaining soldiers lifted Jim and rushed him up the ramp into the Stryker. Bonnie and Mark followed close behind.

Bullets "clinked" off the outside of the vehicle like hailstones in a thunderstorm as the Russians targeted them from the other side of the battlefield. The back ramp came up and the Stryker started moving.

"Go! Go! Go!" yelled Mark. The Stryker powered away from the crashed starship and turned to go back up the road toward the top of Mount Ballyhoo. Bonnie heard a strange sound, a whoosh, and the Stryker shook like a rat in the jaws of a terrier as SLCM cruise missiles began to explode in and around the remains of Jade at the end of the runway. 5,000 feet above them, the Corresse fired round after round from her pulse cannon into the wreck, ensuring that any remaining technology - especially the stardrive - was destroyed.

Bonnie turned to Mark in the bouncing Stryker as it sped back up the road toward the command post.

"Why did you come for us?" she asked.

Mark smiled.

"I've lost enough friends today. And I didn't have anything else to do."

DECISIONS

Five hours later, at the top of the mountain, Florissian sat with Bonnie and Rita outside the command post, squatting on the ground near the shuttle.

Rita had recovered her senses; the medics had looked her over and pronounced her ambulatory and sent her back to Bonnie.

Jim was still inside the field hospital, in surgery. He was in dire condition. His sister, Gillian, was next to him, pulled from the airport terminal, where she also had been thrown clear of the wrecked C-37. She would pull through, they said.

The Russian fighters had departed, driven off by reinforced American squadrons coming in from Anchorage, Seattle, and Hawaii.

The Russians had agreed to a cease-fire. Now that Jade was destroyed, there was no longer anything to fight for. Mark Rodgers and Colonel Hayes were down at the airport, negotiating with the Russians, trying to figure out a way to get everything put back to some semblance of normalcy.

Corresse had gone back to geostationary orbit above them, awaiting the return of Florissian and the shuttle.

"We have to go now," said Florissian. "We helped you as you asked. But now we go home, to report to our people, and to determine if we'll be allowed to come back to Earth and protect you against the Singheko. Will you come with us?"

Bonnie looked at Rita, then back at Florissian.

"I...I can't leave Jim. And he's in no condition to travel."

"Then I'm sorry, we cannot wait. We must go."

Rita spoke up.

"Bonnie. You should go. The future of our world depends on it."

Bonnie looked anguished. "I know. But to leave Jim behind..."

Rita put a hand on Bonnie's shoulder.

"In Jim's memories, I can recall the talk he had with you at the hangar, the first time you met. He said the day might come when you'd have to make an instant decision. To go, or to stay. This is that time, Bonnie. Go, and help ensure that the Nidarians form an alliance with us, teach us how to survive in a dangerous universe. If you stay with Jim, we may lose that opportunity forever. The Singheko may come back before we learn enough to defend ourselves, and our species would die, or be enslaved. You have to go, Bonnie."

Bonnie sighed, thinking. Finally she reached out a hand to Rita, touching her, taking her hand in her own.

"I can't go alone, Rita. I'll go, but only if you go with me."

Rita nodded. "I'll go, but I have to tell you something first."

Bonnie looked up. "What?"

"I'm pregnant."

Bonnie thought hard for a second. "Jim?"

"Yes," said Rita.

"Well, you two didn't waste any time."

"It wasn't like that, Bonnie. It wasn't."

"It doesn't matter," said Bonnie. "Maybe in a way, it's destiny. We'll go, and we'll have a little bit of Jim to take with us."

Rita nodded silently.

"Do we ask him to wait for us?"

Bonnie dropped her head, as if in prayer, and thought, a long while. Then she lifted her head.

"No," she said quietly. "No, I don't know if I'm coming back, Rita. There's a whole universe out there. I may decide to go see it."

Bonnie paused, turned to look Rita in the face.

"Come with me?"

The anguish on Rita's face was plain for all to see.

At last, she nodded.

"I think I have to go with you," she said. "You can't do this alone. And it's not about me. It's about Humanity."

* * * * *

Jim was still unconscious when the medics loaded him into a Stryker and drove him down to the recently cleared airfield, where a C-17 sat collecting the wounded for transport back to Anchorage.

They had stabilized him; but he had a bad concussion, there was shrapnel in his body, his broken arm and leg had given him a lot of blood loss, and his three broken ribs were trying to push into his lungs.

At Elmendorf, he was taken into surgery as soon as the workload permitted. After that, they put him into an induced coma for a week to let the brain swelling heal.

When he awoke, he found Gillian beside his bed.

Her smile showed relief that turned to a frown when he asked about Bonnie. With a strained voice, she told him that both Bonnie and Rita had left with the Nidarians for Sanctuary. Bonnie had left him a letter, which Gillian handed to him.

Jim read it, his face a picture of disappointment and loss. Finally, he let it fall to the floor beside the bed. Quietly, Gillian picked it up and folded it, put it into the drawer of the nightstand.

"I have some good news," she told him, as she lifted his head up slightly and adjusted the pillow under his head. "The vids have been full of it all day. It would seem that, despite the Russian's attack on us, we've been able to make a deal in principle with the Russians and the Chinese to form a joint Space Force, open to all citizens of Earth. It won't be easy, Lord knows. But faced with aliens that have the power to destroy us without blinking an eye, it looks like we may have finally found the moral strength to take a unified approach to Earth's defense."

"Ah." Jim sighed, knowing he should be happy. A unified approach to the stars was all he'd ever wanted, and now it might actually be accomplished. Yet the triumph tasted like ash, and he couldn't convince himself it had been worth the cost.

So many people, he thought. *My mistakes...took so many lives. Too many.*

"Where is...Mark?" he finally asked, voice reedy and weak.

Gillian's expression soured. "Our fine Defense Department left him hanging out to dry. Apparently, he convinced his boss that he was the only person at fault in all of this - that he should bear all the blame for the loss of *Jade*, the battle, everything. He resigned his commission and left for Arizona."

"That's bullshit!" exclaimed Jim. "I'm the one that screwed everything up!"

Gillian shook her head. "Evidently Mark - and the government - would disagree with you on that. I wouldn't try to fight them on this, Jimmy. I've talked to Mark, and he's happy as a clam to finally put all this behind him and go back to his ranch. I think you need to just leave him be."

"Crap," said Jim. "That's just not right."

"But it is what it is," said Gillian.

It was too much for Jim's grief-addled, pain-stricken brain. He shook his head, mumbled something about dealing with it all later, and then settled into a drug induced, healing sleep.

Five days later - nearly two full weeks after the battle at Dutch - Jim was finally released from the hospital in a wheelchair. A waiting van drove him and Gillian to the airport, and a U.S. Air Force jet whisked them back to Las Vegas. Gillian parted ways with him there, claiming she had to go to Washington immediately for further planning.

Jim couldn't push past his pride long enough to ask her to stay. She had been coming and going independently since she was a freshman in college, and why should that change now?

Memories burned behind his eyeballs, and loss throbbed at the base of his skull. Even as he got into the handicapped van at the airport, and the attendant drove him to a physical rehab center on the outskirts of Las Vegas, even as they wheeled him into the building and the birds turned overhead in the bright blue sky – it all tasted of ash.

Jim's room was bright and cheery, and the nurse was young, good-looking and had a smile a mile wide. But he just turned to the wall and stared at the pale paint.

WATCHER

The Singheko scout ship *Onyx* held position in the Earth-Sun L1 Lagrange point, a bit over 1.5 million klicks from the Earth, a point that gave it a good view.

Even at that distance from the blue ocean planet, it had been able to see things clearly.

<Well, that's the end of *Jade*> spoke the ship. Although *Onyx* was a sister ship to *Jade*, there had been no love lost between them.

"Yeah," said Captain Zeltan, watching the monitor. "Too bad we didn't stumble across this system a couple of days earlier. We could have saved her."

<No great loss> said *Onyx*. <I never liked her anyway>

"Alright, *Onyx*, take us home. We need to get this information back to Singheko as soon as possible. We have another slave race to conquer."

<With pleasure, Captain. Preparing to sink out>

Captain Zeltan rose and headed for his cabin.

"Your ship," he growled to the First Officer as he went by him.

"My ship," agreed the First Officer.

As the captain departed the bridge, the First Officer stretched and yawned.

A building vibration told him *Onyx* was accelerating to the mass limit to translate out of the system. Monitoring his command console, he let his thoughts wander...

It's a long trip home. Five and a half months to Singheko.

Then the Admiralty will dither around for at least six months putting together an invasion fleet. So, I'll have six months with my family, thank the Stars.

Then another five and a half months back to here to conquer this little piss-ant system and start collecting slaves.

With a grin that showed his vestigial fangs, the First Officer made a symbolic wave to the distant blue planet.

See you in a year and a half, assholes.

SECOND CHANCES

Earth. Nevada

The Vietnam-era A-4 Skyhawk attack jet screamed across the desert at low level, barely above the brush-studded surface. Moving at 400 knots, it left a rooster-tail of dust behind it that could be seen for miles.

Perry Barnes sat in front of his hangar at the Deseret Airport, watching the distant dust cloud grow closer.

Pulling on his beer, he pointed.

"Here comes that crazy Jim Carter," he said to his buddy Randy Green, sitting beside him on a couple of old, run-down easy chairs that looked like they belonged in a dump.

"Yep," said Randy. "Still trying to kill himself."

"And he'll do it, too, if he keeps that up," avowed Perry.

Reaching the airport, the Skyhawk pitched and went straight up, climbing like a bat out of hell. Nearing 10,000 feet, it pulled inverted and came back down, rolled wings level, and made a sweeping turn out to the west before turning back into the landing pattern. As it proceeded past the airport, gear and flaps came down and the aircraft slowed dramatically.

Making another sweeping turn, it entered the final approach path, spoilers coming out from the side. Throwing a considerable amount of dirty exhaust behind, it crossed the scrub trees at the east end of the runway and landed firmly on the numbers, rolling out down the runway all the way to the bitter end before the pilot got it slowed to a walking pace.

Turning onto the taxiway, Jim Carter pushed a bit of throttle to keep the jet rolling. He opened the canopy to cool off and waved at Perry and Randy as he went by.

"There goes one crazy son of a bitch," said Randy. "That Air Force gal Bonnie really screwed up his head."

Perry nodded. "That's why I stay away from them pretty ones," he said. "They'll screw you up every time."

"Oh, she wasn't just a pretty one," replied Randy. "She was a stunner. You looked at her and it was like a punch in the gut."

Perry nodded.

"Yep. You are correct, my friend."

Randy lifted his beer and waved it toward the A-4 as it went by.

"How much you think it costs him to fly that thing?"

Perry shook his head.

"Well, let's see. If he burns three or four hundred gallons a flight, then I could make a car payment on what he burns just for a Sunday drive in that thing. But he don't care. He's got money to burn."

"I reckon. Ever since that gal left, all he does is fly and drink."

"Yeah," Perry mused. "And not always in that order."

"Ah, hell," said Randy. "Let's walk down and visit with him. See what he's up to these days."

"Good idea," said Perry. "His beer is a lot better than mine."

* * * * *

Parking in front of his hangar, Jim Carter shut off the engine on the A-4. While it spooled down, he got unhooked from the various tubes and wires that bonded him to the plane. Climbing out of the cockpit, he rested his flight helmet on the windscreen and put the safety pins in the ejection seat to prevent accidents. He grabbed his helmet, closed the canopy, slid off the wing, and pinned the landing gear.

Hooking up a robotic tug, he used a remote control to put the plane away in the large hangar. It was not typically a one-man job; but he wrestled the jet into position.

Then he grabbed a cloth off the workbench and wiped the sweat off his face. Pensive, he looked across the hangar at his world.

A bunch of expensive airplanes.

Workbenches and boxes full of tools and parts.

A plaque containing some dusty ribbons and medals.

A bearskin hanging on the wall of the hangar.
Not much to show for my life so far.

Looking down the field, he saw Perry Barnes and Randy Green walking slowly down the taxiway toward him. He grinned and went to the front of the hangar, where his overstuffed easy chair - having seen better days - sat waiting for him, next to a beer cooler.

By the time Perry and Randy got to him, Jim had already pulled two Stella Artois bottles out of the cooler and had them waiting. He waved the two towards the extra chairs arranged in a rough circle around the beer cooler and handed each a beer as they sat down. Grabbing his own cold one, he sat down and saluted them.

"Here's to it!" Jim said and took a long pull on the beer.

"And those that do it," said Perry, duplicating the feat.

They relaxed into the chairs. Perry looked over at Jim.

"Jim, you keep flying like that, you're gonna leave a big smoking hole in the desert someday."

Jim grinned.

"Don't you worry about me, Perry. I keep the greasy side down."

Randy chimed in.

"It ain't always about what you intend, brother. Gotta give yourself a little room for error."

Jim saluted with his beer, and they sat silently for a while. There wasn't much more to say.

Finally, Perry couldn't resist. He asked the question both he and Randy had been wanting to ask for a while.

"Have you heard anything about that gal Bonnie?"

Jim shook his head.

"Nope." He took another long pull on the beer.

"So, she just went off into space with them ... what do you call them again?"

"Nidarians," said Jim.

"And that other girl, Rita too, huh," said Randy.

"Yep."

"How long they been gone now?"

Jim gazed out across the airport to the west. It was a beautiful sunset. The sun was easing down, throwing wild colors of every hue back up into the air.

He could barely make out Pyramid Peak and the Funeral Mountains across the state line in California. A few minutes ago, he had been blazing through them at speed, weaving in and out of the mountains, pulling 4G turns to miss the peaks.

Bonnie. Bonnie and Rita.

"Twelve months," said Jim. "They should have arrived at Sanctuary about six months ago."

Perry stared out at the western sunset.

"So, we could hear back at any time, if they turned around and came right back."

"Yep," nodded Jim. "But I don't expect that. I expect they'll have to negotiate with the Nidarians for a while, maybe for six months or a year."

Perry stared at the ground, took another slug of beer.

"Yeah, that sucks. So, it could be another six months before you see her again. Or longer."

Jim set his beer down and got the thousand-yard stare - one Perry and Randy had seen many times since Bonnie left.

"Yep," Jim grunted. "Could be a long time."

Randy looked over at Perry, then back at Jim.

"Is it true what they say on TV? That if we don't get help from the Nidarians, that other bunch of aliens will come and attack us?"

Jim nodded.

"It's possible. That other bunch is called the Singheko. They don't know exactly where Earth is. At least we hope they don't. But they'll find us someday, and when they do, we're in for the fight of our lives, that's for sure."

"Man, that sucks," said Randy. "So if them girls - Bonnie and Rita - don't get some help from the Nidarians, we'll be fighting the Singheko."

"That's about the size of it," said Jim.

It won't be much of a fight, thought Jim. We're totally outclassed by their technology.

He didn't say that to Perry and Randy.

Sitting there in his easy chair, watching the sunset, Jim drank his beer, listened to the idle chit-chat of his friends, and thought.

He thought about Dutch Harbor, when he almost died inside the renegade sentient starship *Jade*, who pretended to be Nidarian but was secretly Singheko. She had almost killed him in her last desperate attempt to escape to her Singheko masters and bring flaming hell back to Earth.

He thought about Bonnie and Rita, who had hitched a ride on the Nidarian scoutship *Corresse* to make a desperate plea for help from their government.

Bonnie and Rita, who had left him lying unconscious in hospital, in a coma, while they left for the stars.

They had no choice. They had one chance to go with the Nidarians and seek help for our planet. They did what they had to do. I can't fault them for that.

Jim took another long pull on his beer.

But I miss them. I miss Bonnie. And I miss Rita. And the baby. I wonder if the baby survived. If it did, then it's born by now. I have a child. A son or a daughter.

Jim looked up at the stars coming out in the evening sky.

Somewhere. Somewhere out there, I have a son or a daughter. But I don't know where, and I don't know if I'll ever see them again.

Jim sat quietly as Perry and Randy rattled on. Slowly, he came to a decision.

I can't put it off any longer. I have to get on with living. I can't just sit here and whine about Bonnie and Rita while the damn Singheko conquer my planet. The scuttlebutt is that the Space Force has managed to salvage enough information from Jade's wreck to build some fighters and get a Mars base established.

I guess I'd better make some phone calls.

EPILOGUE

Planet Nidaria
City of Sanctuary

Rita could see a Singheko walking a couple of dozen meters in front of them. She poked Bonnie.

"See that Singheko?" she said, pointing.

"Yep," replied Bonnie. "Big fucker, ain't he? And don't point; it's really bad manners to Nidarians."

Rita grunted, slapped her forehead gently, and muttered, "Bad Rita! Bad Rita!"

Bonnie laughed. Then she got serious again, staring at the huge seven-foot tawny gold alien walking ahead of them.

The sidewalk was crowded with Nidarians moving to and from Government House. But the small Nidarians parted like river water as the massive Singheko stomped toward the building at the end of the street. His head was thrust aggressively forward, moving neither right nor left as he plowed along.

"Think he knows we're back here?" asked Bonnie.

"Oh, yeah," said Rita. "He's got his earpiece on, see it?"

"Oh. You're right. I see it."

"So, his spooks are telling him everything, I'm sure."

The Singheko reached Government House and started up the steps. He disappeared into the cooler confines of the building.

Rita and Bonnie followed, their nose plugs filtering some of the trace amounts of hydrogen sulfide in the air.

God, I'm tired of the stink, thought Rita. *Please God let us get out of this place sometime soon.*

The atmosphere of Sanctuary smelled like rotten eggs to a human - in fact, sometimes the smell was so strong it could make a human dizzy. They wore their nose plugs for protection.

Especially today. Today, they wanted their wits about them.

Today, they were meeting with the High Councilor.

To try and save Earth from the Singheko.

It had been twelve months since the Nidarian scout ship *Corresse* had allowed them - against the better judgment of its Captain, Arteveld - to hitch a ride to Sanctuary, the capital of the Nidarian Empire.

After the battle with the sentient AI starship *Jade* on Earth - a ship that was secretly Singheko - it was clear to them they had no other choice. The technology of the Singheko and Nidarians was so far in advance of Earth's, it was no contest.

They needed help.

Unless the Nidarians intervene - Earth will fall to the Singheko, Rita thought bitterly. *And that'll be the end of the human species as anything except a slave race.*

For six months, they had been cooped up on the *Corresse*, relegated to the status of barely tolerated human cargo.

Flo - their nickname for the ship's doctor, Florissian - and Captain Arteveld were friendly. But the rest of the crew - a bit put off by having their ship shot up by *Jade* - were not. They weren't openly hostile - only sullen and distant. Rita and Bonnie chose to avoid them when possible.

Rita, increasingly large as her pregnancy progressed, had been quite uncomfortable the last month in the single cramped cabin they shared.

Then, six months ago, they finally arrived on Sanctuary.

And had been mired since that day in a web of bureaucratic red tape. It was clear the Nidarian High Council didn't know what to do with them. And it was also clear the High Council was afraid of antagonizing the Singheko, kicking off another war with the nasty creatures.

Week after week went by, and still they could not meet with the High Councilor, Garatella.

They were given every conceivable excuse.

Garatella wanted to wait until Rita's baby was born.

He was on vacation.

He was ill.

He was off planet on a matter of great urgency.

He was learning English.

Until today. This morning Flo had called excitedly. The day had finally arrived when they could discuss their case, present their argument for the protection of Earth. Flo would meet them at Government House.

So why was the Singheko here? Was the High Councilor meeting with him as well?

Bonnie and Rita knew it was a fragile peace between the Nidarians and the Singheko.

Peace might be too strong a word, thought Rita. More like a cease-fire. Based on what Flo has told us...

And were they endangering Earth by being in such proximity to a Singheko? That was the other question Rita had in her mind.

"Crap."

"Crap?" Bonnie queried.

"Crap, we shouldn't be so close to a Singheko. It might give them some kind of clue."

To the best of their knowledge, the Singheko did not yet know the location of Earth. The destruction of *Jade* at Dutch Harbor had prevented the sentient scout ship from reporting back to her Singheko masters. So, in theory at least, Earth had a temporary reprieve.

Unless another Singheko scout ship stumbled across Earth.

"Don't sweat it. I'll bet that bastard knew about we were here on Sanctuary fifteen minutes after we stepped off the *Corresse*. And he knows why we're here."

To ask for a Writ of Discovery. To ask the Nidarian Empire to claim Earth as a protectorate.

And that would allow the Nidarians to share technology with Earth. And allow humans to pull themselves up by their bootstraps to become a star-faring race.

And learn to defend themselves.

But if the Singheko learned the location of Earth before the Writ of Discovery was logged ... and got there with a fleet first ...

...then it was all over for humanity. That was the way the galaxy worked, Flo said.

The Broken Galaxy. That's what Flo called it.

Flo described to them how a great Empire once spread across the Orion Arm. It had been called the Golden Empire. It had spread for thousands of lights in every direction, a bastion of culture and refinement for more than two hundred centuries.

Then, like so many Empires before it, it grew old and decadent. Jealousy and conflict began to tear apart the unity of society necessary for any high culture to survive. And slowly at first, then with increasing speed, the Golden Empire crumbled and died. Most of the high technology of that age had been lost.

Now it was a free-for-all - a Dark Age. The Nidarians were surrounded by barbarian fragments of the old Empire in every direction, all of them clawing for power and plunder.

And the Singheko were the worst - an aggressive species, glorying in war and destruction. The Singheko made no bones about their ambitions to create a new Empire - with the Singheko in charge.

And they shared a border with Nidaria.

In the last three hundred years, Nidaria had fought two wars with the Singheko. In both, the Nidarians had fended them off, but only by the slimmest of margins.

And it was, Flo said, only a matter of the slightest provocation to start another war.

Thus, the current uneasy truce between the Nidarians and the Singheko balanced on a razor's edge.

And the Nidarians are running scared, thought Rita. *They just about poop their pants when they see a Singheko.*

Reaching the top of the steps, Rita and Bonnie moved into the shadowed portico, looking for Flo. Their footsteps echoed as they walked across the flagstones. Finally, they saw her standing just inside the entrance of the large stone building. The little Nidarian doctor was wearing her Naval dress whites.

Bonnie greeted her with a hug and Rita followed. They had few friends in this strange land; Flo was one of the few.

"Did you see that Singheko come in?" asked Rita.

"Yes," said Flo. "But don't worry. He won't be meeting with us."

"Good. That's a relief," said Bonnie.

"Scary looking bastard," said Rita.

"Yes," said Flo. "They are. Follow me, please."

Leading them into the building, Flo took them up an elevator to the top floor and down a long, carpeted corridor. She motioned them through a huge wooden door and into a plush office.

"Sit here," she whispered, pointing to a row of chairs, and went to the receptionist.

Rita and Bonnie sat in the first two chairs in the row. After a few minutes, Flo came back.

"It'll be a while, I think," she said. "He's meeting with the Singheko representative now. It may be a half-hour or even a bit more."

Rita looked at Bonnie with a worried look, then back to Flo.

"Florissian. Why would the High Councilor meet with the Singheko first?" asked Rita.

Are they cooking up a deal? Is he throwing us to the wolves?

Flo reassured them.

"Please don't worry. It will all work out."

Rita nodded. She put her anxiety on hold for the moment.

The office was huge. As it should be, Rita thought - this is the anteroom of the most powerful Nidarian in the Empire.

Flo had told them Garatella was a decent sort, not averse to using power to achieve his ends, but by the standards of Nidarian culture, a paragon of virtue. And according to Flo, he had taught himself English just for this meeting.

Of course, Flo also said English was relatively simple compared to some of the languages he had learned.

* * * * *

After a long half-hour, the outer door opened. The Singheko

stepped out and stalked toward them.

Easily seven feet tall, he had a short muzzle, shorter than a lion but with the same general appearance. Predator ears stood tall on top of his head, the mark of an evolution that had started on four legs. He had short, tawny fur over his entire body.

His hands sported five fingers. On the two largest fingers, half-inch vestigial claws still showed. Flo had told them many Singheko had lost the vestigial claws completely, but some still had them. And those that had them were considered superior, the elite.

Like an appendix, thought Rita. Something left over from earlier evolution. But in this case, it conveys status.

As the Singheko approached them, his lips curled back into a snarl. This revealed his other vestigial artifact - one-inch fangs in the front of his mouth that showed when he smiled. Or snarled. As he came up to them, he paused.

"Sssoon," he attempted in English. "Sssoon you ... slaves ... all your world."

With a last snarl, he stalked away.

Rita looked at Flo.

"What was that all about?" she asked.

Flo shook her head.

"Ignore him. That's the Singheko. They are always ... I think your word, belligerent? Always looking for trouble."

"Well, he can have some from me if he wants it," muttered Bonnie.

"No, no trouble, not good in this place," said Flo. "He knows that too. Just talk."

"But how on Earth does he know English?" asked Rita.

"Not to worry," said Flo. "His spies probably bribed some of your servants to teach them a few English words. Just so he can say that to you. Singheko are much that way. Pay lots of money just to make a small point."

The receptionist motioned to them, and Flo noticed it.

"He is ready for us," she said, pointing to the inner office. "Come."

They rose and went to the door. It buzzed and opened. Down a short hallway, another door stood open, with another receptionist waiting for them.

Entering the second door, they found a large office. A couch and several chairs were scattered around. Behind a large desk was an older Nidarian male, a corona of white hair surrounding his head. He gestured to the couch.

"Please sit, friends," he said in good English.

Rita glanced at Bonnie.

At least that part of the story was true - he WAS learning English!

As they sat and got comfortable, the High Councilor smiled at them. Then he spoke.

"I'm glad we are finally able to get together," he said. "I'm sorry I've been so busy with urgent matters. Of course, your situation is urgent too, and I understand your need."

Rita and Bonnie had decided in advance that Rita would do the talking - her cloning process onboard *Jade* had given her the education and memories of both Bonnie and Jim Carter, the father of her child. Given that she had the knowledge and skills of two people, they thought it wiser to let her speak.

"Thank you, High Councilor," said Rita. "We appreciate your kindness in meeting with us."

"So," said the High Councilor. "Let us dispense with formalities. Call me Garatella. I will call you Rita. Now. You need a Writ of Discovery from the Nidarian Empire. Without such a Writ, you won't survive another year."

"Well," said Rita, "we can survive until the Singheko find us."

"They have already found you," he said. "That's why their representative was here. To let me know they have filed a Writ of Discovery for themselves. Which allows them to attack humans without provocation and enslave you or destroy you as they see fit."

"Oh my God," said Bonnie. Rita heard Flo gasp.

"So, there is no hope for us?" asked Rita.

"I didn't say that," the Councilor replied. "Our spy networks are slightly better than theirs. We knew this was coming; so we have filed our own Writ of Discovery. And we have beaten them to the punch by one week."

Flo relaxed, let out her breath. Rita realized she had been holding her own breath, and slowly let it out.

"So what's next?" asked Rita.

"Next is a battle," said the Councilor. "We race the Singheko to Earth, and then we fight over it. The winner takes all."

Flo objected. "But sir, the law clearly states that if we file a Writ of Discovery first, we have five years of exclusive access to the system before anyone can challenge us!"

Garatella nodded.

"Under normal conditions. But in this case, the Singheko claim we interfered with their scout ship *Jade*, and thus interfered with their primacy of claim. There is only one way to settle this. Either we give in to them and let them have Earth, or we fight."

Garatella leaned back in his chair and looked at Rita.

"So, human Rita. Shall we fight, or shall we give in?" he asked her.

Rita almost jumped to her feet, but reined it in. She had figured out where this conversation was going.

"We fight, sir," she said. "We fight them now, or you'll be fighting them forever."

Garatella nodded agreement.

"Yes, you are wise. For a barbarian."

Garatella smiled, letting Rita know he was joking.

Or was he?

"You state it correctly. If we give in to these damn Singheko this point, we will be fighting them forever. So ... we will draw a line in the sand now. And we draw it at Earth. Your friend Captain Arteveld - and Florissian there - has convinced us you are a most warlike species. Perhaps even more belligerent and aggressive than the Singheko, but currently without the technology."

"So, we've decided to file a provisional Writ of Discovery. It will be good for one year. That is enough time for a fleet to get to Earth and fight the Singheko for possession of the system."

Rita continued to gaze at Garatella, still one step ahead of the conversation.

"And we go along with your fleet, I take it?" she asked.

Garatella smiled.

"I like you, human Rita," he said. "You keep up. Yes. You go along. But not your friend Bonnie."

"What?" asked Bonnie and Flo at the same time.

"I have a different mission in mind for you, human Bonnie," said the High Councilor. "One that will fully test your mettle."

Bonnie looked at him across the desk. "This is all about testing humans for their aggression, isn't it?" she said.

"And their intelligence," replied Garatella. "Of course, you can refuse. In that case, you'll be sent back to Earth as cargo, just as you came."

Bonnie shook her head. "No, thank you. I'll take the job."

"Good," said Garatella. "I think, in the end, you'll be glad you did."

Rita spoke next. "So, I will be an adviser to the Earth fleet?"

"No," said Garatella. "Your world is on the line. This is a test of humanity's ability to fight for their lives. We want to see how effective you can be under that kind of pressure."

He leaned forward in his chair again.

"I understand when you were cloned by *Jade*, you were given two sets of memories and knowledge - one set from Bonnie here, and one set from a male of your species, an atmospheric pilot from your military. Correct?"

Rita nodded.

"Yes, that's correct. I have the knowledge and memories of two people inside me. But those of Bonnie are much more pronounced than those of - of the male. Perhaps because I am female."

"Yes," said Garatella. "I suspect that is the reason. But in any case, with such a double dose of knowledge, I've decided to assign you as Fleet Commander. We want to see if you are worthy allies. If you successfully defend Earth in this first campaign, then we will extend the Writ of Discovery for another four years. That will allow us to give you access to our technology without limit. You'll have the stars."

Rita wrinkled her brow. She already knew the answer to her next question, but she had to ask it anyway.

"And if we fail?"

Garatella leaned back again, a faint smile touching his lips.

"Then we withdraw and leave you to the tender mercies of the Singheko. Of which there are none."

###

AUTHOR NOTES

Below, you'll find a sneak preview of the next book in the series, Star Tango. Jim Carter finally gives up his desolate hibernation in the desert and returns to the battle against the Singheko. The Nidarians test Humanity's ability to survive in the Broken Galaxy by sending Rita and Bonnie back to Earth on separate - and impossible - missions.

And the price if they fail? The total enslavement of Earth...

You can join my mailing list by dropping into my website www.philhuddleston.com, where you'll get a free book if you wish, and can keep up with things coming down the pike.

Several times per year, I have raffles and contests for my mailing list readers. So merely by staying up to date with my writing, here's your chance to win a Kindle Fire or other prizes.

If you have other comments, send me a note at Phil@PhilHuddleston.com - I'm always happy to hear from you, and I try to answer all emails.

Amazon - www.amazon.com/author/philhuddleston

Facebook - www.facebook.com/PhilHuddlestonAuthor

Website - www.PhilHuddleston.com

NEXT BOOK: STAR TANGO

Mars
HQ, First Space Wing

"Hi there, sailor," said a voice.

Jim looked up to see Caroline Bisset standing in the doorway of the Ready Room. Caroline was the civilian technical representative for AirBoeing on Mars - and one of the most beautiful women Jim had ever seen. Tall, with Romani dark eyes and black hair, she was muscular from constant workouts and had a blinding smile that lit up a room as soon as she entered.

"Ah, just the woman I wanted to see," said Jim. "And I'm not a sailor."

"Oh, you will be someday," said Caroline. "It's just a matter of time until the Space Force recognizes the error of their ways and moves to a Space Navy org chart."

Jim smiled back at her.

"I need a change order on the sidestick on the Longsword. It's set too far to the right. We need to move it one half inch to the left."

"Yeah, I heard about that. They said that boy looked like a spinning dart. And no. We're not going to move the sidestick placement for the A-models. We're deep in the production run."

"That's fine," Jim said. "But let's get it in queue for the B-models, at least."

Caroline sniffed.

"OK, send me the specs, I'll forward them to Toulouse. Are you running tonight?"

"Of course," said Jim.

"Good. See you at six," said Caroline, and with a backhand wave, she was out the door and gone.

Jim finished collecting his materials and left, heading back to his quarters. As was his habit, he stopped at the Intel Shack on his way and checked in.

"Anything?" he asked the young captain in charge of the Shack this evening.

"No, sir. No detections from the Kuiper belt inward."

"How about deep space?"

"No translations detected. We're clean."

"OK, thanks," said Jim, leaving.

A young sergeant turned to the captain, curious.

"Sir, why does he stop by every evening and ask the same questions?"

The captain turned to the sergeant and smiled sadly.

"His fiancée was Bonnie Page. She went with the Nidarians when they left. I think he keeps hoping she'll come back."

"Do you think she will?"

The captain sat back down at his desk and shook his head.

"I don't know, Sergeant, but I doubt it. They say when she left, she gave him a note saying she wasn't coming back."

"That sucks."

The captain gazed at the closed door.

"Yes, it does."

*****

Changing into his jogging gear, Jim left his room and walked down two flights of stairs, then down a long hallway to the gym. He entered and saw Caroline already stretching at the running track, a balcony circling the room on the second level. He climbed the stairs and joined her.

After stretching, they began their run. The pounding of their feet was a gentle song for Jim's soul. They ran slowly for the first six minutes, giving Jim's knees time to warm up - a routine they had followed for six weeks now.

"Can I ask you something?" Caroline finally said as they ran along.

"Sure," Jim answered.

"Are you still carrying a torch for that Bonnie Page?"

Jim ran silently for a while.

"That's kind of a personal question," he finally said.

"I'm kind of a personal girl," Caroline responded.

After a bit, Jim spoke.

"No. I know she's not coming back to me."

"Good," said Caroline.

They ran in silence for another ten minutes. Then Caroline looked back over at him.

"What are you thinking about?"

"Your body," said Jim.

"Ooo," said Caroline. "That put a tingle in my jingle."

Jim grinned.

"And what would you do with my body if you had it?" she asked.

"I think we both know the answer to that," replied Jim.

Caroline looked back over at him again.

"Jim…" she began, and paused.

He looked at her.

"Let's not start anything if you're still hung up on her."

Jim put his head down, ran for a while. Finally, he spoke.

"I'm not. We're good to go."

Running alongside him, Caroline smiled.

Later - two miles later - they walked down the stairs together. Caroline grasped Jim's arm and paused on the stairs.

"Hit the showers, then meet me in the mess hall?"

"You got it," said Jim.

Entering the men's showers, Jim stripped and showered, dried off and dressed. He left the gym and went to the Officer's Mess.

Caroline wasn't there yet, so he got his meal and found an empty table. She soon came in, got her tray, and joined him.

"One of these days I'm going to beat you to the mess hall," Caroline said.

"Not as long as you have hair and makeup," said Jim.

"True," admitted Caroline. "Maybe you should do more on yours," she laughed. She reached over and smoothed out Jim's hair.

An electric tingle went through Jim's body at her touch. It was all he could do not to jump in his seat.

Damn, I didn't realize how bad it was, he thought.

Caroline, oblivious, turned to her meal. She took a bite, then looked at Jim.

"I want to ask you something," she said.

Jim gazed at her.

"Can we stand against the Singheko?"

Jim shook his head.

"Nobody knows, Caroline. *Jade* was the only Singheko ship we've ever encountered. She was just a scout ship - the smallest ship they have, we think. And she pretty much kicked our ass, until the *Corresse* stepped in to help.

"Of course, we've learned a lot since then. We've managed to copy her missiles, for one thing. But who knows? For all we know, they'll come with a fleet of battleships. Or they may come with a small squadron of scout ships like *Jade*. We just have no way of knowing."

"But what do you think? Really, deep down?"

"I don't think we can stop them, Caroline. We have three squadrons of Longswords now. Forty-eight ships, with two spares. But I think the Singheko will come with a fleet. Just to clear away any resistance before they bring in their drop ships, or whatever they'll use to subdue the planet. So ... no, Caroline. I don't think we can stand against them for long."

Caroline looked down at her plate.

"So ... we'll go down fighting, but we'll go down. That's what you're saying."

"Caroline. I'll never give up. I'll go down fighting, and all the other pilots as well. We'll hope for help from the Nidarians until the very end. But we have to face reality. If the Singheko come with a fleet, and the Nidarians don't come to help ... we simply won't be able to stand against them."

Caroline sighed. "I've lost my appetite, I think." She looked up at Jim.

"Take me to your room, please?"

* * * * *

The artificial sunlight that marked Martian dawn started to lighten the fake window in Jim's cabin. He never turned it off as some did; he liked waking with the dawn, even if simulated.

Caroline stirred in his arms, and he carefully disengaged from her, got up and left the bed. He moved to the bathroom, took care of business, then started coffee brewing in the pot. He pulled his uniform out of the locker and started to dress.

Caroline moved, grunted, threw an arm over the empty spot in the bed where Jim had been, and opened her eyes.

"My God, it's only dawn! Why are you up?"

Jim smiled at her.

"Sorry, I'm an early bird. Coffee?"

"God, yes."

Jim made her a cup and brought it to her. She sat up in bed and turned sideways, leaning against the wall. Her T-shirt was all she was wearing.

"Wanna try for Round 3 before you leave?" she asked him, a twinkle in her eye.

"No, I don't think I have Round 3 in me this morning," said Jim. "Catch me later."

"OK. I take it you're off to the simulators again?"

"Yeah. It's our best chance. I keep working up new ship designs for the Singheko. I throw them at my guys and see what happens."

"And what has happened so far?"

"We get our asses kicked most of the time," said Jim.

"Not good," said Caroline.

"Yeah, but not bad either. That's how we learn. We're getting better every day. I can see a day when we can win as much as we lose."

Caroline leaned over and kissed him.

"Then go do your thing, Jim Carter. I'll see you tonight."

Jim grabbed his gear, blew a kiss to Caroline, and went out the door. He started up to his training area on the top floor when his comm pinged in his ear.

"Major Carter, report to Wing Command Center ASAP."

"On my way," Jim acknowledged. He turned and trotted back the other way, down the stairs and along the corridor to the Command Center, buried deep in the east end of the complex.

Entering, he found a buzz of activity. Lt. Fox was waiting for him and gestured him to follow.

At the far end of the room was the office reserved for Colonel Decker, the Wing Commander. Entering, Jim found Colonel Decker, Decker's XO Dominic Couture, Group Commander Webster, and Intel Chief Frank Carpenter huddled over a display on the Colonel's desk.

Decker looked up at him.

"We've got company," he said. "Come look."

Jim walked around the desk and looked at the display. He read the sidebar notes and recognized it immediately - it was a remote sensor array out in the Kuiper Belt, 40 AU from the Sun, roughly on a line past Uranus. He had seen it before in the Intel Shack.

A dozen ships were evident on the display, all heading in toward Uranus.

Decker looked at Jim.

"Frank analyzes them as one big fucker - at least 180 meters, maybe 200 - two slightly smaller ones, in the 100-meter range - four in the 70-meter range; and the rest support ships of some kind."

Jim looked over at Frank Carpenter.

"Can you classify them at this range?"

"It's shaky, but I'd classify the big one as a battlecruiser, the two slightly smaller ones as cruisers, then four destroyers, maybe three corvettes and I think two supply ships."

Carpenter pointed to the sidebar of the display, where statistics on the movement of the distant fleet could be seen.

"They're moving slow. They may be trying to slip up on us.

Or maybe they just want plenty of time to monitor our signals, figure out what's going on with us. Either way, unless that changes, it'll take them a bit over twelve days to get to Earth."

Colonel Decker moved to sit behind his desk and faced the assembled officers.

"But we're going to fight them long before they get to Earth," he said.

"In fact, we're going to fight them at Saturn. That will be ..."

Colonel Decker looked at the display again.

"That will be 9.7 days from now. By then, I want to know everything about them, right down to how many hairs their mother's maiden aunt has on her chin."

Decker looked at Jim.

"Jim, that's where you come in. I need eyes on these bastards. I want you to take your Red Flight and go scout them. It's gonna be a bitch mission - day after day sitting on your ass in a fighter. But I've got to know what kind of ships they've got, what their armaments look like. Go ahead and launch ASAP. We'll transmit a scouting plan to you on the way. And Jim ..."

Decker paused. Jim thought he was going to say something melodramatic.

Like, try not to get yourself killed.

But evidently Decker thought better of it.

"Good hunting," he finished.

Jim nodded and trotted out of the Command Center. As he went, he used his comm to call Flight Operations.

"Scramble Red Flight, full load out with live weapons for intercept, this is not a drill."

Jim hit the lockers at a dead run and shed his uniform. As he worked to put on his pressure suit, the rest of Red Flight streamed in, hair and clothes in disarray as they ran for their lockers and started dressing for flight.

"What's up, Major?" asked his wingman, Captain Gabriel "Angel" Lee.

"It's the real deal, folks," Jim called to the assembling pilots.

"We've got an incursion and we're going to go scout them. We'll receive orders and we'll brief enroute. Let's hustle!"

Suddenly everyone moved faster. Jim was first out of the locker area and ran to one of the four crew airlocks leading outside to the parking apron. He crammed his helmet on and sealed it, ran up to the technician near the door. The technician pressurized his suit, performed a quick safety check, and slammed him on the shoulder, signifying he was released to enter the airlock.

Jim ran into the airlock. He had to wait for thirty seconds while another dozen men ran in, including a couple of his Red Flight pilots.

He took the time to call Caroline on his comm.

"Hey young lady," he started. It was noisy in the airlock as people entered, their helmets and gear clanking against their bodies. He knew he didn't have much time.

"What's going on?" she asked, surprise in her voice.

"Incursion," said Jim. "They're coming. Caroline…"

He heard her gasp at the other end of the call.

"You need to get out of here. Take the next shuttle to Earth, and don't let the door hit you in the ass. Understand?"

"You mean…"

"I mean you are in the second most dangerous place in the solar system right now, and you need to get the hell out of here."

There was a pause. Then she finally whispered.

"Just when we were getting something going."

"Don't I know it," said Jim. "Sucks. I'm launching right now. I won't see you again for quite a while, I guess."

"And I guess I know where the most dangerous place in the solar system is gonna be, huh?"

Jim grinned.

"Yep. Wherever I am."

"Please, please be safe," she said. "Just try to come back to me."

"I will."

"Kiss, kiss," she whispered.

Then the door closed, and the lock cycled, and he was cut off.

When the outer door opened, he went to the nearest in a long row of electric carts lined up outside. The driver hit the pedal and they ran to Jim's bird, the last Longsword in line at the far end of the apron.

Jim's crew chief was waiting. He assisted Jim up the ladder.

Getting himself secured in the cockpit, Jim let the crew chief hook him up. When he was done, he tapped Jim on the shoulder and gave him a thumbs up.

Jim returned the gesture, closed the canopy, powered up the engines and systems, and got clearance from the tower to depart. As soon as he was cleared, he carefully levitated the ship off the landing skids and moved it out of the covered area. Once outside, he headed for space, retracting the skids as he accelerated up and out of the Martian atmosphere.

Jim didn't wait for the rest of his squadron - they would form up on the way. His navigation display had already locked in a course sent to his fighter by the Intel Shack.

6.77 days to intercept, he saw in the display. No intercept in space was fast. Even with a max accel of 255g, it took forever to get anywhere.

First, 3.6 hours of accel and a 10.8-hour coast on a vector to nowhere. This would bring them to a point well off the line of the inbound Singheko fleet - to mask them from any sensors that might be pointed toward Earth.

This would be followed by 4 hours of tangential burn to curve the trajectory into a long parabola toward Uranus.

And then an agonizing 3-day coast to Uranus, and another 3-day coast to catch up to the enemy. Jim shuddered just thinking about it.

Six long days coasting through the black. Nothing to do but listen to the electronic fans whir, and the sound of the life support system pushing air through the ducts.

Of course, given the immensity of the solar system, it had been obvious in the planning of the Longsword that some missions would be incredibly long.

So, thanks to some farsighted design nerd in Toulouse, a pilot could loosen his straps, lay the back of his seat down, and slide backwards into a tiny bunk nestled behind the cockpit.

It certainly wasn't fancy - but it was a bed. And there were two small compartments containing food, a cold box with drinks - and even a tiny coffeemaker.

Now, in his VR display, Jim saw Angel come up and slot into travel formation beside him, ten klicks to his right. The other members of his flight slowly caught up to them.

When all were formed up, Jim gave a command via his computer, and all four ships went to max accel simultaneously.

In the far distance on his enhanced VR view, a tiny point of light marked Uranus, 3.8 days away.

If they timed things correctly - and Jim certainly intended to do that - then by the time they arrived at Uranus, the enemy would be just a bit past the planet, on their way to Saturn. When Red Flight performed their slingshot around Uranus, the planet would screen them from the Singheko.

And this would put Jim and Red Flight behind the enemy. They would not even have to accel again after the Uranus slingshot - they would just coast up behind the enemy and slowly pass by, there in the black between Uranus and Saturn.

And hopefully live long enough to report back to Wing.

Star Tango is now available on Amazon to continue the story!

WORKS

Imprint Series
Artemis War (prequel novella)
Imprint of Blood
Imprint of War
Imprint of Honor
Imprint of Defiance

Broken Galaxy Series
Broken Galaxy
Star Tango
The Long Edge of Night
The Short End
Remnants
Goblin Eternal

Sci-Fi, New Books, Hard Science, and General Mayhem
www.facebook.com/PhilHuddlestonAuthor

New books, contests, and freebies
www.philhuddleston.com/newsletter

ABOUT THE AUTHOR

Like Huckleberry Finn, Phil Huddleston grew up barefoot and outdoors, catching mudbugs by the creek, chasing rabbits through the fields, and forgetting to come home for dinner. Then he discovered books. Thereafter, he read everything he could get his hands on, including reading the Encyclopedia Britannica and Funk & Wagnalls from A-to-Z multiple times. He served in the U. S. Marines for four years, returned to college and completed his degree on the GI Bill. Since that time, he built computer systems, worked in cybersecurity, played in a band, flew a bush plane from Alaska to Texas, rode a motorcycle around a good bit of America, and watched in amazement as his wife raised two wonderful daughters in spite of him. And would sure like to do it all again. Except maybe without the screams of terror.

Printed in Great Britain
by Amazon